Angus smoothed one long strand of hair from her shoulder. "I didn't imagine it."

"Imagine what?" Her clear eyes searched his.

"How beautiful you are. Or how good we are together." He kissed her.

Savannah blinked, slowly stiffening in his arms. He felt it, saw it—the way she was withdrawing from him.

"What's wrong?" He ran his finger along her jaw.

"Nothing." Even her voice was distant.

"You can tell me." He tilted her chin up until their eyes locked. "I'm a good listener."

"I know." Savannah pressed her eyes shut. "I should go."

"You can be honest with me." He hoped she would be.

She opened her mouth, then closed it. She was really struggling. "What if it's hard to hear?"

Were those tears in her eyes? "I can handle it."

Dear Reader,

Welcome back to Granite Falls. The little town has seen quite a population boom since book one. We're not done yet. You've visited the McCarrick brothers and their cutting horse ranch in previous Texas Cowboys & K-9s books. This time, Angus McCarrick is our leading man. He likes his life as is and swears he's not the marrying type, but our heroine, Savannah Barrett, might change that.

As the daughter of one of the wealthiest and most influential families in Texas, Savannah has grown up trying to live up to her father's expectations. Having a one-night stand with a dreamy mystery cowboy is the most out of character thing she's ever done. But that one unforgettable night leaves her with lifelong consequences. Pregnant. With triplets.

Angus wants to do the honorable and right thing for the babies, but Savannah wants more. Can her pregnancy lead to real love, a family and the whole package? Or are she and Angus destined to co-parent their triplets from two very different worlds?

I hope you enjoy Savannah and Angus's story and that you'll come back to Granite Falls soon!

Happy reading,

Sasha Summers xoxo

An Uptown Girl's Cowboy

SASHA SUMMERS

Recycling programs
for this product may
not exist in your area.

ISBN-13: 978-1-335-59449-5

An Uptown Girl's Cowboy

Copyright © 2023 by Sasha Best

For questions and comments about the quality of this book, please contact us at CustomerService@Harlequin.com.

Harlequin Enterprises ULC
22 Adelaide St. West, 41st Floor
Toronto, Ontario M5H 4E3, Canada
www.Harlequin.com

Printed in U.S.A.

Sasha Summers grew up surrounded by books. Her passions have always been storytelling, romance and travel—passions she's used to write more than twenty romance novels and novellas. Now a bestselling and award-winning author, Sasha continues to fall a little in love with each hero she writes. From easy-on-the-eyes cowboys to sexy alpha-male werewolves to heroes of truly mythic proportions, she believes that everyone should have their happily-ever-after—in fiction and real life.

Sasha lives in the suburbs of the Texas Hill Country with her amazing family. She looks forward to hearing from fans and hopes you'll visit her online: on Facebook at sashasummersauthor, on Twitter @sashawrites or email her at sashasummersauthor@gmail.com.

Books by Sasha Summers

Harlequin Special Edition

Texas Cowboys & K-9s

The Rancher's Forever Family
Their Rancher Protector
The Rancher's Baby Surprise
The Rancher's Full House
A Snowbound Christmas Cowboy

Harlequin Heartwarming

The Cowboys of Garrison, Texas

The Rebel Cowboy's Baby
The Wrong Cowboy
To Trust a Cowboy

Visit the Author Profile page
at Harlequin.com for more titles.

Dedicated to those willing to fight for their happy endings. Keep up the good fight!

Chapter One

"It's my birthday, too."

Savannah stared up at the starry sky, blinking furiously. "I know, Chelsea." Her twin sister didn't have the best track record for keeping plans but this was different. At least, it should be. A sisters' night to celebrate their birthday. An evening at Gresham Hall. Some yummy dinner while The Rustler's Five, their favorite band, played, then spending the night at the elegant West Mill Inn and getting spa treatments tomorrow. "Chels…this was your idea." An idea they'd agreed to months ago. It *was* their birthday.

"I know. I know. Rain check, okay? I'll make it up to you, so don't be mad, okay?" Chelsea pleaded. "Please, please, please."

Savannah could never stay mad at her twin for long— they both knew that. But she wasn't ready to forgive and forget just yet. "Can you blame me?"

"You'd understand if you met him." Chelsea's swoony sigh had Savannah shaking her head.

Her sister loved falling in love. Staying in love, however, was a different story. And, though Savannah never said as much, Chelsea's relationships were more about attraction than real love. It was a long shot, but she had to try. "What about taking a rain check with him? Asking him—"

"Damien."

"—Damien if he can wait one night?" Savannah waited. And kept waiting. The longer Chelsea stayed quiet, the more frustrated Savannah became. If her sister did delay things with Damien and go ahead with their plans, she'd be sullen and pouty and the whole evening would be ruined. Basically, the evening was ruined either way. "Never mind." She took a deep breath. "Have fun with Damien and I'll see you later."

"Oh, Pickle, you're the best." Chelsea squealed. "There isn't a better sister in the whole wide world, I know it. Why don't you try to have some fun tonight? It'd be easy to do. Just smile and laugh and be charming—you're a hottie, too, y'know? Take a page from my book and find yourself some hottie of a cowboy eager to give you a *really* happy birthday."

"Yeah, sure." Savannah had never and would never.

"I'm serious, Pickle. You need to learn to cut loose a little. Orgasms are good for you."

Savannah's sigh was all irritation. Twins or not, they were two entirely different women.

"Your loss. Okay, I'll bring a big cake home and we can eat it all when you get home tomorrow, okay?" But she hung up before Savannah could answer.

"Happy birthday." She turned to head back inside the dance hall—and slammed into a wall. Her phone fell, hitting the wooden porch with a thud. But the hands resting on her shoulders informed her she'd collided with a very broad chest—not a wall. Even if it was rather wall-like—as chests go. "Sorry." She stepped back, mortified.

"Excuse me, ma'am." A deep voice. Smooth and warm.

Savannah looked up. The tan felt of his cowboy hat cast a bit of a shadow on his face, but she could make out a strong jaw lined with a close-cut auburn beard.

"My fault." He touched the brim of his cowboy hat before stooping to pick up her phone and offering it to her.

"No, it was mine…" She took her phone. "Thank you. I wasn't watching where I was going. Distracted… I mean, I was distracted."

"Bad news?" He nodded at her phone.

"Um…" She shrugged. "Yeah." But she wasn't going to let Chelsea stop her from enjoying her night.

"Sorry to hear that." He sounded sorry, too. Which was sweet.

"Thanks." She blew out a slow breath, trying to rally. "Not really bad news. Not in the grand scheme of things. My sister. She just… We had plans for tonight and she canceled. She does that—a lot. At the last minute. I don't know why I'm surprised. It's our birthday. We're twins, so I guess I thought… Hearing it out loud, I sound pretty selfish." She stopped, realizing she'd just shared way too much information with a complete and total stranger. "Anyway."

He tipped back his hat then, giving Savannah a clear view of his handsome face. The first thing Savannah noticed were his eyes. Warm and brown with just the right number of lines at the corners to imply he was good-natured. Beyond that…well, he was ridiculously handsome. Very…manly. One might even say sexy. Well,

Chelsea would say it. Chelsea would get that look, that *He's mine* look. Savannah never thought about a man like that. Until now.

Get a grip. With an awkward smile, she headed rapidly toward the door before she could make things worse.

Inside Gresham Hall, the low rumble of the crowd and blast of air-conditioning cleared her brain. She was upset. Emotional. Irritated. Disappointed. Heck, mad even. Her reaction to the bearded cowboy was fueled by *all* of *that*. Not that there was anything wrong with her appreciating a good-looking man. He was. She did. And that was that.

She made her way to the table they'd reserved along the edge of the dance floor. Chelsea had insisted on paying for the premium table. She'd wanted to be up close to see the band. Now Savannah squirmed in her seat. Alone. Up front. She'd never felt more exposed in her entire life.

"Ready for a drink?" The waitress was young and perky, her cleavage dangerously close to spilling out of her low V-neck T-shirt. "Or are you waiting for the rest of your party?"

"It's just me." Savannah forced a smile. "I'll take a white wine."

The server's brows rose. "Sure." She eyed the empty chair. "Can I take this? We're expecting a full house."

"Of course." Maybe having the empty chair gone would make this less awkward?

"Great." The server lifted the chair. "I'll be back with your wine."

Savannah nodded, watching the chair and the server disappear into the crowded room. Was this really what she wanted to do for her birthday? Sit here, alone, drinking? Wasn't that plain sad? She could go. If she left, she could go to the hotel, put on her comfy pajamas, watch *New Girl* on Netflix, and order room service. She should go. Except she really wanted to hear The Rustler's Five. *Dammit, Chels*. She tapped her manicured nails across the wood-top table as she started making a mental pros-and-cons list. Bottom line, if she left, she might not get a chance to see her favorite band live again—at least not anytime soon.

"I couldn't help but notice you, darlin'." The words were slurred. "You're too pretty to be sittin' here alone."

Savannah glanced at the man leaning a little too far into her personal space. Unlike the handsome cowboy she'd encountered on the porch, this man was an overt creeper—his focus entirely on her chest. Ugh. This was one of those times when she wished she was as good a liar as Chelsea. "I'm not alone."

He smiled, using his thumb to point back over his shoulder. "Then why did I see your chair get carried off?"

She frowned. "I'm not interested."

"Well, that's because you haven't given me a chance." The man rested both hands on her table. "Give me five minutes and I can change your mind."

Savannah considered the man. He was handsome enough. He was groomed and pressed, with a fresh shine on his boots. Appearance wise, there was nothing wrong with the guy. "While I appreciate your enthusiasm, you can't change my mind."

"No?" He chuckled. "I'd hate for you to miss out. Hell, I'd hate for us both to miss out. How about I go get myself a chair and we talk about this?"

"No. Thank you." She stopped drumming her nails, sending him her most glacial stare. It normally did the trick. Normally.

"I never back down from a challenge, darlin'." He winked. "You're all feisty and I like that."

Was he serious? It's not like she was using big words.

She glanced around the room, looking for a quick exit. She didn't have the patience for this. But her gaze landed on the hottie cowboy from outside. He was watching her. Correction, he was watching the sleazy cowboy talking to her. And hot cowboy wasn't happy. When his eyes met hers, he stood and headed her way and all Savannah could hear was Chelsea's advice ringing in her ears. "Cut loose. Have some fun."

But then sleazy cowboy was taking her hand and, ick, rubbing his thumb along the inside of her wrist—and what happened next was mostly a blur.

Angus had never liked Jason Tilson. He was a fast-talking, self-inflated piece of shit that lived for the hunt and loved to talk all about his conquests. At the moment, Jason was laying it on thick with the sad-eyed woman who'd almost knocked him on his ass not ten minutes ago. And it bothered him. Something fierce. He didn't know the woman from Adam, but he couldn't sit there, knowing it was her birthday and she was alone, and leave her prey to a sonofabitch like Jason Tilson.

That was why he slipped off the barstool, grabbed a spare chair from a table he passed and headed toward where she sat. He didn't know what the hell he was doing, but Jason was taking her hand and the look on her face told Angus everything he needed to know. He was too far in to stop now.

"Jason." He grabbed the man's shoulder and spun him around.

"Gus?" Jason shook off Angus's hold. "You mind?"

"Yep." He set the chair down with a resounding thud. "She does, too."

Jason looked at the woman, who was watching them

with wide eyes, and then back at him. "You and her are...
together?"

"Maybe. Maybe not. What's it matter?" Angus stepped
closer.

Jason bowed up. "It matters 'cause you're interrupting
our conversation."

Angus gripped the front of the man's shirt. "The conversation is over."

"Gus." The woman was up, her hand resting on Angus's
arm. "I don't need anyone fighting for me."

Angus released Jason.

"Bye, Jason." She waved, then sat.

Jason smoothed his shirtfront and snapped, "You
coulda said something."

"I did, several times, but you were having a hard time
understanding the concept of no." The woman crossed
her arms over her chest. "*No* should have been enough.
Gus shouldn't have had to step in to make you listen."

Angus couldn't sit. He was glad she was getting the
chance to speak her mind but even more pissed by what
he was hearing. He couldn't help but say, "You owe her
an apology."

Jason didn't like that one bit.

"Go on." He gripped the chair back.

"I'm sorry." The words were dripping with sarcasm,
but Jason turned on his heel and made his way back to
the bar before Angus could do or say anything more.

"This birthday just keeps getting better and better." The
woman sighed. "Thanks for that." She was studying him.

He nodded, uncertain what that look meant.

"You want to sit?" She nodded at the chair he'd carried
over. "Ward off any more unwanted advances." There
was a ghost of a smile on her full red lips.

He sat, doing his damnedest not to stare. Here he'd

tried to be chivalrous and chase off that scumbag Jason.
She likely wouldn't appreciate him giving her a once-
over. But she was beautiful. As soon as she'd walked
into him, he'd been a little starstruck by just how pretty
she was. In a soft way. Fragile. Classy and elegant. Untouchable for a man like him. "We'll have to come up
with a signal so I know what's wanted and unwanted."

She did smile then. "Oh, good point. Don't want the
welcome ones scared off." She leaned forward to rest her
elbows on the table, meeting his gaze. "Thank you, Gus?"

"You're welcome." His chest felt tight. Damn, but she
was something to look at. "You know my name. What's
yours?"

A strange expression crossed over her face. It was no
more than a handful of seconds but whatever she was
thinking looked like a weighty decision. "Chelsea." She
twisted her long hair and pushed it back from her shoulders. "My name is Chelsea."

The server arrived with a big glass of white wine.
By the time he'd placed his order, Chelsea had already
knocked back a third of her glass. Maybe the whole thing
with Jason had upset her more than she was letting on.

An awkward silence hung over the table until the
server came back with his beer. She kept looking his
way, blushing, and sipping her wine. And he didn't know
what to make of it.

"Happy birthday, Chelsea." He toasted her.

She had a blinding smile. "Thank you. Here's to having a fun evening." She tapped her glass to his beer bottle.

"Cheers to that." He took a healthy swig of his beer.

Her phone chirped so she pulled it out of her purse.
One look at the screen, her smile disappeared, and her
phone was shoved back into her purse.

After a long stretch of silence, he asked, "All good?"

She finished off her wine. "Family. My father." She took a deep breath, her eyes traveling over his face before she went on. "He's on the controlling side of things. Okay, he's very controlling. My sister and I planned this without telling him and he's not happy about it."

Angus could understand a father being disappointed about missing his daughters' birthday. "Did he have something special planned?"

She shook her head, her long brown hair swaying. "Oh, yes—but not for our birthday. He's hosting some dinner party for his big important friends tonight. Momma has a migraine—she gets them a lot when Dad has a dinner party—so he needs me to come play hostess. You know, smile and nod and refill drinks." She peered into her empty wineglass. "I'm very good at it, too. Being charming."

"I'm sure you are." Angus got the feeling she had some talking to do. Surprisingly, he wasn't against listening.

"My sister has managed to ensure he'll never call her for help—they don't get along. At all. My twin does what she wants, when she wants, no matter what."

"Like tonight?" He couldn't help but be hurt on her behalf.

"Yes. Like tonight. Sometimes, I envy her. You know? What would that be like? To do what you wanted?" A new glass of wine appeared and Chelsea took a sip. "The thing is, I get how lucky I am. I've never wanted for a thing in my life. Material things. It's my parents' way of showing us they love us, I guess. By buying us things. Sometimes I wish they'd carve out some time for us— just the family." She took another sip. "Of course, my sister says the four of us together for more than an hour would lead to disaster, so..." She shrugged.

He and his brothers hadn't grown up with a bunch of

stuff, but they'd had loving and affectionate parents. Family dinners and chores, supporting each other's football or baseball or rodeo events, and working the horses at the ranch. They were all in it together. He couldn't imagine growing up any other way—especially not the way Chelsea was describing.

"I'm sorry, Gus. You're being so sweet to me. If Ch— my sister was here, she'd tell me I was being a real downer and to lighten up, so…" She smoothed her hair back from her shoulder and looked at him. "I'm going to try that. So, I'm going to say something a little uncomfortable now." She swallowed. "I just have to get up the nerve."

Angus sat up, his curiosity piqued.

"You're single?" Her gaze met his.

"Lifelong bachelor. That's the plan."

"I think you're incredibly attractive." She took a sip of wine.

"The feeling is mutual." Which didn't do her justice. "But I'm not so sure if the wine might be clouding things."

"No." She drew in an unsteady breath. "I thought so on the porch. I thought so before the wine got here. I do think the wine gave me the courage to say it out loud." Her gaze was glued to his mouth. "I'm not drunk, Gus. I know what I'm doing and saying."

His grip tightened on his beer bottle. "That's good to know."

The music started but he didn't move. As long as she was looking at him like that, he had no interest in anything else. He'd never been so drawn in, so eager to burn in the fire she set deep inside of him. She was mesmerizing. Beautiful. And she wanted him. There was no denying or pretending otherwise.

"Dance with me?" She held her hand out to him.

The moment his fingers threaded with hers, he knew

he was done for. He wouldn't be driving home tonight or in any rush to get on the road in the morning. As long as Chelsea wanted him around, he'd stay. Holding her close on the dance floor set his every nerve on end. He lost himself in the feel of her. Her sweet softness. The scent of her. The way she fit against him.

"Gus?" she whispered.

"Hmm?" With her head resting against his chest, he suspected she could hear his heart pounding away.

"Thanks again." She sighed and looked up at him. "I think this is going to be the best birthday ever." Invitation burned in those dark eyes of hers.

His hand pressed flat against her back and he drew in a slow breath. If he didn't do something to diffuse the tension between them, he was going to kiss her in a way that might not be acceptable for a public dance hall. "I don't have a cake and I left all my birthday candles at home, but you can still make a birthday wish, if you've got one?"

She smiled broadly, her hands sliding up his chest to wrap around his neck. "My birthday wish? That's easy." She stood on tiptoe and pulled his head down to hers. "You."

"Don't waste your wish on that." He murmured against her lips. "You've already got me."

Her lips clung to his and Angus forgot about the music and the band and the other people on the dance floor. Kissing her was all that mattered. And when she made a little groan of pleasure, dammit all, he didn't want the song to end.

Chapter Two

Four Months Later...

"I can't marry you." Savannah loosely tied the snow-flake-print apron around her vanishing waistline.

"Before long, you're not going to be able to hide... that." Greg, her closest friend, pointed at her stomach.

"My stomach? Is it that bad?" She ran a hand over the swell, sighed, and tugged the apron in place.

"Of course, it's not bad." Greg hugged her. "I don't think it's bad. But you know your parents aren't going to see it that way."

"Tell me something I don't know." Savannah turned. "Where are the sprinkles?"

"Here." Chelsea handed her the jar with red, white, and green sprinkles. "You could do worse than Greg, Pickle. He's cute. And rich. And he loves you." She picked up one of the cookies Savannah was decorating and took a bite. "These are so yummy."

"And for the fundraiser." Savannah wiped the back of her forearm across her forehead. "So, stop eating them. Unless you plan on helping me bake?"

Greg eyed Chelsea. "I can't tell if you were just insulting me or supporting me?"

Chelsea shrugged. "Me neither." She took another bite of cookie. "I'm only eating one more."

"Chels, I'm serious. For every one you eat, you have to decorate." Savannah frowned as her sister devoured a perfectly decorated gingerbread man.

"You know you don't want me to decorate cookies." Chelsea wiped her hands together. "I'd traumatize the children."

"Whatever." At least they were done talking about her pregnancy. Every day for the last month, Chelsea or Greg would bombard her with questions she had no answers to. Namely, what was she going to do? It was a question she had asked herself multiple times daily since she'd learned she was pregnant. She wasn't supposed to be able to get pregnant. Ever. She'd grown up with irregular periods and been diagnosed with polycystic ovary syndrome. Her obstetrician had told her the only way she'd ever get pregnant was with reproductive therapy.

Yet, here I am. Pregnant.

"Your new hair. Did I miss the big reveal?" Greg asked, eyeing Chelsea's shock of white-blond hair. Greg was one of the few people that dared to go toe-to-toe with her twin sister. His father handled her father's legal affairs—which meant he'd been a fixture in their home for as long as Savannah could remember. They'd practically grown up together. Once Greg passed the bar exam, he worked for his father—which meant he worked for her father, too.

"Did you see a mushroom cloud over the house on

your way here?" Chelsea grinned. "No worries, you'll get to be here, front row, for the fireworks." She adjusted her oversize elf hat. "Maybe I should show them my hair right after you tell them you're pregnant?"

"Dad would have a heart attack." Savannah pressed the snowflake cookie cutter into the last little bit of dough. "I know you two don't get along, but you don't want him to drop dead."

Chelsea's eyebrows rose. "Where is daddy dearest?"

"In the barn." She put the cookie cutout on the cookie sheet and carried the tray to the oven. "The new horses are here."

"The overpriced horses we have no use for?" Chelsea reached for another cookie.

"Stop!" Savannah snapped, slamming the oven door. "Not another bite. I mean it."

Chelsea held up her hands. "Pregnancy sure has made you grumpy. You should eat a cookie. Depriving those babies."

"It's definitely babies?" Greg asked, eyeing her stomach with renewed concern.

"You mean, it hasn't changed since she found out a month ago? Yep." Chelsea held up three fingers. "She'll be as big as a house in no time."

Savannah shot her sister another look and set about making another batch of cookie dough. Every year, she made take-home treats for A Night with Santa. It was a fundraising event for the No Child Hungry charity that her family cosponsored. It was a charity close to her heart, one she'd advocated and worked with during her time in the pageant world.

"You know Daniella and Becky will make the rest tomorrow." Chelsea was eyeing a star cookie. "That is what they get paid to do, Pickle. So why are you in here slaving away?"

"Because having the cooks make the cookies doesn't feel, I don't know, homemade? Besides, it's the one thing they will let me cook. And I need some holiday spirit." But really, it was because she was restless. If she didn't keep herself occupied, she was overwhelmed. Her future was rushing toward her, and she couldn't come up with a plan that worked. She always had a plan. Always. This, she hadn't planned for.

It wasn't like she could pretend this wasn't happening. So far, she'd managed to camouflage her slight baby bump with layers, but that wouldn't work for much longer. The house they all shared was massive, and they were all preoccupied with their own lives, but even her father would eventually notice she was the size of a whale. From the way it was going, that would be sooner rather than later. She could already feel the babies moving. They were real. Busy. Growing inside her. And, ready or not, they were coming.

"Hey." Greg took her hand. "I'm serious about this. Marry me."

It was sweet, very sweet. That was Greg. One of the good guys. Which was why she couldn't marry him. "And if you meet your one true love?" Savannah fanned herself and leaned against the kitchen counter.

"Unless pigs start flying and Hell freezes over, there's nothing to worry about." Greg's one love had left him at the altar and turned him into a cynic. He said love was the first step in a marathon of torture and pain. "I'd rather spend the rest of my life with someone I respect and like."

"And you'd win major brownie points with Dad." Chelsea took the star cookie. "Last one, I promise."

Savannah threw a pot holder at her sister.

"I've never pretended I didn't have ambition." Greg shrugged. "He'd help me get into the DA's office, it's true.

But, if you marry me, I can make sure he goes easy on you."

"Maybe I should marry you. I need more help in that department than Savannah." Chelsea wiped some of the frosting off with her finger. "Is this a new recipe? I want to bathe in this stuff."

Savannah let the two of them carry on. While they picked and prodded at one another, Savannah stifled a yawn. She was so tired. One of the things she was having trouble with was fatigue. Like bone-deep exhaustion. She'd always been a doer, but now one of her favorite things to do was nap. Or take a bath. The clock said it was almost six, so there wasn't time for a nap before their standing seven o'clock dinner. But a bath...

"Can I count on you two to keep an eye on those?" She pointed at the oven. "The timer's set." She couldn't stop the yawn this time. "I'm going to take a bath."

"We got this." Chelsea gave her a thumbs-up. "I won't eat them all."

"I've got this." Greg squeezed her shoulder. "Try to relax, Savannah. Stress is bad for you."

She nodded as she left them in the kitchen. Her parents wanted to make sure that there were no illusions about their status, so her family home was big and audacious. Momma came from old oil money, and Dad was part of the Austin Cougars pro football family dynasty. But Dad wasn't satisfied with riding on his family's coattails. No, Richard Barrett had been a mayor and judge and, if he had it his way, in two years he'd land himself a prestigious position in government. From the custom leather furniture to the big game hunting trophies he'd had mounted and displayed throughout the home, the Barrett name represented wealth and excess, and her father was proud of that.

By the time she'd climbed the grand staircase and headed down the east wing to her suite, she was dragging. She turned on the oversize bath, poured in some citrus bath salts, and turned down the overhead lights to a nice, soothing glow. But once she was chin-deep in bubbles with her head resting on her bath pillow, her brain started throwing out questions.

What was she going to do?

One night. One mistake. And now everything had changed.

There was no way to find Gus. It was impossible to track the name Gus—nothing else. And even if she could, would he want to have anything to do with her or the babies? They'd talked enough to know that they were from different worlds. Chances were, her father wouldn't let Gus within five feet of her—let alone his Barrett grandchildren. It was probably for the best that Gus wasn't a factor.

She closed her eyes and, for a few minutes, let herself think about the night she'd had with her sexy bearded cowboy. Never in her wildest dreams could she have imagined anything as pleasurable and intense as what they'd shared. But, more than that, they'd talked. She knew how close he was with his brother. That his father had passed on and his mother lived with her sister in North Carolina. She knew he loved horses more than just about anything. And she knew he had a big, barrel-chested laugh that had made her smile until her cheeks hurt. His big, rough hands had made her feel loved and cherished. How could she consider that, her time with him, a mistake?

"He was a good guy." According to the pregnancy book she had hidden under her bed, talking to the babies was good. "Your dad. He was a cowboy. A big, sweet, tender giant who made all my birthday wishes come true." Her fingers traced along the swell of her stomach before she pressed her palms flat. "There you are." She smiled at the flutters and twists she felt in her belly. "Enjoying our bath?" She rested her head back and sighed. "Let's enjoy a few more minutes of peace and quiet before your aunt Chelsea starts tonight's dinner off with a bang."

Her parents, specifically her father, were ridiculously overprotective. Dad couldn't handle not being in control of a situation—or a person. Momma had tried to explain it was his love language, but Savannah knew that wasn't a thing. Over the years, she'd learned to pick her battles. It was easier to live at home than move into an apartment of her own and have his round-the-clock security trailing after her and tracking her every move. She took after her mother, preferring to avoid her father's temper. Chelsea, on the other hand, lived to make their father's blood pressure skyrocket. Like now. Bleaching and chopping off her hair? Dad was going to flip. She took a deep breath. "Maybe I should listen to your aunt? And tell them all about you three tonight?" But the last time she'd listened to Chelsea, she'd wound up spending the night with her hottie bearded cowboy. And that hadn't exactly worked out the way she'd expected. "Maybe not."

Angus wasn't a fool. He'd donned a freshly starched shirt and jeans, polished up his best boots and trimmed his beard so it was respectable. It wasn't that he didn't always take pride in his appearance—he did. But the Barrett family was old money and having them as a client would open doors for McCarrick Cutting Horses. If he needed to put on his Sunday best to impress Richard Barrett, he would—the man was Texas royalty.

"They're fine-looking horses." Richard Barrett was a talker. "The best. I won't settle for anything less."

Angus had noticed that for himself. Since he'd driven down the long, tree-lined drive leading toward the Barrett home and beyond, to the barns, every detail screamed *money*. Which, for someone like Richard Barrett, likely equated to the *best*. "I wouldn't bring them to you if they weren't." Angus rested his arms on the top rung of the impressive pipe corral. He wasn't blowing smoke, though. He wouldn't sell a horse if it wasn't in peak shape; his reputation hinged on it. "They're the best. Sharpest. Agile. Instinctual. They'll serve you and your herd well."

"I'll hold you to that." Mr. Barrett clapped him on the shoulder. "How about you come up to the big house for dinner? We could put you up in one of the guest rooms while you're training us on commands."

"I don't want to inconvenience anyone." It would be a lot nicer staying here than some motel for the next two nights. Besides, it'd be nice to see how the other half lived. Getting to rub it in his brother Dougal's face only sweetened the deal.

"I wouldn't have asked if it was." Richard smiled. "Tonight will only be a small family dinner. A few close friends, is all."

Angus kept stride with the older man as he led them from the barn. The Barrett homestead was more like a mansion. In truth, it resembled a fancy hotel more than anything. With staggered pitched rooflines, a turret or two, columns along the front, and windows lining both floors. What made it more daunting was the amount of white Christmas lights framing the home. An illuminated wreath hung from every window and several Christmas trees were strung with white and blue lights along the drive to the house. "You've an impressive home, sir." Which seemed nicer than saying it was a little much.

"I do." Mr. Barrett chuckled. "Only the best." He opened one of the heavy wooden doors and stepped aside. "Come on in, son."

Angus took a quick look around and almost tripped over his own feet. If he thought the outside was a little much, the inside was…well, it *was* too much. First thing he noticed were the hunting trophies. A lion. An-honest-to-goodness lion was stuffed and mounted, midleap, onto the back of a running big-horned animal. "Is that a—"

"Kudu." Richard pointed at the animal. "*That* was a good hunting trip. You like hunting?"

He wasn't a fan of trophy hunting, but he'd keep that to himself. "I don't have much time for it." Angus hoped that was a neutral enough answer.

"You should make time." Richard pointed up. "That one was hard getting out of the mountains, let me tell you."

Angus glanced up at the bighorn sheep mounted on a clump of decorative rocks jutting out of the wall of the massive room. "I bet." How much did that cost? Not only to have the animal stuffed and mounted, but to have a fake mountain built into your wall to display the animal? The McCarricks were comfortable, but this? Well, this was another level of money—one he couldn't wrap his mind around.

"Richard?" a woman called from the bottom of the stairs. "Who is that, dear?"

"Lana, this is Angus McCarrick, of McCarrick Cutting Horses. He brought our new horses all the way here himself, to train us and make sure we were happy. Angus, this is my beautiful wife, Lana."

"It's a pleasure, ma'am." There was an air of frailty about the woman that had Angus gently shaking her hand.

"You're most welcome." She smiled. "You're staying for dinner?"

"We will put him up while he's here. Two or three nights," Mr. Barrett added. "I'll get Savannah to tell Mary to get him a room ready."

"I'll tell Mary." Mrs. Barrett argued. "Savannah's having a moment to herself."

"What's the matter with her?" Mr. Barrett was frowning.

"Nothing is the matter, Richard." Mrs. Barrett sighed. "But *I* can tell Mary." She smiled at Angus then. "Excuse me, won't you."

"Drink?" Mr. Barrett led him through two iron-inlaid wooden doors. "It's not easy living in a house full of women, let me tell you."

Angus didn't respond, inspecting the room with interest. There was a fireplace on the far rock wall. The snap and pop of the fire echoed in the cavernous room. Even with the holiday decor, abundant white lights, and a towering Christmas tree decorated in all white and silver, the room felt cold. "Whiskey? Scotch?" He glanced at him. "Beer?"

If he was going to play with the big boys, he needed to drink like the big boys. "I'll have what you're having." Which could be a big mistake.

While Mr. Barrett was pouring the drinks, others arrived. Pete Powell and his son, Greg. Pete, it turned out, was Richard's oldest friend and lawyer. Greg was following in his father's footsteps. Lana returned to assure Richard that she'd taken care of things with Mary, whoever that was, and Angus's nerves were starting to relax when Richard Barrett's eyes bulged out of his head and he yelled, "What the hell did you do?"

Angus froze, as did everyone else. A quick sweep of

the room saw Mrs. Barrett and the elder Powell were staring over his shoulder in shock. Greg Powell, on the other hand, looked like he was trying not to laugh.

"Let me guess, you don't like it?" This, from a voice behind Angus.

"No, I don't." Richard Barrett's face was an angry shade of red. "You look—"

"Like Pink? The musician? You know who that is, don't you, Dad? That's what I was going for." There was amusement in the woman's voice. "Oh, we have company? Isn't anyone going to introduce me?"

Angus turned slowly, avoiding any sudden movements. Whatever was happening, he wasn't about to get sucked into any drama. This deal was too big—too important. But the moment he saw what—who—was causing the commotion, Angus froze.

No breathing.

No heartbeat.

Nothing.

Because it was her.

"Chelsea Barrett." She was walking toward him, smiling, like she'd never laid eyes on him before.

Angus was reeling. Was this a joke? Did she really not recognize him? His pride stung something fierce. For him, their night together had been anything but forgettable. He swallowed. Hell, she'd tempted him to consider something more—and that never happened. After an hour of sleep, he had woken to the sound of the motel room door shutting. He had wrapped the sheet around his waist and pulled open the door to see her climbing into a cab and driving away. He had stood there, like a damn fool, willing her to look back. As if that would have somehow changed something. It had been a one-night thing. That was all. But it had been one hell of an unforgettable night. Or so he'd thought.

"And you are?" Chelsea was smiling up at him—still *no* sign of recognition on her face.

But, up close, she didn't look exactly the way he remembered her, either. Besides the super short, white-blond hair, there was something *different*. "Angus McCarrick." He shook her hand. Something was definitely different. It had to be her, didn't it? She was so familiar. But she wasn't as soft. Not her body, her eyes. That was it. Her eyes were different.

"Sorry I'm late." Another voice.

Angus was too busy studying Chelsea Barrett to care.

"You missed Dad's freak-out." Chelsea pointed at her father, wearing a familiar smile. "He's still red, but I don't think we need to worry about a heart attack or calling the paramedics."

"Chelsea." Lana Barrett scolded. "That's not funny. You know your father needs to be careful of his blood pressure."

"You okay, Dad?"

"Yes, Savannah." Richard Barrett took a deep breath. "I'm fine. I should be used to your sister's antics by now." He sighed. "Angus McCarrick, of the highly recommended McCarrick Cutting Horses, meet my other daughter, Savannah. Also known as Miss Fort Worth, Miss Texas, and Miss Southwest."

"Obviously she's the good twin," Chelsea added.

Then it clicked. Chelsea was a twin. Every single inch of him tightened as he turned. He knew it before he saw her. But once their eyes met… It was her. Exactly as he remembered her. Beautiful and willowy and right there—triggering a barrage of memories from their night together.

And just like that, he was aching for her. Not good. Not good, at all.

But, damn, it was a relief to see her react. She recognized him. Boy, did she. Her fleeting smile, so sweet, before her expression shifted to sheer panic. All the color drained from her face so quickly, Angus found himself moving toward her. Too bad Greg, the clean-cut junior lawyer, beat him to it. Angus didn't miss the way lawyer boy protectively draped his arm across her shoulders. Or the way he murmured something for her alone. If that wasn't staking a claim, he didn't know what was.

"I'm fine, Greg," Savannah whispered, her spine stiffening enough to have lawyer boy's arm slip from her shoulders. For one second, she looked directly at him. The message was loud and clear.

Keep your mouth shut.

He got it. He did. He wasn't about to make things awkward by announcing they knew each other. No way, no how.

"It's nice to meet you." He took a very deep breath. "Savannah." He didn't miss the slight tremor in her hand as she took his.

Sonofabitch. The jolt was there—as strong as he remembered. From her sharp indrawn breath, she felt it, too. Good, dammit. He'd spent the last few months trying to convince himself that their night together had been nothing special. One touch, taking her hand, and it was clear he'd been lying to himself.

"Welcome, Mr. McCarrick." She let go of his hand, flexing her fingers.

"Angus will be staying with us the next few days." Richard Barrett clapped Angus on the shoulder again, his voice booming. "Showed up with three of the prettiest horses I've ever seen. Being the professional he is, he's staying until the boys and I've mastered the commands and such. Make sure the horses are a...good fit."

It was the reminder he needed. This was an important business deal for him and his brother. Angus wasn't worried about the horses. Richard Barrett, he wasn't so sure about. Now that he knew who the man was, everything Savannah had told him was enough for Angus not to like the man. But this was business and he needed to set that aside if he wanted to have the all-important Barrett name endorsing McCarrick Cutting Horses. Business was business.

"I know you, Dick. It won't take long." Pete Powell chuckled. "You're more stubborn than a mule. Once you make up your mind about something, it's done."

Angus nodded, doing his best to tune out Savannah—of how close she was. Yet not close enough. *Dammit all.*

"It's time for dinner," Lana announced.

This is gonna be a hell of a long dinner. He followed Mrs. Barrett from the big room down the hall to what Angus suspected would be another big, impressive and intimidating room.

"I don't envy you." Chelsea trailed behind the group, watching him and Savannah. "*Training* Richard Barrett? Yeah, no. Good luck with that."

He had no response for that. Savannah smoothed her hair from her shoulder and he could almost feel the silky strands sliding between his fingers or falling forward, over his chest and shoulders.

"Whatever this is, you need to cool it," Chelsea whispered, making sure only the three of them could hear her.

Angus paused, frowning. *What the hell?*

"Don't say a word. Twin thing." Chelsea tapped her temple. "You two, cool it." She pointed back and forth between them. "Come on, Pickle." She took Savannah's hand.

Savannah nodded and headed into the room without a backward glance. It left a familiar hollowness in the center of his chest. He didn't like it. He didn't like any of this. Except for finding Savannah again. That part was good. Or was it? She didn't exactly seem happy to see him. Then again, it had to be awkward to have her one-night stand showing up on her doorstep, hobnobbing with her father. That was all it had been. A one-night stand. And that night was long over.

And yet, risky or not, he couldn't help but wonder what would happen if the two of them wound up alone. Would she acknowledge the spark between them? Would she want to experience even a sliver of the pleasure they'd shared that night? He sure as hell did. One thing was certain, Savannah Barrett was worth the risk.

Chapter Three

Savannah pushed the apple pie around on her plate. Tonight's nausea had nothing to do with her pregnancy and everything to do with the fact that her gorgeous bearded cowboy was sitting directly across the table from her.

He was here. Here. At her family dinner table. Gorgeous and bearded. Flesh and blood and 100 percent untouchable.

Thankfully, she had years of practice at being a hostess. Smile. Nod. Act interested. Read the room. Keep conversation flowing. Laugh—but not too much or too loudly. In general, be charming. She was good at it, normally. But tonight, she couldn't seem to get her footing.

Gus—Angus—was doing just fine. He was completely unfazed by her presence. While she sat there thinking how ridiculously handsome he looked in his tan button-down oxford, he was laughing and chatting and eating his dessert as if he hadn't made her cry out from orgasm.

Chelsea kicked her, again, under the table.

Because I'm staring.

"Done?" Chelsea asked, nodding at Mary, who was hovering at Savannah's shoulder.

"Oh, yes, thank you, Mary." She leaned back so Mary, the evening maid, could clear her dessert plate.

"No problem, Miss Savannah." Mary smiled as she took the plate, her voice low as she added, "You didn't eat much. If you want anything later, just let me know."

"That's kind of you." Her stomach churned at the idea of food. All she wanted was the peace and quiet of her room.

"How long have you been in the cutting horse field?" Greg asked Angus.

Savannah knew this already. Angus's family had been raising and training cutting horses since his family settled in Texas, generations ago.

"My family's been raising horses since they came over from Scotland. It's in our blood. My grandmother used to say we had kelpie blood." Angus shrugged. "My grandmother loved Scottish folklore."

"Have you ever been to Scotland?" Her mother was charmed.

Because he is charming. The thick, tousled auburn hair. The well-groomed beard. The flashing eyes. *Oh, give it a rest.*

"No." Angus shook his head. "I hope to, one day."

"What's a kelpie?" Chelsea propped herself up on an elbow, fluttering her eyes at Angus.

It was Savannah's turn to kick her sister under the table.

"Ow—um…" Chelsea shot Savannah a death glare and shifted in her chair, out of Savannah's range. "I'm not familiar with the term."

"A water horse." Angus's warm brown eyes glanced

at her. "Most of the legends are meant to warn children away from water and single women away from charming strangers out to trap you."

"Good advice." Her father seemed louder than normal. "Advice you two should heed." But he seemed to be talking directly at Chelsea. "It's not easy being the father to daughters, let me tell you."

Chelsea rolled her eyes. "But, Dad, how else am I supposed to meet my soul mate and have a bunch of grandbabies to carry on the family line?"

Her father wasn't amused. "If you were interested in finding your soul mate, I'm sure your mother and I would come up with some decent candidates."

"Gosh, thanks, Dad, but I'm not sure that's how you meet your *soul mate*." Chelsea sighed and sat back in her chair.

"There's no such thing." Richard Barrett nodded. "A partner. A reliable, loyal, like-minded partner is better than some romanticized ideal. You're old enough to realize that and stop wasting your time on men that would never make a good husband."

"According to you," Chelsea pushed back.

Mr. Barrett grumbled something under his breath, then said, "According to anyone with half a brain—"

"Do you have siblings, Mr. McCarrick?" her mother cut in.

"I do. My brother, Dougal. We're partners in the family business." Angus's smile made Savannah's insides go soft. "We butt heads now and then. As families do, sometimes."

Dougal was Angus's best friend—someone Angus loved dearly. Like she loved Chelsea.

"Hear, hear." Pete Powell chuckled. "At the end of the day, family is all that matters."

"It is." Angus nodded. "Family first."

He said it with such conviction, Savannah's heart clenched. Family first. His family. She resisted the urge to cover her stomach. *His* family.

Savannah glanced at her father. Though he liked to say he worked as hard as he did to provide for his daughters, that was more an excuse. Her father was an ambitious man. He wanted the name and power and money. He needed it. The Barretts were already in that top 1 percent, but it still wasn't enough for him. That had nothing to do with making sure she and Chelsea were financially secure.

"And carrying on the family legacy." Her father tapped on the edge of the table. "You girls have quite a mantle to carry. Responsibility and prestige and hard work. Whoever you pick will have to toe the line. I know my girls won't let me down."

"On that note, Savannah and I have a podcast to listen to." Chelsea stood. "'Night, Mr. Powell, 'night, Greg. Mr. McCarrick." She waved.

Savannah stood, too, grateful for her sister's out. "It's been a lovely evening. Good night." She couldn't resist taking a last look at Angus. His warm brown eyes were waiting for her. His smile had those just-right crinkles at the corners of his eyes in full force.

If they'd been alone, she'd have gone around the table and climbed into his lap. *Wait, no.* She wouldn't. Surely... Yep, she totally would. Not exactly the most reassuring realization to make, but there it was. The way his focus shifted to her mouth, she suspected he'd let her climb onto his lap and use his big strong hands to hold her in place.

"Come on." Chelsea slipped her arm through Savannah's and tugged her from the dining room.

Savannah waited. Her sister wasn't one for keeping

her thoughts to herself. But they made it all the way to Savannah's room before Chelsea opened her mouth.

One word—that said so much. "Gus?" Chelsea leaned against the closed bedroom door.

Savannah nodded.

"Shit." Chelsea pushed off the door. "You okay?"

Savannah shook her head. Okay was not how she was feeling.

"You going to tell him?" She flopped onto Savannah's bed. "I mean, I won't blame you if you don't but…"

She sat beside Chelsea, smoothing her cream silk blouse over her stomach. "I should. He is the father." Telling him would turn an already complicated situation into an impossible one. "But Dad…"

"Would probably castrate him." Chelsea sighed.

"Gee, thanks, Chels." Savannah pressed her hands over her face. "That makes everything easier."

Chelsea took one of her hands. "Sorry. You know me, I can't help it." She squeezed her hand. "He seems like a really nice guy. Like he might be dad material, you know? And he's so *hot*."

"You noticed?" She nudged her sister. "I noticed, you noticed." She lay back on the bed beside her sister.

"What?" Chelsea glanced at her. "He *is* hot. But he's yours."

"He is not mine." She rested her hand on her stomach and concentrated on the fluttering, rolling movement there. He was *theirs*. Their father.

Gus—Angus was a nice guy. A sweet, hardworking, family-loving, beautiful manly-man. A man who was the father of her babies. She drew in an unsteady breath, tears stinging her eyes. What sort of person would keep a father from his children? Could she live with that? She knew the answer before she'd finished thinking the question. "I have to tell him."

"You want me with you?" Chelsea asked, squeezing her hand again.

"No." She squeezed back. "I can do it."

"You're not worried about getting...distracted?" Chelsea rolled onto her side. "You know." She bobbed her eyebrows. "'Cause he's hot. I'll keep my fingers crossed for you. You know, working off some stress would be good for you."

"Oh, Chelsea." Savannah couldn't help but laugh. "Hot or not, learning he's going to be a father isn't something I'd consider foreplay." And, no matter how hot or tempting he was, she had to tell him about the babies. Climbing into his lap or falling into his bed was not an option. No way, no how, no matter how much she might want otherwise.

Angus had spent an hour pacing his room before he'd given up and taken a shower. She wasn't coming. Unless he wanted to spend the night going door-to-door, he couldn't exactly go find her. He was pretty sure that was the fastest way to get his ass kicked out of the Barrett household.

The shower was stocked with fancy bottles of shampoo and body wash, exfoliating cream and foot scrub. He read the back of the bottles and used them all. His feet had never been officially scrubbed before but it felt damn good. *Who knew?*

He stepped out onto the bath mat, wrapped a towel around his waist, and wriggled his toes. "I'm going to have to get some of that." He took the bottle of foot scrub out of the shower and headed into the bedroom.

"Hi." Savannah, in a white nightgown with her hair falling down her back, was sitting on his bed.

He stopped. "You're here." *No shit, genius.*

She nodded, her gaze bouncing from his chest to his face and back again. "I... I wanted to talk."

She was here, that was all that mattered. "Not to stop me from stealing this?" He held out the foot scrub.

Her smile was worth it. "No. Feel free. Have it." There was laughter in her voice.

He eyed the bottle. "Now I don't have to feel guilty."

"Guilt-free foot scrub." She laughed then.

"Question. Why does your sister call you Pickle?"

"Oh. She had a speech thing when we were little. She used to say dill instead of deal, stuff like that. She went around telling people that we were twins and that made me a big deal. My speech therapist would ask, is Savannah a big dill pickle or a big deal? She thought it was funny so it's become my nickname."

"Huh. Well, okay then." He shrugged. "So, you're not here to talk about this." He set the foot scrub on the side table and sat beside her on the bed. "What are you here to talk about?"

"Um..." She cleared her throat and took a deep breath. "You and I... You're naked."

And she was pretty damn distracted by his chest. He didn't mind. He kinda liked the way she was looking at him. A whole hell of a lot. "I just got out of the shower."

"Right." She forced her gaze up. Dammit. The hunger in her eyes had him gripping the bedcover. "The foot scrub," her voice was soft and husky.

"Screw the foot scrub." He leaned forward, cradling her face in his hands. "I was hoping you'd come."

She leaned into him. "I had to."

His lips brushed over hers, pulling a groan from deep inside his chest. "You taste as sweet as I remember."

She was up on her knees as she slid her arms around his neck. "You remember?"

"Every damn thing." His lips sealed with hers, parting her lips and breathing her in. He felt it the minute she melted into him, her hands sliding up and into his hair and holding him close. He moved, sliding his arms around her waist and lifting her up and onto his lap.

He couldn't get enough of her mouth. Full and soft lips moving over his with a frenzy he understood. Her fingers twined in his hair, tugging him closer still. Her breathing picked up as she straddled him.

The crush of her breasts against his chest had him groaning again.

As hungry as he was for her, he wanted to slow things down. Some little voice in his head told him she'd wanted to talk… Talking wasn't going to happen as long as her nails were sliding down his back.

Her hands gripped the towel around his waist. She wriggled, an impatient grunt slipping from her lips and into his mouth. They could talk later.

His hands slid up the silky softness of her thighs, sliding her nightgown up as he went. The gown needed to go. She leaned back for him to pull it up and off and toss it aside. His memories hadn't done justice to her lush curves. The slide of her bare breasts against his chest had him throbbing against her. The curve of her ass fit his hands as he settled her close against him.

"Gus." She stared down at him, nodding. "Please."

"You're sure?" he rasped, barely able to hold back.

She arched her hips against him. "Please."

They came together suddenly, both of them moaning at the depth and force of the fit. He loved her moan. He loved the way she clung to his shoulders as she thrust against him. It was hard and hot and fast—without control or hesitation. That was what haunted him. How free she was. Savannah had no inhibition. She gave him pure pleasure, holding nothing back.

It didn't take long for his release to build. He wanted to hold on and make things last, but one look at her face, driven and clouded with desire, made that impossible. He gripped her hips and thrust into her, the power of his release emptying his lungs and draining his body. She bit into his shoulder, arching into him until she was shaking. He held on to her as her soft, broken cry rolled over him.

He lay back on the bed, pulling her gently beside him and tucking her against his side. He needed a minute to calm his heart and steady his breathing. Hell, he needed more than a minute. Loving Savannah wrung him out—and he had no complaints.

"I… I'm sorry," she gasped.

"I'm not." He turned his head, burying his nose in her hair.

She laughed softly. "No…me neither."

He hugged her close. "Happy to hear that."

She sighed, going soft against him. "Angus."

"Savannah." He ran his hand down her back. "Savannah suits."

"Chelsea didn't?" She looked up at him.

"Savannah is a better fit." He smoothed one long strand of hair from her shoulder. "I didn't imagine it."

"Imagine what?" Her clear eyes searched his.

"How beautiful you are. Or how good we are together." He kissed her.

She blinked, slowly stiffening in his arms. He felt it, saw it—the way she was withdrawing from him.

"What's wrong?" He ran his finger along her jaw.

"Nothing." Even her voice was distant.

"I call bullshit."

Her smile was reluctant, but she didn't relax.

"You can tell me." He tilted her chin up until their eyes locked. "I'm a good listener."

"I know." She blinked rapidly, then pressed her eyes shut. "I should go." She looked the way she had when she'd told him her name was Chelsea. Like she wasn't sure what to say.

"You can be honest with me." He hoped she would be.

She opened her mouth, then closed it. She was really struggling. "What if it's hard to hear?"

Were those tears in her eyes? "I can handle it." At least, he hoped he could handle it. He wasn't so good with tears. He propped himself up on an elbow.

"Angus…" She tugged his towel up to cover her. "I…" She stood, stooped for her nightgown, and tried to put it on without dropping the towel.

He stood. "Let me help."

"No…" She stepped back. "I can do it." The towel fell and her hands dropped to her stomach.

Angus watched her cheeks go red, but couldn't understand why she was fumbling with her gown or acting so jumpy. It wasn't like he'd never seen her naked before. He had—and thoroughly enjoyed every inch of her. She had a beautiful body.

There was a soft knock on the door. "Angus?" It was Chelsea.

Savannah shook her head and held her finger up to her lips.

He picked up the towel off the floor, waited for Savannah to hide in the bathroom, and cracked his bedroom door. "Hi."

"Hi." She shook her head. "I know she's in there." Her

words ran together. "I'm a little tipsy. I'm also hoping you two have finished your business because my dad is up and drinking, and he's been known to poke around. Because, you know, he's an ass."

"Seriously?" Angus knew Richard Barrett was a dick, but this was still a surprise.

"Yep. Wait, are you telling me it's unusual for a father to do bed checks on his adult daughters?" Chelsea feigned surprise. "Anyway, I've come to rescue my sister. Don't you know Savannah is a perfect child? I, on the other hand, know ways of sneaking around undetected by our self-important father."

"I'm here." Savannah slipped past him into the hall-way. She looked more frazzled than ever.

"Look at how messy your hair is." Chelsea giggled. "Let me guess, the talk didn't happen?"

"You're drunk, aren't you?" Savannah was frowning at her sister.

"A little." Chelsea held up her thumb and forefinger to illustrate.

Savannah looked horrified. "We should go."

"I told you." Chelsea gave him a head-to-toe look. "You got distracted—not that I blame you. You're going to have to tell him eventually."

What the hell does that mean? "Savannah—"

"Will be here tomorrow." Chelsea tugged Savannah's hand. "And he'll be dressed, so talking will be more likely to happen."

"Chelsea, could you please shut up," Savannah all but hissed. "Angus, tomorrow… We need to talk."

"I got that," he murmured, beyond confused. "Just answer one question. You *are* okay?"

Chelsea nudged Savannah. "You're right, he is sweet."

He didn't know what to make of the look on Savannah's face.

"Just tell him." Chelsea nudged Savannah back. "He can sleep on it and it'll give him time to calm down."

That didn't help the mounting pressure in his chest. "Okay, tell me."

A loud thump caused all three of them to jump.

"Hurry up. It's easy, Pickle. You say, I'm pregnant, and that's that," Chelsea whispered. "And, yes, *you* got her pregnant. Savannah is like a sex camel—she can go a long *long* time without sex. Excluding you." She grabbed Savannah's arm and pulled her stunned sister after her. "Close your door," Chelsea called back.

Angus closed the door and stood, frozen in place. Pregnant. Savannah was pregnant. Sonofabitch. With his baby. His. He slid down the door to sit. A baby. He was going to be a father. Him. It was a lot to take in.

And then there was Savannah. She was worried—so worried she'd hesitated to tell him. It ate at him. What exactly was she worried about? That he'd want nothing to do with the baby? Or that he would? How the hell was he supposed to sleep without knowing that?

Chapter Four

As far as long nights go, Savannah was pretty sure last night had been the longest night in the history of long nights. Not only had her sister dropped her news on Angus, she'd had to take care of Chelsea. She'd had to press a cold washcloth to her sister's forehead as Chelsea heaved up what must have been a bottle of whiskey before they both crawled into Savannah's bed to sleep. Rather, Chelsea slept. Savannah tossed and turned and tried to come up with something to ease her panic. So far, she'd had no luck.

The sun was streaming into her bedroom when Chelsea finally moved, groaned, and pressed a hand over her eyes. "Don't hate me," Chelsea murmured. "I know I screwed up, big-time."

"You did." She was too tired and frustrated to sugarcoat things.

Chelsea rolled to face Savannah, moaning. "You look awful."

"If you're trying to make amends, maybe start with something kind or flattering or not rude." Savannah turned her head on the pillow to look at her sister. "You look pretty rough yourself."

"You're gorgeous… But your eyes are all puffy and dark." Chelsea frowned.

"Surprisingly, I couldn't sleep."

"It's my fault." Chelsea scooched closer, draping her arm around Savannah and resting her head on her shoulder. "I'm sorry. I'm so, so sorry. It just came out."

"You were drunk." Savannah patted her sister's arm. Drinking was something Chelsea did. Like their dad. And neither of them handled their liquor well.

"I was." Chelsea nodded. "But still. I… I just blurted it out."

"I know. I was there." And she'd replayed the look on Angus's face most of the night. He'd been shocked, which was expected, but they hadn't stuck around for much else. Chelsea had been right, their father—also on a bender—had checked in on them not five minutes after they'd collapsed in Savannah's bed.

"Poor Angus." Chelsea moaned again. "Can you imagine how he feels? First, seeing you again was a surprise—but a good one, I'm sure. Then finding out you're pregnant with his kid—kids. I mean, talk about a hell of an evening."

Savannah couldn't stop the tears from coming then.

"Oh, Pickle." Chelsea hugged her tighter. "I'm not helping."

"No," Savannah sobbed. "You're not."

"Breakfast," Momma's cheery voice rang out as she backed into Savannah's bedroom. "Oh, goodness." She stood, breakfast tray in hand, staring at the two of them. "Whatever is the matter?"

"N-nothing." Savannah sat up, wiping at the tears, and hoping her mother hadn't heard anything. "I have…a migraine." Her mother was a frequent sufferer of migraines and would be instantly sympathetic, not suspicious.

Chelsea sat up, too, gripping her head and mumbling several expletives.

"That's not nothing." Their mother put down the tray and sat between them. "That's horrible. Would you like me to draw you a bath? That helps me sometimes."

"A bath would be great." Savannah kept wiping at the tears.

Momma smiled as she reached up to tuck Savannah's hair behind her ear. "I'll pull the curtains, too. Light doesn't help. And I'll make you some ginger tea. I swear it'll settle your stomach." She swallowed. "I mean, I always get nauseous when I have a migraine so—"

"Me, too." Savannah had a hard time meeting her mother's eyes.

"I'm here." Chelsea leaned against their mother. "I need attention. I feel bad, too."

Their mother laughed. "Migraine?" Momma disapproved of drinking. She felt so strongly about it, their parents now had separate bedrooms. Admitting to a hangover wasn't going to earn Chelsea a bit of sympathy from their mother.

"Let's go with that…" Chelsea sighed as their mother draped an arm over her shoulder.

"I think you two are too big to take a bath together, but I can get one going in your room if you like, Chels?" With a kiss on each of their foreheads, Momma stood, pulled the curtains closed, turned on one lamp in the far corner, and headed into Savannah's bathroom.

"We have the best mom." Chelsea sort of collapsed on

her side, her head in Savannah's lap. "You're going to be just like her," she whispered.

Savannah ran her fingers through her sister's short do. "I hope so."

When it came to mothering, she was the best. She'd been hands-on when they were little and she made a point to have special time with them now. From afternoon tea in town to shopping trips and spa days, she always made them both feel loved and cherished. If, however, their father was in the mix—she seemed to fade into the background. Chelsea said it was because Mom knew he'd talk over her and ignore what she said, so she didn't try anymore. It hurt to see Momma diminish herself for him.

"There's toast there." Momma pointed at the tray, wiping her hands on a towel. "Might not hurt you to have a piece before you get in the bath."

Savannah didn't argue. She nibbled on the dry corner and hoped her stomach would behave while Momma was still in the room.

"I'll be back with the tea in a bit." Momma held her hand out. "Come on, Chels, let's get your bath going, too."

"Oh, goody." Chelsea moved in slow motion as she stood. "Then, a nap?"

"Hopefully you two will be up for having lunch." Momma slid her arm around Chelsea's waist and, carefully, led them to the door. "Your father has a few of his Rodeo Board pals coming over. He wants to show off the new horses and give that nice young man, Angus McCarrick, some introductions."

Angus would appreciate that. In all their hours talking that long-ago night together, he'd mentioned his desire to grow their operation. He had a real passion for horses. He'd been animated when he'd talked about that moment of connection with a difficult horse or seeing a horse in sync with their rider and precipitating what came next. She couldn't remember ever feeling that way—about anything.

"Try to rest, Pickle." Momma blew her a kiss as she pulled the door shut behind them.

Sitting alone in a dark room didn't do much to brighten her mood. She lay back on her bed and rested her hands on her stomach. "I'm going to have to face him, you know?" She closed her eyes to concentrate. The flutters and rolling were faint and unpredictable. She was looking forward to more reassuring concrete solid kicks and movements. Whether or not this pregnancy was expected, she was happy she was going to be a mother. It was the rest of it that had her so terrified and uncertain. Her parents. Angus. What her life would look like once the world knew.

Dad might actually have a heart attack.

Her whole life, she'd gone out of her way to make her parents proud of her. Her father, especially. To earn one of his real smiles, a rarity, had filled her with such pride. The older she got, the fewer and more far between those real smiles became. He seemed to get harder and more jaded with each passing year. He stopped caring about their school events and birthdays—unless someone he deemed important or influential was going to be there. Her pageants were important, giving him exposure and more connections. He was disappointed that she wanted to give them up. *Now there's no choice.*

It was foolish to think that she could bring out the father of her childhood, but she couldn't let go of the idea that, somehow, someway, he was still inside. Chelsea told her to get over it and accept that their father was now an outright asshole. But trying to win his smile and approval had turned into a habit she didn't know how to break. Finding out about her pregnancy would probably take care of that.

Then she remembered. "The bath." She pushed off the bed and hurried into the bathroom. The bubbles were piled high, but the water wasn't spilling over the sides yet.

The smell of lavender and eucalyptus should have been soothing, but instead her stomach flipped and Savannah ran for the toilet to throw up her dry toast breakfast.

Considering Angus hadn't got much sleep, things with Mr. Barrett and his top ranch hands went well. He had no choice but to set all thoughts of Savannah and the pregnancy aside and focus on work—for now. Richard Barrett might be a proud sonofabitch, but he was smart enough to understand that learning the commands would make him look good in the saddle. Once the older man's well-dressed friends started showing up to watch, looking good was of the upmost importance to Mr. Barrett. It helped that the horses were well trained and responsive. He'd handpicked these four horses for that reason.

Angus spent the morning rubbing shoulders with a judge, a congressman, an investment banker, and others who served on the board of the Fort Worth Rodeo Board with Mr. Barrett. They weren't all ranchers but most of them liked to pretend they were—and they had the money and inclination to buy the tools of the trade even if they didn't really need them. That included cutting horses—which Angus would be all too happy to provide.

He'd planned on staying with the horses and working through any questions or concerns the ranch hands might have for him, but Mr. Barrett steered him in the direction of the big house, along with his guests.

"Y'all go on ahead into the den. Barb has some snacks

and drinks set up, and Lana will be along shortly, with the girls." He pointed the way.

Girls as in Savannah? His chest collapsed in on his lungs as he glanced toward the stairs.

"I figure we should settle our accounts before we settle down for lunch? I like to get the money out of the way." Mr. Barrett clapped Angus on the shoulder. "If that's agreeable with you?"

Business. He took a deep breath. *This was business.* Whatever was going on with Savannah could wait another ten minutes, surely. "Yessir."

"Good. Then let's head to my office."

As soon as he crossed the threshold of Mr. Richard Barrett's office, Angus understood what it meant to be intimidated. It was intentional, of course. If he wasn't so out of sorts, he'd probably have found the number of deer heads, antlers, and tusks mounted on the wall behind Mr. Barrett's imposing desk funny.

"Have a seat." Mr. Barrett indicated the single chair opposite his desk before going around the massive wooden desk to sit. He pulled a checkbook from a desk drawer and glanced at Angus. "I'll make the check out to you."

Angus stared around him. He'd never be comfortable in this environment. Impersonal. More a showplace than a home. He sat and tried not to fidget.

"Impressive?" Mr. Barrett nodded, his gaze sweeping the room. "Like you, I've worked hard to get where I am. I respect a hardworking man. A driven man, putting in the sweat equity and time to ensure their success, is rare nowadays. But it takes a shrewd businessman to recognize a golden opportunity and grab it, before that opportunity passes them by." Mr. Barrett ripped the check out and held it toward him.

He took the check, read the number, and almost fell out of his chair. Something hard and cold settled in the pit of his stomach.

"You take that and the guarantee that you'll get more high-dollar clients than you could ever imagine." Mr. Barrett sat back in his chair, his steely eyes hard. "You take that, end things with my daughter, and never speak to her again. That means no further contact with her or her children of any kind. Ever. Everyone comes out ahead." He paused. "Otherwise, you'll head home with your horses and no check. Whatever claim you make on Savannah's children will land you in court. I'll use my arsenal of lawyers to keep things tied up until you're bankrupt, with nothing and no one to show for it."

By the time the man was finished talking, Angus could hear his blood roaring in his ears. The check was shaking because his hands were shaking. His throat was too tight to breathe, let alone speak. Richard Barrett was trying to pay him off? The man was giving him a seven-figure check to walk away from Savannah and the baby he'd just learned he was having? He set the check on the desk and stood, his mind ping-ponging back and forth until he was dizzy. He kept coming back to one question. Over and over. "Does Savannah know about this?" Did he really want to know the answer?

Mr. Barrett's grin was hard. "What do you think? Let's just say Savannah has entrusted me to…take care of this. It's my job, Angus. I'll always take care of her. What was it you said? Family first? I couldn't agree more." He tapped his fingers on the edge of the desk. "You show-ing up was unexpected. She's marrying Greg Powell— you met him—that's all arranged. He's a good man. He cares about Savannah a great deal. He'll take care of her and their family in a way you never could." He patted the edge of his desk. "You need some time to think it over?"

Hell no. The only thing he needed time for was to climb over the damn desk and knock the smug smile off Richard Barrett's condescending face.

"I want you to think long and hard about what I'm saying here. You're a decent man. I can see that. You might feel obligated to do right by her." Barrett used air quotes around the word *right*. "But that would take away any future she has. She's meant for more than being a wife and mother. She's got aspirations and dreams. She wants to make a difference in the world. You can't give her that. And the children? Here, they'll have the best schools. Travel. You name it. Their lives won't begin and end with a ranch full of horses. A real father would want to give their children the world, not limit their opportunities."

Richard Barrett was evil. A bastard. So why the hell did the man's words make some sort of twisted sense? The man wasn't lying. He did want what was best for his child—

There was a knock on his office door, followed by Lana Barrett saying, "Richard, darling, lunch is ready."

Angus couldn't move. He was frozen. His hands, white-knuckled, gripped the arms of the chair. If he let go, he couldn't be accountable for his actions. He was fuming. Raging. Breaking.

"On my way." Richard stood and came around the desk. "Join us for lunch when you're ready. Judge Frye is keen on getting a horse for his daughter. I'm sure you have just the right one." He patted Angus on the shoulder and left, the click of the door echoing in the deafening silence of the room.

Angus stared straight ahead, past the antlers and tusks and glass-eyed deer heads out the window to the bright green fields beyond. Green fields—because they were watered. Because nothing here was real or natural. Because there was enough money to make things how Barrett wanted them, not how things were meant to be.

Did that include Savannah?

Barrett said as much. He was taking care of it for her—it, as in him. But, dammit, last night she'd said she'd wanted to talk to him. She'd come to his room to talk to him. She'd wanted him…and she'd made love to him.

It didn't add up. The girl he'd spent the night with had poured her heart and soul out. Her constant pursuit of perfection and her fear of failure—because of her father. She was a romantic and wanted the white picket fence and all that and believed loyalty was important. Meaning, she wouldn't have slept with him if she was engaged to Greg Powell.

If the girl he'd spent the night with had only lied about her name. What if it had all been a lie?

Before he went off half-cocked, he needed to calm down. Was he seriously considering taking the check and the opportunity Richard Barrett was offering him? How could he walk away and pretend he wasn't going to be a father? It went against everything he stood for. Family was everything.

Then there was Savannah. This talk they needed to have. If there was even the slightest chance that he and Savannah could be a family, they owed it to the kid to try, didn't they?

If Barrett did what he said with the whole possible financial ruin thing, it would make things a lot harder for him, for Savannah, and their family.

Damn Richard Barrett.

He stood, his gaze landing on the check. He'd never seen that big a number in his life. If he worked hard every day for the rest of his life, he'd never earn that number. Few could. Richard Barrett hadn't even blinked.

He pulled his phone from his pocket and dialed his brother, Dougal.

"Hello?" Dougal answered. "Do I need to come bail you out?"

"The day's still young." Angus ran his hand over his head. "I don't think you can get me out of this."

"Talk." Dougal wasn't a big talker.

"You remember the girl? The Rustler's Five concert?"

"The one you haven't stopped talking about?" Dougal sighed. "Lemme guess, you ran into her."

Angus chuckled. "And she's pregnant."

The line went completely silent.

"Her dad, our big client, Richard Barrett, offered me, us, two and half million dollars and business referrals if I walk away." He swallowed, his anger choking off his words. Until now, he'd been too shocked to fully appreciate the full offensiveness of the man's proposition.

Still silence.

"I didn't knock him on his ass," he ground out, imagining just how gratifying that would have been.

"You didn't?" His brother was pissed. It took a lot to get Dougal pissed. "I'm impressed."

"He made it pretty damn clear business would suffer if I didn't take his offer. He's a real sonofabitch." It helped talking through it. Sort of. His anger had been in check before.

"What are you going to do?" Dougal's voice was pitched low with anger.

He knew. It was easy. He wasn't that man. "I can't walk away." He ran his hand over his head. "I need to talk to Savannah. Hopefully, she'll be more reasonable than Barrett."

Dougal grumbled something under his breath. "Away from the father."

Angus nodded, taking in the view again. "Our way of life is likely to be an adjustment for her." She'd grown up with maids and every material thing at her fingertips. He and Dougal still burned toast and drank two-day-old coffee warmed in the microwave. There was dog hair on the furniture and his favorite recliner had duct tape around the arm to hide the hole his little dog, Gertie, had made when she was a chew-happy puppy.

"Don't start getting ahead of yourself. Talk to her first." Dougal sighed. "I shoulda come with you."

"I'll be home soon enough." Angus took a deep breath. "How's Willow doing?"

"She's fine. She's a tough ol' girl." The only time Dougal sounded that gentle was when he was talking about his big black Lab, Willow. She'd been out with Dougal, clearing brush, and chased a rabbit into a clump of cactus—getting a snout full of needles and one close to her eye. The vet said she'd heal up fine, but Angus told Dougal to stay home anyway—his brother would be too worried about the dog to be of much use.

Angus was quick to offer up reassurance. "Like you said, she's tough."

"That she is." He cleared his throat. "Don't let that bastard rattle you. You do what you know is right and I'll back you."

Angus breathed out a sigh of relief. It wasn't a surprise to hear Dougal say as much, but he'd needed to hear it all the same—especially if his actions did impact their livelihood. "See you tomorrow."

"Yep." And Dougal hung up.

Angus shoved his phone into his back pocket. How the hell was he supposed to sit through lunch without causing a scene? He'd never been one to sit on what he was feeling. Hell, working with Barrett and his friends this morning had been hard enough—worrying over Savannah, the pregnancy, and all that was left unsaid. That was before Barrett had gone and showed his true colors.

He ran his hand through his hair, took a deep breath, and let himself out of Barrett's office. He followed the rumble of conversation down the hall, but couldn't bring himself to go inside. If he was going to keep a cool head, he'd be wise to keep his distance from Richard Barrett—for now, anyway.

Lana Barrett came around the end of the hallway, saw him, and stopped. She gave him a long, thorough inspection—one that made him suspect she knew exactly what was going on—before she asked, "Not hungry, Mr. McCarrick?"

"I was taught to clean up before sitting down at the table. Especially a table as nicely set as yours, ma'am." He hesitated, wishing Savannah had shared more about her mother.

"I appreciate that, Mr. McCarrick. Manners are overlooked too often these days." She didn't reach for the door or move; she was still studying him.

He tested the water. "Is there something you want to ask me, ma'am? I'm an open book."

"I do have a question, Mr. McCarrick, but it might be a bit personal." She waited for him to nod. "My husband talked to you about what I told him?"

He hesitated. "And that would be?"

She lowered her voice. "That you are the biological father of my grandchild?"

He nodded.

"And, what, exactly, did he say?" She crossed her arms over her chest.

Well, damn. "He made it clear what my options were."
He wasn't sure how to go on. For all he knew, Mrs. Barrett had been the one to tell her husband what to say. She
didn't come across that way, but Angus wasn't feeling all
that confident in his people-reading skills.

"Let me guess, my way or the highway? My husband
usually gets what he wants." Her eyes, so like Savannah's,
narrowed.

Not this time. Of course, it wasn't up to him. That was
why he needed to talk to Savannah. Alone. To know what
she wanted. He hoped like hell she'd give them a chance.

She went back to studying him. "I've never seen my
daughter light up the way she did when she first saw you,
Mr. McCarrick. I'd like to think well of you."

"I'd like that, too, ma'am." He hoped like hell he wasn't
making a mistake as he went on, speaking from the heart.
"I'd like to do right by Savannah—by my baby—if she'll
have me."

Chapter Five

"Your daddy says we should be expecting a wedding invitation soon?" Judge Frye whispered.

Savannah had years of experience when it came to keeping her features blank but pleasant. "Oh? That's news to me, Judge." She hoped her smile wasn't as brittle as it felt. "Normally, that means an engagement."

He chuckled. "We're all expecting you and Powell Junior to marry, naturally."

Naturally.

"You two have been thick as thieves since you were both knee-high to a grasshopper." He kept on chuckling. "That boy needs to hurry up before some other fella comes along and catches your eye."

Not likely. How many men would be excited to court and marry a pregnant woman? A woman pregnant with triplets, no less? She had yet to see how the babies' father was going to react to the fact there was three of them—

after just finding out he was going to be a father... For the fifth time, her gaze swept the table. Still no Angus.

"Greg is a dear friend." Which was true. "Would you like more potato salad?" She held her breath and offered the carnival glass serving dish. The smell wasn't sitting right with her stomach. Then again, not much did.

"Don't mind if I do." Judge Frye took the dish and added a large serving to his plate.

Thanks to Momma, she'd had breakfast in her room. While she'd appreciated the time to herself, she'd missed a chance to see Angus. Seeing him was key. She had no idea what he was thinking or feeling after Chelsea had dropped the news on him. Now he was nowhere to be found and she couldn't help but worry. Well, add to her worries. Worrying was all she'd done since she'd come home from her doctor's office with a black-and-white set of grainy ultrasound photos and a bottle of prenatal vitamins.

Momma came and went, dishes were cleared, and new courses brought in, Chelsea kept testing Dad's patience, and just when Savannah had almost given up hope, Angus walked in. *Finally.*

"Sorry I'm late." Angus took a seat next to Chelsea. "Didn't feel right sitting down at such a fine table without cleaning up first."

"I'll have a plate made up for you." Momma stood and left, all smiles.

Her attempts not to stare at him were an utter failure.

He was so handsome. Sitting among her father's friends, he stood out. He didn't spend his days with trainers and stylists and wearing high-dollar clothes to fit a part. He earned his physical prowess through hard work—he was confident in his own skin and his abilities and, oh, so sexy. Just thinking about the touch of his hands on her skin sent a shiver along her skin.

"Your wife is quite the hostess. And as lovely as ever." Judge Frye lifted his cut-glass iced-tea tumbler in honor of their mother.

"I'm a lucky man," Dad agreed, his gaze falling briefly on Angus.

Savannah didn't miss the look. It wasn't a good look. It was hard—and full of judgment. The kind of look she'd seen on her father's face when he was discussing something unpleasant. It set a jagged knot in her throat and her stomach churning.

"How did it go with the horses?" Chelsea shot Angus a dazzling smile. "Was Dad a difficult student?"

"It went well." Angus smiled back. "Your father knows how to handle himself. No fear—a horse can sense that. They're intuitive animals." He leaned back as Momma set a food-laden plate on the table before him. "Thank you. I hadn't meant for you to go to any trouble, Mrs. Barrett."

So sweet and considerate. That was Angus. Angus, who wasn't looking her way.

"No trouble at all." Momma returned to her seat. "Richard's father used to say hard work deserves a good meal."

"My mother would agree with that." Angus ate with gusto—never once acknowledging Savannah.

All she needed was some sign. The teeniest hint as to what he was thinking would help. Or had last night's news so upset him that he couldn't look at her? Maybe he'd pack up his things and go? That would make things easier. *And 100 percent awful.* She speared a green bean on her plate, but couldn't bring herself to eat it.

Conversation drifted from upcoming charity events to football stats and more. Try as she might, Savannah couldn't concentrate on any of it. She smiled and nodded when there was a pause, but for all she knew smiling and nodding was the last thing she should be doing. When dessert was over, her patience was at an end.

Thankfully, Chelsea's twin senses must have been tingling, because she was up and announcing, "Momma, Savannah and I have a mani-pedi to get to. You gentlemen enjoy your afternoon."

This was news to her, but she didn't argue.

It took fifteen minutes for the three of them to extract themselves from the dining room, but Chelsea was a woman on a mission.

"Crap on a cracker, those men can talk." Chelsea was shaking her head.

"Chelsea, that's not very nice." But Momma was smiling.

Chelsea snorted. "Momma, if you think that was bad, be happy I didn't say what I was really thinking."

"It did seem like the longest lunch." Savannah glanced back at the dining room door, feeling a flicker of guilt for leaving Angus to fend for himself.

"Poor Angus McCarrick will earn whatever connections he makes before he leaves tomorrow." Chelsea voiced what she was thinking.

"Don't you worry about Mr. McCarrick." Momma looked quite pleased with herself. "I sense he's made of sturdy stock."

"You do?" Maybe it was the way her father had been sizing up Angus, but Savannah was picking up on a few things herself.

"What are you up to?" Chelsea tugged the both of them into the small study and carefully closed the door behind them.

"Whatever do you mean?" Momma's brows rose but her cheeks were stained pink.

Savannah sat, her nerves too frayed to hold back a second longer. "Momma, you know. I know you know."

"I suspected. You don't get sick, Pickle. You've been so tired. And you've been wearing looser clothes." Momma sat opposite her. "And then I overheard the two of you talking. I know."

"Shit." Chelsea perched on the coffee table between them.

"And Dad knows?" Savannah forced the words out.

"He does." Momma's smile faltered then. "I… I panicked. I'm sorry. I should have talked to you two first. I was just so…so surprised."

"*Wait.* Dad knows? Whoa, whoa, whoa. How is Angus alive?" Chelsea leaned forward, staring at their mother in shock.

"Let's not worry about your father for the moment." Momma patted Chelsea's knee before turning to Savannah. "What I really want to know is what you want, sweet girl. What's in your heart?"

Savannah held her breath, her mother's question pressing in until she blurted out, "I don't know. I don't. But I want the babies."

"Babies?" Momma's eyes widened.

"Three." Chelsea held up three fingers—on both hands. "One, two, three."

"Yes. I see." Momma blinked. "Goodness. Are you all right? Are they all right?"

"Yes. So far, we are all good." Savannah took a deep breath. "I want them very much. I'm happy I'm expecting and that I'm out of the first trimester and they're safe." She cradled her stomach. "But I don't know what's best for them or me or if I'll be a good mother. And how can you tell me not to worry about Dad? He's…Dad. He's already telling people to expect a *wedding invitation* for Greg and me."

Momma reached up and tucked a strand of hair behind Savannah's ear. "Sweetie, let's back up. You being happy is the best place to start."

"And what do you mean you don't know if you'll be a good mother? You've been mothering me since we were in the womb." Chelsea snorted.

Savannah shot her sister a look.

"Huh, I guess that's not exactly comforting?" Chelsea giggled. "It's not your fault I'm compelled to rebel against Dad."

"And you do it so well, sweetie." Momma smiled at Chelsea.

That had all three of them laughing.

"Your sister and I will go get a mani-pedi. You go on out to the barn until you get a chance to talk to Angus. He'll be packing up to head home tomorrow." She shook her head. "Call me old-fashioned, but I believe the two of you need to work through what's best for all of you. Not me, not your father, not Chelsea, or Greg. We might all think we have the best of intentions, but this is one of those times when only you and Angus have any say-so in what happens next. And, whatever that is, I will support your decision. No matter what your father says or does. You hear me?" She drew Savannah into a strong embrace.

"Who knew you were such a badass, Momma?" Chelsea hugged them, too. "You know you can count on me, Pickle."

Savannah held on to the two people closest to her heart. Until now, she'd felt alone and lost. Then again, until now, Momma had tended to hold her peace and follow Dad's lead. She was so glad her mother had chosen now to speak up.

"Now, we'll all leave together." Momma stood, smoothing out the front of her houndstooth-print wool skirt. "As soon as you're ready."

Savannah grabbed her purse and left with them. They dropped her at the barn and headed off into town while she settled into the hayloft to jot notes for her talk with Angus. She wanted to be clearheaded and well-spoken when he showed up looking all manly and irresistible. Whatever else was between them, the attraction was undeniable. Or was it? Maybe learning she was pregnant had killed his desire. He hadn't spared her a single glance through lunch. *Stop.* There was no point speculating what he was or wasn't thinking. Until she spoke to him, all she was doing was making things worse. *I'll find out the truth soon enough.*

Angus sat on a hay bale, legs propped up, whittling on a piece of wood, biding his time. He'd packed up his saddle and tack. The trailer had been washed. He'd made sure the wheels were good and checked all the gauges on the truck, too. He'd run out of things to occupy himself with, but he wouldn't wake Savannah. She was too peaceful. She needed sleep. She and the baby. His mother used to go on and on about how hard her pregnancies had been on her—if she was sleeping, she needed it. He'd wait.

He was flipping through the newest *Ranch & Farm* catalog for the third time when she finally yawned and rubbed her eyes.

"Angus?" She sat up then, eyes wide and startled.

"Hey, hey." He dropped the catalog. "Didn't mean to scare you."

"No, you didn't. I was waiting for you." She blinked, running a hand over her hair.

"You were? That's a relief." It was, too. He was clinging to the hope that Richard Barrett had said all he'd said to scare Angus off—that he hadn't been speaking for Savannah.

"Believe it or not, I don't normally take a nap in the barn." Damn, but he could look at that smile all day.

"I would." He stood and moved to her side, sitting on the blanket she'd spread out over the hay. "As haylofts go, this is pretty comfy."

"Is it?" She sounded nervous.

He *was* nervous. "I'm guessing you want to talk?" His eyes met hers. "About…the baby." He stumbled over the word.

"Babies," she whispered.

His heart, already clipping along at above average rate, skidded to a halt. "Come again?"

"Babies." She spoke a little louder now but there was a definite waver in her voice. "More than one. Three, actually."

"Three?" He'd never squeaked before. Not once. The word definitely resembled a squeak. He cleared his throat and tried again. "Three." Three was a hell of a lot more than one. Or two. He had two hands. Three meant he'd be outnumbered. It was pretty damn terrifying. "Three," he murmured again.

She nodded, her smile fading. "Does it make a difference?"

"No. It's a surprise. All of this… But, no." He rubbed his hands on his thighs to stop himself from reaching for her. "Not at all."

She stared at his hands long and hard. "I… I thought maybe you'd panicked and left—"

"Oh, I am panicking." He chuckled. "Trust me. But I figure we're in the same boat there."

She nodded.

They were quiet then. It was an easy silence. The horses knickered and snorted below. The ranch hands were talking somewhere a way off. The call of a dove and a finch or two sang from the nearby oaks. After a time, his heart wasn't about to launch itself out of his chest.

"I guess I should talk first?" Savannah's eyes met his. "I'm not certain where to start or what to say. I've been trying to figure out what's the best, the right, thing to do."

He nodded. "And I wasn't part of that equation until now."

"It's not that I didn't want you to be." She turned a bit so she was facing him. "I didn't know where to start or how to look for Gus with the kind eyes and strong shoulders." She shrugged.

Strong shoulders and kind eyes, huh? Is that how she thought of him? He could live with that. "But you would have looked for me? If you'd known my name?" Her answer was important to him.

She didn't hesitate. "Of course. You have every right to know and be a part of…this. If that's what you want. I'd never force you to… I'd understand if you don't."

He could breathe easier now.

"Is that what you want?" She was looking nervous again.

"I'm not trying to dodge the question, Savannah. But I'd like to know what you want, first. You told me you don't have your thoughts and wishes taken into consideration all that often. Now that I've met your father, I see what you mean." He paused. "No disrespect to him…" Hell, he had nothing but disrespect for her father but he didn't want to influence her.

"That's very considerate of you. He is a man of strong opinions."

Her father was a pile of cow shit, but he'd keep that to

himself. The less Barrett was involved in this conversation, the better. "I think this is one of those times when your opinion comes first." He waited, crossing his arms over his chest.

"I was told I'd never have children—not without medical intervention. And even then, it was unlikely. I was devastated. I want a big family. I've always wanted a big family." She shook her head. "Anyway, I went to the doctor last month expecting the worst. And then I found out I was going to be a mother. It was such a surprise. The best surprise." She was all but glowing now, her smile so big it warmed him up through and through. "It's a gift, you know? I'll try to be the best mother I can be." Her joy was palpable. And beautiful. "But I guess I'd always assumed babies, if there were any, would come after I'd found my…husband. Or partner. It's what I want. The whole package deal—a husband, kids, all that. Well, what I wanted."

Did she realize she'd taken his hand? "I get that. I think that's what most people want." He glanced down at their hands, noting how silky-soft and small hers was. His was big and coarse and rough. The contrast was stark.

"We're strangers," she whispered.

"Almost." He ran his thumb along her wrist. Her shiver set him on fire. "I know a few things about you."

Her words were halting. "But our lives are so different."

Which was true. "I do have a question."

She nodded.

"It's been said a time or two that there's already someone special in your life." Namely, Greg Powell. "Is this true?"

Her hand pulled free and she stood. "Are you… I wouldn't sleep with *you* if I was involved with someone else." Savannah Barrett, angry, was a sight to see. She was fuming, staring at him with such contempt.

He was smiling as he stood. "Good." Richard Barrett was a dick.

"You… Are you…" She sputtered. "Are you involved? I'm not interested in being the other woman."

"I would never ask you to be. There are a few things I consider unforgivable, Savannah. Cheating is one." He paused. "I was told you were marrying Junior Powell. I figured I'd clear that up."

"Oh. *Oh.*" Her features smoothed. "And, you're not… you don't have a someone special?"

"No. Lifelong bachelor." *Shit.* He hadn't meant to say that. Not when he knew what needed to be done. "Well… Now, I guess I do. I have three very special someone specials." He nodded at her stomach. "I want to be a part of their lives."

Savannah stared up at him. "You would?"

"If that's what you want?" He sighed. "We can figure this out, together. We are in this together, after all. I want to do right by you—by my babies. I meant it when I said family comes first."

"What does that mean?" It was a whisper.

"It means…" What? He couldn't give her the picture-perfect family she wanted. He didn't love her. She didn't love him. "Come home with me. Let's do the right thing." It was hard to say what came next. "Let's get married. Try to make it work for them." He heard how unsteady he sounded, but there was no help for it. Marriage hadn't been part of his five-year plan—if ever. He liked his life as it was. *Now that's all going to change.*

"Marriage?" She didn't look happy. Not one little bit.

He pressed his hand to her stomach. "We're a family now." It was that simple.

"I… I don't want to get married because I'm pregnant, Angus." Her hand pressed over his, the swell of her stomach filling his palm. "I get that you want to do the right thing, but I want the real thing. Us, getting married now, ensures that won't happen."

Which wasn't what he wanted to hear. He didn't *want* to get married. But no matter what happened, he didn't want his kids thinking they didn't give it their all to be a family. No matter what Barrett said or did, Angus had to live with himself and that outweighed any threat the man had thrown at him. "Where does that leave us?"

"On the same team. You want to be involved. I want you to be involved. We…we co-parent?" She looked just as uncertain as he felt.

"Co-parent?" He shifted from one foot to the next. "Can we co-parent at my place?" He was pretty damn sure Barrett would make it impossible if she stayed here.

"I think that sounds like a good idea." It was a small smile, but it was a smile. She held out her hand. "Shake?" Her gaze drifted across his mouth.

He grinned. "I'd prefer a kiss." These babies weren't the only thing that bonded them. There was desire, too. A hell of a lot of it.

She smiled. "Deal." She slid her arms around his neck and stood on tiptoe. "Will we co-parent with benefits? Like friends with benefits?"

"I'm open to negotiations." He chuckled. "We are the ones setting the rules, aren't we?"

"Yes." It was a light kiss. "Yes, we are." There was no denying her hunger for him. She melted against him and he welcomed it.

He didn't know what the future looked like, but they were in it together. He'd do his best by her, his best by their children, and listen to and respect her wishes. Respect wasn't love, but it was something. And, if they were going to stand a chance, the sooner they started building a foundation, the better.

Chapter Six

Angus wanted to do the right thing. She should be happy. She should have expected as much. He was a good guy. He'd done the honorable thing and proposed. And it made her want to cry. This wasn't how she'd pictured her proposal. Of course, she hadn't pictured being pregnant with triplets when she was proposed to, either.

But he was kissing her now—which was enough to short-circuit any real thought beyond the feel of his mouth on hers and his hands firm against her back. She'd never been this happily consumed by touch before. Not just physical, either. All he had to do was look at her and she was a boneless mass of quivering want. She should be embarrassed. Instead, she held on and enjoyed the scratch of his facial hair.

When the kissing stopped, he held her close. His thickly muscled arms felt just right around her. And, for the first time since she'd left the doctor's office, it was easier to breathe.

"This went really well." Her words were muffled against his chest.

"You were expecting something different?" His tone was low and soothing.

"I didn't know what to expect."

He held her away from him, his auburn brow furrowing.

"Okay, fine, I was expecting you to pack your bags and leave." She winced.

"I'm glad to disappoint you." He was frowning now, his arms sliding from her waist. "It does sting to hear how you thought I was going to react."

She held on to his arm. "It's not a reflection on you. More me, really." She backpedaled furiously. "I wouldn't blame you for leaving. Between learning I was pregnant, which is a lot, and my dad with his 'all about the Barrett family' speech at dinner, being significant and blah, blah, blah. How he has a specific future in mind for me—"

"Like you marrying Powell Junior." Angus was watching her. "Or someone like him. Not like me."

"Like that, yes. Which has nothing to do with you." She went on. "It's him. He's…he's so caught up in the way *he* sees things. *His* plans. I was worried he'd talk to you before I could and, I don't know, get you to see things his way? He tends to get what he wants." She winced again. "I'm making him sound like some sort of mafia kingpin or something."

"Or something." The corner of his mouth kicked up. "Mafia kingpin, huh?"

She rolled her eyes. "I don't know what the right term is. Obviously."

"How would your father convince me to do what he wanted?" Angus was watching her closely.

"Maybe he'd make you an offer you can't refuse sort

of thing?" She knew it was a bad joke, but she was only partly teasing. "I'm kidding. Sort of." She took a deep breath. "I don't know. I don't want to know. He's a jerk, but he is my dad."

Angus's expression softened then.

Her hand caught his. "I'm still not sure that came out right, Angus. I didn't mean to imply anything about you. I'm sorry."

"Like you said, we're near strangers. It'll take time for us to figure each other out." His eyes crinkled from his smile. "Words are easy. Actions are what matter."

And just like that, he was sexier than ever. *Is that possible?* It would seem so. She resisted the urge to fan herself.

"What?" One brow cocked. "What's that look mean?"

"Look?" She blew out a deep breath.

"That look." He pointed at her. "The one you're wearing right now."

Normally, she was good at hiding her feelings, so his calling her out caught her off guard. "Honestly?"

"Always." He nodded. "That's something else. I'd rather hear the truth, even if it's not easy to hear or say. Agreed?"

She nodded. *Don't say it.* She couldn't say it. People didn't actually say things like, "I think you...you are incredibly...sexy." And, yet, now she'd said it. Her cheeks were on fire.

"Oh?" He ran his finger along her lower lip. "Well, since we're being honest... Every time I look at you, I want you more."

She leaned into his touch. "We have that in common." The idea of falling into the hay with him right then and there sounded oh-so appealing.

"We do." He shook his head, but he was grinning. "As

much as I'd like to kiss you, I think there's more talking to be done first."

"There is?" She'd rather do some kissing.

"Deciding we want to give this a chance is one thing. How we go about it is another." He cleared his throat, his own cheeks pinkening. "I'd really like us to get married, Savannah."

She opened her mouth to argue, but he kept going.

"If we're committed to making this work, then we should do it right." He said it as if it was the next obvious step.

There it was again. That word. *Right.* It set a lump in her throat. Why did the word have to be so *wrong*? "But marriage is…" Forever. Permanent. Legal.

"A commitment." He ran his fingers through his hair. "I don't want you, or anyone, thinking this is a game or some temporary thing. If we go into it thinking that, it's not real. I have every intention of being there for my kid—kids. I want them to know we gave it our all. They deserve that."

She was reevaluating his sexy status all over again. As in, confirming he was the sexiest man in the known universe—and probably beyond. Men didn't talk this way. At least, she'd never encountered one that did. Angus spoke his mind in a way that stirred her body and her heart. He made a powerful argument. "I can't, Angus. We can't. We can do right by our kids without sacrificing any chance of future happiness. A future that includes real love."

The muscle in his jaw clenched tight.

"I understand what you're saying. I do. But what if we get married and you meet the love of your life? Or I meet the man of my dreams? Then what? We let that opportunity pass us by because we're doing the right thing? I can't do that, Angus. I don't think it's wrong to want to be loved."

His nod was reluctant.

"You should want the same. You said your parents were happily married."

"They were," he murmured. "But I hadn't thought about getting married, Savannah. I never thought I was the marrying type. I like being a bachelor." He shrugged.

Which made his willingness to marry her all the sweeter. She was more than a little overcome. The last twenty-four hours had been one long roller-coaster ride of emotions. Up and around, upside-down and backward. Every once in a while, she knew which way was up. Now was not one of those moments. It took effort to get the words out. "I will not marry you, Angus McCarrick." She swallowed, so nervous she was shaking. "Because you don't want to get married, and I want to marry for love. And, just because we're going to be parents, doesn't mean we have to give up on what we want."

"You're one stubborn woman." But there was a reluctant smile on his face.

"I'll take that as a compliment." She was still shaking, but she smiled back at him. "So, no marrying. Yes to going home with you so we can get to know each other and figure out this whole co-parenting thing."

"I believe you said something about co-parenting with benefits?" He was grinning now.

"I did." Her cheeks were hot. "I can't believe I said that." Further proof that he brought out her wild side.

"I'm glad you said it." He ran his fingers along her cheek. "No debating that one."

She shivered from the touch, leaning into him. "We're good? We have a plan?" Why did her voice waver? This was what she wanted.

He nodded and stepped closer, pulling her back into his arms. "It's going to be okay, Savannah." He ran his hand down her back. "Like you said, we're in this together. A team. Whatever happens, it will be okay."

She rested her head against his chest. His heartbeat was steady and strong—like his arms around her waist. It'd be all too easy to get used to this. Straightforward communication. Honesty. Strength. But they'd have to be strong enough to stand up to her father. As terrifying as that was, what choice did they have?

She glanced at her phone to check the time. "Time's almost up. Chelsea and Momma covered for me so I could talk to you without Dad interfering. I'm supposed to be getting a mani-pedi with them." She eased from his hold. "Chelsea's loving all the spylike stuff." She took a deep breath. Momma would probably be on his side—disappointed that there were no wedding bells in the imminent future. She'd make her understand. Chelsea would support her. But would that really help? Her brain was already spinning. "Are we leaving in the morning?"

"I'm packed and ready." He nodded. "If you think you need more time—"

"No. I'll be ready to go. We can tell him, everyone, tonight at dinner?" She hoped having the whole family present would help rein in her father's reaction. Her eyes were stinging then. It was too much to hope her father would support their decision. Unlike Momma, he should be thrilled they weren't planning a wedding. "Going with you will give us the time to figure things out on our own. Dad... Well, you know Dad."

"He might not want to hear it, but this isn't about him." He tilted her chin up. "This is what you want?"

Without a doubt. "It is."

The crunch of tire on gravel was unmistakable.

Angus let her go and peered through the hayloft door. "Looks like your ride is here."

She ran a hand over her hair and smoothed her champagne-colored tunic over her long, stretchy straight skirt. "Any hay anywhere? I don't want Chelsea's imagination running away with her."

The corner of his mouth quirked up again. He made a slow circle around her, plucking one piece of straw from her hair. "You look beautiful." He pressed a hand to her stomach again. "I'll see you all soon."

The sight of his hand on her stomach had her eyes stinging again. He was right. Maybe everything would be okay. She stood on tiptoe, kissed his cheek, and hurried down the stairs and out the barn door to her sister's waiting SUV.

"How did it go?" Chelsea asked the moment she'd closed her door.

"It went well." She blew out a deep breath. "I'm going home with him tomorrow."

"No shit?" Chelsea gasped.

"Chelsea, please." But Momma sounded pleased. "Is that all? And where is home? How far away will you be?"

"I don't know." They'd been so focused on coming up with a plan that the details had slipped by. "I'll find out. But, yes, that's it, Momma. For now."

Momma's sigh was disappointed.

"Probably a good idea to get out of town." Chelsea glanced at her in the rearview mirror. "You're not going to be able to hide your baby bump for long."

"What about Christmas?" Momma's voice was tight. "That's only two weeks away."

"I know." And she was sad she'd miss the holidays with her family. "But I'm going with Angus tomorrow. It's for the best. In case Dad—"

"Blows his top? Loses his cool? Explodes?" Chelsea stopped. "Sorry."

"That's very sensible, Savannah." Momma reached around to take her hand. "We can talk and check in over Skype or whatever. It won't be the same as having you here, but I respect your decision."

Thankfully, Momma sounded calm and resigned. Chelsea was Chelsea. And Angus was being about as perfect as a man could be. If her luck held, Dad would see that this was what she wanted and respect that. She stared out the window, her spirits sinking. Her father had never respected her wants or wishes. What made her think he'd start now?

Angus surveyed his appearance in the mirror for a final time. He hadn't intended to take extra care trimming up his beard, starching his shirt and jeans, and making sure his boots were oiled up, but he was glad now. He didn't give a damn what Richard Barrett thought of him; he'd lost the right to Angus's respect the minute he'd pulled out his checkbook. But he respected Lana Barrett, Chelsea, and Savannah—and he was staying under the man's roof.

Tonight was important. He wanted to look like a man capable of providing for Savannah and the babies. Not on the level that Barrett could but, dammit all, she and their kids would never want for a thing. It was important Savannah's family knew as much.

No matter what Barrett said or did, Angus was determined to keep his temper in check. Barrett could protest and rail, but this was about Savannah and his children and their future. As long as he remembered that, Angus would have no problem keeping his cool.

Of course, it couldn't just be the family that night. Pete

Powell and the not fiancé, Greg, were already sipping drinks and making small talk with Richard and Chelsea. Lana saw him and offered him a beer, giving him a bright, encouraging smile. But it was Savannah that drew his eye. She looked every bit Texas royalty. Maybe getting married was a bad idea. How would they have been able to make it work?

"Angus." Richard gave him a tight smile. "Glad you could join us for one last meal."

"I appreciate the hospitality." He patted his stomach. "Pretty sure I've put on a pound or two from the food."

"Whatever." Chelsea snorted. "I bet you have a six pack. Or an eight pack."

"Well, that's not awkward." Savannah shot her sister a look.

Chelsea shrugged. "What? I'm just saying what we're all thinking."

"No." Greg Powell shook his head. "No offense, Angus, but I wasn't thinking about your abs."

"No offense taken." At this point, he was pretty sure bringing up Savannah's pregnancy would be less awkward than their current conversation.

"Let's sit down to eat, shall we?" Lana waved them to the table. "Try to behave, Chelsea."

"We could talk about the weather?" Chelsea mumbled, winking at Angus as she sat next to him. "How long does it take you to get home?"

"About six hours." And he was ready to get home, with Savannah, away from the tension and judgment that clouded the air of the Barrett dining room.

"You travel a lot?" Powell Senior asked.

"No." He thanked the maid that filled his glass with iced tea. "A lot of clients like to come out to the ranch, take a tour, and pick up their horses. When we deliver, we try to set up several stops all at once, and my brother and I take turns."

"That sounds efficient." Lana placed her napkin in her lap.

"Work smarter, not harder." Angus repeated one of his grandfather's favorite sayings.

"A sound philosophy," Powell Senior agreed.

"Is your brother married?" Lana asked.

"No, ma'am. It's just the two of us." For now.

"A bachelor pad, eh?" Barrett shot him a narrow-eyed look.

"I hope you're all hungry." Lana glanced around the table. "Chef prepared grilled snapper, mushroom risotto, and a spinach and bacon salad."

"It smells delicious." Greg sat back as a plate was set before him.

It did and Angus was starving. But the food on the plate had been arranged with such care that he almost felt guilty eating it. Another reminder of what Savannah was used to. Not just food on a plate, more like art on a plate.

"Daniella, our chef, knows her way around the kitchen." Barrett leaned forward and picked up his fork. "She should, for what we're paying her."

And there it is. Barrett never missed an opportunity to slide money into the conversation.

"Pickle?" Chelsea whispered, her tone pulling Angus's full attention to Savannah.

Her skin was green. "I'm good." She took a sip of tea. Then another. She wasn't good and she wasn't fooling anyone.

"Not a fan of snapper?" Barrett asked around a mouthful of food. "You're the one that's always saying we need to eat healthy and now you're not going to eat it?"

Savannah took another sip of tea and set her glass

down, eyeing her plate with trepidation. Now she was green and sweating.

"You don't look so good." Angus didn't give a rat's ass what anyone else thought.

"I'm fine." She gave him a reassuring smile.

"You need a minute?" Chelsea was up, pulling Savannah's chair back.

"Sit down, Chelsea. Savannah said she's fine." Barrett waved his fork at her.

"I think you need to make an appointment with the eye doctor, Dad. All anyone needs to do is look at her to see she's *not* okay." Chelsea didn't bat an eye.

Angus couldn't help but admire Chelsea's spirit. And her loyalty to her sister.

"That's enough, Chelsea." Barrett set his fork down. "If Savannah needs to excuse herself, she can excuse herself. She's old enough to make her own decisions."

Finally, one thing he and Barrett could agree on.

"Speaking of which." Savannah patted her upper lip and chin with her linen napkin. "I have some news." She looked at him.

Here we go. Angus smiled and gave her a nod. Now was as good a time as any.

Barrett must have seen the exchange because there was an unmistakable warning to his words. "Whatever it is can wait until our guests leave and we can discuss it privately."

"We're all family here." Chelsea smiled, perching on the arm of Savannah's chair and taking her sister's hand.

"Chelsea," Barrett barked. "Did I ask for your opinion? Stay out of it."

"Richard, dear, please stay calm." Lana glanced at her daughters.

"Angus and I are leaving." The words burst out of her. "I'm going with him tomorrow."

It was deathly quiet in the room. No one moved.

"Over my dead body." Barrett sat back in his chair, his face going a deep red. "I don't know what you're thinking, Savannah. If he wants to marry you, you know why? You're rich. Texas is a 50/50 state. It's a win-win for him." He drew in a deep breath. "I'm assuming your hormones have clouded your judgment." He pointed, more like jabbed, his finger in Angus's direction. "I'll say this once. You cannot and will not marry *this* man."

Savannah winced at the ferocity of her father's words.

"Way to be a dick, Dad." Chelsea was staring at her father, mouth open.

Angus was stunned. Barrett was going to slander him that way? After the bastard had tried to pay him off? He couldn't sit there and say nothing. "While I understand your concerns, Mr. Barrett, Savannah and I have discussed this—"

"Stop talking." Barrett's voice was low and harsh. "I don't want to hear you speak. Not now, not ever. Get out of my house."

"Richard." Lana stood. "Be reasonable."

"I am the only person being reasonable here, Lana." Barrett glared at his wife.

"Maybe we should leave you to sort this out on your own." Pete Powell sat his napkin on the table.

"No need." Barrett picked up his fork. "This discussion is over. McCarrick, you have five minutes to leave or I'll call the police."

Angus was shaking with anger as he stood, but he kept his peace. Savannah was stuck in the middle of this. He needed to be strong for her—not wasting time thinking about putting the smug sonofabitch in his place. Leaving was the right call. There was no changing the man's mind. Not now, at least.

"Angus, wait." Savannah came around the table to his side. "I'm coming with you."

He held his hand out, offering her a reassuring smile as she took it.

"Dad, I'm sorry, but this isn't about you." Savannah's hand was shaking in his. "This is about me and Angus… and our babies."

Barrett was up, slamming his hands down on the table with such force everyone jumped. "No, you're not, Savannah. Getting you pregnant doesn't make him a father. I guarantee you, he can't give you and your baby the best. Whatever this is—" he gestured between them "—it won't last. You'll wind up alone. You can count on it. You know I'm right."

Angus was seething, fuming, but Barrett was making enough of a scene without him adding more drama to it. "I'll take care of them." The reassurance was for her, no one else.

"Get out." Barrett hit the table again. "Dammit. I'm calling the police." He pulled his phone from his pocket.

"Dad, what the hell is wrong with you?" Chelsea moved to put a hand on her mother's shoulder.

"Let's go." Savannah tugged him to the door, trembling so badly he slid his arm around her waist.

"If you walk out that door, you're no longer my daughter." Barrett sucked in a deep breath. "I mean it, Savannah. I won't bail you out when this falls apart. This is your last chance to make the right choice."

Angus stared at the man in shock. He'd known he was an asshole, but this? This was unforgivable.

"Richard. What are you doing?" Lana was shaking her head. "Don't do this."

"I won't stand by and support our daughter throwing away her life." Barrett looked at him with pure scorn.

Damn the man. Damn him for putting Savannah in this position. He was the stubborn ass laying down the law without any regard for Savannah's feelings. Now he was throwing her out like a piece of trash? His selfishness was breaking his daughter's heart and Angus hated the man for it.

Lana Barrett burst into tears.

"I…" Savannah was clinging to his hand, leaning into him. Every breath was ragged and uneven. "I'm sorry, Momma. Chels." She looked around the table. "I apologize for the drama, Mr. Powell. Greg."

"You don't need to apologize for a thing," Angus murmured. "You're doing great."

Barrett moved quickly, coming around the table with a guttural roar. It was pure instinct that had Angus pushing Savannah behind him. He had just enough time to brace for the solid punch Barrett landed against his jaw. His head snapped back, pain shooting along up the side of his face, but he stood his ground. No matter how strong the urge was to flatten the sonofabitch, he wouldn't strike back. For Savannah.

"Mr. Barrett." Greg Powell was between them, placing both hands on Richard Barrett's chest. "Sir."

"Dad!" Chelsea sounded pissed.

"Richard." Lana Barrett had a hand pressed to her chest, her voice trembling. "How could you?"

But all that mattered was Savannah. She was staring up at him with tears in her eyes. "Are you okay?" It hurt to smile, but she needed it so he did. "We should go."

Angus steered her from the dining room, down the hall, and out the front door. It was only when they were in his truck that her tears came. He slid over on the seat, pulled her into his lap and held her close so she could cry herself out. Her grief cut deep. Family was family. They were supposed to stand by you, no matter what.

He rocked her gently, wishing he could fix this. "He spoke out of anger. He'll regret it." Damn fool.

"I… I…" She sobbed.

"I've got you." He pressed a kiss to her temple. Barrett had just made things a hell of a lot less complicated, as he'd left Savannah with no choice but him. "*We* are a family now, Savannah. I'll always have your back." He meant it, too. Savannah and his babies. "Let's go home."

Chapter Seven

Savannah was exhausted. Her eyelids felt heavy and her head ached. It was quiet—no rhythmic road sounds or Angus humming. She was in a soft bed. Angus's scent. She rolled over, burying her face in the pillow as her hand searched for him. The bed was empty so she forced her eyes open.

Light came from an open door on the far side of the room. A completely unfamiliar room.

Angus was sound asleep in a large recliner beside the bed. His head was cocked back and his mouth was open, his low snore steady. He wore a white undershirt and boxers, his bare feet propped on the edge of the bed. A quilt draped over his legs and pooled on the floor beneath him.

Either her eyes were playing tricks on her or the quilt moved. She leaned closer to the edge of the bed. The blanket moved again. A dog? The scruffy black head emerged from under a fold in the blanket. It was a little dog. Terrier-mix, from the look of it. It had wiry black hair and a tail that curled back over itself. Ears perked up, the dog cocked its head to one side and stared up at her. It had an underbite, one tooth sticking out playfully. The dog whined, standing and stretching so the blanket slid off.

"Who are you?" Savannah whispered, smiling at the frantic wag of the little dog's tail.

"Gertie." Angus's voice was low.

Gertie leaped onto Angus's lap, the tail wagging at light speed.

"I didn't mean to wake you," she whispered.

"I was awake." He yawned. "Sort of."

"I'm guessing we're here? Your home?" she whispered again, smiling at Gertie's attempts to cover Angus's face with doggie kisses.

"Our home." He smiled at her, scratching Gertie behind the ear. His hand all but dwarfed the little dog's head. "Gertie wanted to be the first to welcome you."

The last thing she remembered was Angus tucking his coat around her. She'd been dozing in the truck, the dark road and his humming soothing her to sleep. "You carried me in?" And she'd slept through it?

"You weigh less than a sack of feed." He chuckled, patting Gertie. "And you snore."

"I do not." She didn't, did she?

"You don't." He chuckled. "Hold up." He leaned over and turned on the bedside lamp, a soft light illuminating the room. "Hi."

She blinked, her eyes adjusting. "Hi." Unlike Angus, she was still wearing the clothes she'd left home in. The only clothes she now owned. A crushing weight landed on her chest as every single one of her father's words replayed. Her head hurt. After her sob-fest, she probably had mascara down her face. "I must look like a wreck."

He shook his head. "Beautiful. As always." One thickly muscled arm was tucked beneath his head and pulled his white undershirt tight across his sculpted chest.

He was the one that was beautiful. All she had to do was look at him and she was aching for him. Being hot and bothered over Angus was a vast improvement to being sad. "Bathroom?" She sat up, hoping he didn't see her *look* this time.

"Through there. I'll show you." Gertie refused to move.

"It's all good." She slid off the bed and hurried to the door. "You and Gertie catch up." She closed the bathroom door.

A zebra has fewer stripes than I do. Her reflection was worse than she could have imagined. There were tear tracks and smudges from where she'd wiped and patted and dabbed and made it ten times worse. She looked terrible. She looked sad.

An image of her father, red-faced and with a clenched jaw, had her gripping the bathroom counter. She knew he'd be upset, but nothing could have prepared her for his fury. Nothing. The pressure against her chest almost brought her to her knees. He might be grumpy, arrogant, and a stubborn ass, but at the end of the day, he was her father. He'd said she wasn't welcome back.

You're no longer my daughter.

She could never go home again. She had no home.

It hurt to breathe.

Momma. Chelsea. She didn't even have her phone. There was no way to reach out to them and the distance seemed endless.

"Savannah?" Angus knocked.

"Uh-huh." Savannah took another unsteady breath. Her head hurt from crying. If she kept it up, she'd make herself sick. Poor Angus had dealt with more than his fair share of tears.

"There are towels in the cabinet if you want a shower."

"Sounds good." She sounded pathetic. Maybe a shower would help her feel better?

"It's almost six. How do you take your coffee?" It sounded like he was drumming his fingertips on the door.

She opened the door. "Cream and sugar, please." The concern on his handsome face only increased the urge to cry.

His brown eyes swept over her. "Tell me what to do."

She shrugged, swallowing down the building sob. But Gertie's frantic whining, a few yips, and her paw pressing against Savannah's foot distracted her. When she looked down, the little dog was sitting at her feet, patting her leg with one paw.

"Gertie." Angus grinned. "She's sensitive. Always has been. She can tell when a person is upset. She likes to cheer them up."

"Me, too." Savannah smiled down at the dog.

Gertie stood on her back legs until Angus reached for her. "Come on." Gertie leaped up into his arms. "You worried about Savannah, too, baby girl?" Angus smiled at Gertie's little whine. "I know. I know. I love you, too."

Savannah's heart melted. "She is precious." Which was an understatement.

"She's a mess." Clearly, Angus adored the little dog. "Gertie, you help me take care of Savannah. She's your momma now."

Gertie cocked her head to one side, leaning forward in Angus's arms to snuffle the hand Savannah offered. A few sniffs and she bathed Savannah's hand with kisses. The dog was leaning so far out of Angus's arms that Savannah wound up holding the wriggling bundle of fur. "I'm happy to meet you, too, Gertie."

"Traitor." Angus chuckled. "I can't hold it against her, though. She's got good taste."

Gertie smelled Savannah's cheek and neck and chest, never still.

Angus shook his head. "Come on, now. Let's give Savannah a chance to shower."

Gertie looked at him, then Savannah. With a grunt, the dog flopped onto her back in Savannah's arms—like a baby. Savannah laughed, absolutely charmed.

"Yeah, I know you know you're adorable." He sighed.

Savannah cooed, "Aren't you the most precious thing ever?" She carried the dog back into the bedroom and sat on the edge of the bed, cradling Gertie with one arm and rubbing the little dog's tummy with the other hand. "How can I resist?"

"Watch out. If she senses you're a softie, she'll expect you to carry her around like that 24/7." Angus leaned against the door frame.

"What's wrong with that?" Savannah asked, Gertie's little eyes watching her. "Daddy should carry you around, always."

Gertie's tail picked up speed again.

"All right." Angus was shaking his head. "You two are going to be trouble." Gertie grunted again, the tip of her tongue sticking out of her mouth. "Let's go make Savannah some coffee, Gertie. Let's go." He patted his thigh.

Gertie stretched, jumped from Savannah's arms, and trotted out of the bedroom.

Savannah giggled.

"I like the sound of that. You, happy." Angus patted his hand against the door. "Have a good shower." And then he was gone.

It was really hard for her to focus on anything other than Angus when he was near her. He was so…so Angus. She'd never met anyone like him. She'd certainly never had a man affect her the way Angus did. Now that he was gone, she could properly inspect her surroundings. This was his bedroom. *My bedroom. Our bedroom.*

The king-size bed was comfy. The head and footboard resembled wide, darkly stained fence pickets. Four oversize pillows, soft sheets, and what looked to be a handmade quilt with a log cabin print. From a family member, maybe? She stood and smoothed the covers, fluffing the pillows until she was happy with the result.

An antique chest of drawers sat on the opposite wall with a large mission-style mirror mounted above it. The side tables and quilt trunk under the window were all older and weathered, but full of character. There was only one piece of art—a beautiful painting of a palomino horse, running. All-in-all, the room was welcoming and comfy.

The bathroom was clean and minimal. No bath, which she'd miss, but a perfectly serviceable shower that would do the job. She turned on the shower, stripped off her clothes, and stood under the warm water. The soap smelled like Angus. Woodsy. Fresh. A hint of mint. Invigorating. She lathered up, scrubbing her face free of mascara and tears.

No more tears. No more sadness. No more thinking of her father or his hateful words. This was a fresh start—she needed to go into it with a positive attitude. She owed it to Angus and the babies. She rubbed soap over her stomach. "We're home, babies. Just me, you, and your daddy."

Angus pulled two mugs from the cabinet. "Sugar we've got." He opened the refrigerator and glanced at

Gertie, who was following his every move. "Think milk will do?"

Gertie whimpered.

"Talking to Gertie again?" Dougal came into the kitchen, yawning. "How late did you get in?" Willow, Dougal's black Lab, came trailing after him.

Gertie immediately trotted to Willow, stood on her hind legs, and launched herself at Willow. Willow sat, unfazed by Gertie's playful attack.

"After midnight." Angus shook his head as Dougal took the cup of coffee he'd poured.

"What?" Dougal took a sip. "Two cups." He frowned. "I got the coffeepot ready last night. So, I think what you should be saying is you're welcome."

"Two cups." He nodded at the hall. "She's in the shower."

"Oh." Dougal's brows rose. "Right. How'd it go?"

"Other than leaving without a check for the horses I left behind for fear he'd find a way to land my ass in jail? Bad." Angus gave his brother a very abbreviated version.

"So, you're saying Richard Barrett is an even bigger piece of shit than we'd originally thought?" Dougal's brows were furrowed and his jaw locked.

"Pretty much." Angus pulled another mug from the cabinet. "But she doesn't need to hear that. She needs me on her side, not bad-mouthing her father."

"You're a better man than me." Dougal took another sip of coffee. "What now?"

"Give her a day or two to rest." Angus added one teaspoon of sugar, paused, then added another. "Stress is bad for pregnancy."

"Yep." Dougal nodded. "Might have heard that a time or two in the last year or so."

In the last couple of years, their closest friends had

all married and become parents. It had been interesting to see their group of self-professed bachelors turn into doting husbands and adoring fathers. For Angus, it had been confirmation that he wasn't the marrying type. The amount of stress, constant worrying over the well-being of someone else, losing all of their time to another person or people wasn't something Angus could get on board with. He and Dougal got on fine. Of course, he was there for his family and friends, but at the end of the day, he was accountable only to himself.

Dougal was the opposite. He'd grown up with the love and support of two devoted parents. He wanted the same. A wife and passel of little McCarricks of his own. He'd be a lucky man if he found someone who would put up with his grumpy-ass nature. Dougal had a big heart, but his lack of subtlety and general surliness tended to be too much for most women to look beyond.

What he wanted sort of faded into the background when he thought about Savannah and what she'd been through yesterday. Her own father. Richard Barrett was a bastard through and through. He felt for Savannah.

Savannah, who deserved a good cup of coffee to start her day. He poured a splash of milk into the coffee—then a little more. On top, he added a healthy dollop of whipped cream.

"What the hell are you doing?" Dougal eyed the mug.

"Making her coffee." He shrugged.

"That's not a *coffee*. I don't know what that is." Dougal chuckled and sipped his coffee.

"We don't have cream." Angus nodded at the mostly empty refrigerator. "We don't have much of anything."

"True." Dougal poured himself another cup of coffee. "I guess there's gonna be more than a few changes around here?"

"Not on my account, I hope." Savannah came into the kitchen. "Sorry for the attire." She was wearing the robe Angus's mother had bought for him two Christmases ago—a robe he'd hung on the back of the bathroom door but never worn. She was swallowed in the navy-blue fluffy fabric. "Savannah Barrett." She held her hand out. "You must be Dougal?"

"Yes, ma'am." Dougal shook her hand. "Welcome."

"I made you coffee." Angus handed her the mug, the whipped cream wobbling.

"I didn't know you were a barista." Savannah took the mug. "Thank you."

"I had to improvise." Angus explained, watching as she took a sip.

"It's yummy." She took another sip. "So… What does a day on McCarrick Ranch look like?"

"Up around six." Angus nodded at the clock. It was five fifty. "Coffee." He lifted his mug. "Dougal and I go down to the barns, make sure the guys are up and moving."

"How many employees do you have?" She perched on one of the bar stools.

"Two full-time, two part-time." Dougal leaned against the kitchen counter.

"They've been with us forever so we're more like family. Jack and Harvey might pop in anytime. Jack's got a mile-long beard he takes seriously." Angus chuckled. "He's won a couple of beard awards."

"I didn't know that was a thing." Savannah smiled.

"Speaking of, you're looking a little scruffy yourself. Thinking about entering a competition?" Angus teased his brother.

"Ha ha. Very funny." Dougal sat on the stool next to

her. "Don't ask Jack about it. You'll get stuck listening to him tell you about beard grooming for hours."

Savannah laughed. "I'll remember that."

"Then there's Harvey. He's bald and clean-shaven, so you won't mix them up." Angus poured himself another cup of coffee. "He doesn't say much, either. But we all come up to the house for lunch once or twice a week, so you'll meet them."

"I guess I need to wash my clothes." Savannah glanced down at her robe.

Because the only clothing she owned was what she had been wearing yesterday. Barrett was a shit. "Dougal's got things covered here today. We can go into town, get some shopping done."

"Really?" Savannah glanced between the two brothers. "I don't want to get in the way."

"No, ma'am. I'm the one that runs the place, anyway." Dougal shot Angus a look. "He's too busy starching his shirts and jeans and looking pretty."

Savannah laughed again. "He does always look nice." Her gaze met his before sweeping over him. "Normally."

Angus and Dougal both laughed then.

"I'll make sure to put on clothes before we go into town." Angus shook his head. "You'll like Granite Falls. It's a pretty little town. Even prettier when it's all spruced up for Christmas."

"I love Christmas. Making cookies and decorating the tree and helping with the local toy drive." Savannah's smile faltered. "This year, I'll have to make new traditions."

Angus exchanged a look with his brother. "We'll do Christmas up right this year." He and Dougal didn't do much to celebrate unless their mother and aunt were coming to stay. They knew how to make the holidays special—and were characters to boot.

Savannah finished her coffee. "I can make breakfast if you like? I'm not much of a cook, outside of cookies, but I can boil an egg and make some toast?"

"We can eat in town," Angus offered. "Pretty sure they'll have a decent cup of coffee for you, too."

Gertie circled Savannah's stool, whining.

"Looks like you've already made a friend." Dougal nodded. "My Willow's on the shy side of things, so don't expect her to jump into your arms or make a fuss like that little rat."

"Don't go hurting her feelings, Dougal," Angus sighed, shaking his head.

Savannah slipped off her stool and stooped to pet Gertie. "She's not a rat. She's a princess."

Dougal snorted.

Gertie rolled onto her back for tummy scratches.

"Yeah, real modest, too." Dougal set his mug down on the marble counter. "I'm gonna head out. You two have fun. If I think of something we need, I'll send you a text."

Angus nodded his thanks, making a mental list of all the things he'd need to get. Clothes for Savannah took top priority. A tree, some decorations, and food were a close second. But first, he needed to call in the cavalry. His mother and aunt. Savannah would appreciate having family around. He knew without a doubt his mother and aunt would welcome Savannah with open arms. They couldn't replace her family, but it might ease her homesickness some. And give her some semblance of a happy Christmas.

Guilt wasn't an emotion Angus was familiar with. Until now. Barrett might have been the one to force Savannah's hand, but he was partly responsible. If it wasn't for him, and his and Savannah's night together, she'd still be with her family and enjoying their holiday traditions.

She'd had to give up everything—because of him. He'd do his damnedest to make sure she didn't regret it.

Chapter Eight

Granite Falls was like something out of a storybook. Main Street was lined with garland and candy-colored light-wrapped lampposts. Silver tinsel stars, bells, and snowmen hung from white-icicle-bedecked storefront eaves, and a massive Christmas tree stood, straight and tall, on the lawn of the courthouse. She'd visited several small towns in the Hill Country, but she was certain nothing was as picturesque as Granite Falls. This charming little town was her new home—for now.

"I wouldn't be surprised to round the corner and see Santa." Savannah wandered along the brick sidewalk, admiring the touches of Christmas everywhere. "All that's missing is the snow."

"Well, that's a rarity in these parts. A day or two of ice, maybe. But a real snow? Not likely." Angus glanced her way, like he was waiting for something.

"That's Texas for you. I think we've only had snow once, maybe twice, on Christmas. I'm not one for the cold so it's fine by me." She took a moment to inspect the street. "It's a lovely town."

"Christmas has always been a big deal in Granite Falls." He pointed out several winter and holiday scenes arranged in the picture windows lining the street. "Ever since I can remember, there's a storefront window competition. They take their decorating seriously."

"What's the prize?" Savannah paused in front of one window.

"Bragging rights, mostly." Angus chuckled. "The Granite Falls Family Grocer and the Main Street Antiques & Resale Shop can get pretty worked up over it. It always seems to come down to the two of them." He pointed at the next shop. "As you can see."

Savannah did see. "Oh, my." A small train circled a mini Christmas village while automated reindeer turned their heads and stomped their hooves. In the next window, Mrs. Claus sat knitting and rocking in a rocking chair while the mechanical elves wrapped gifts in shiny wrapping paper. "It's something."

"Morning, Angus." A man stepped outside. "Morning, ma'am."

"Dean." Angus nodded. "This is Savannah. Savannah, Dean Hodges owns this shop."

"It's nice to meet you." Savannah shook hands with the man. "I was admiring your decorations. It's so…so festive."

"Thank you. I can't take any credit for it. My mother takes care of the windows every year." He leaned forward to whisper. "Don't tell her I said so, but I think she goes overboard." He shrugged, smiling. "It makes her happy, so I'm not complaining. What brings you to Granite Falls?"

She wasn't sure what to say. This was Angus's home, and she didn't want to say or do anything—

"I guess you could say she's here for me." Angus took her hand. He seemed genuinely proud—and it warmed her heart through.

"Aren't you the lucky man?" Dean shook his head, but smiled. "Welcome to Granite Falls, Savannah."

"Thank you."

"Savannah's things have been waylaid so you got any suggestions where we can get her outfitted? This is a first for me."

She'd never heard a shopping expedition referred to as being outfitted.

"We've got some things in here. They're a little on the designer end of things. At least, that's what my mother thinks. They're more for the senior crowd." Dean rubbed his chin, scanning Main Street. "I'd go down Austin Street. There's a handful of shops for women—mostly touristy stuff, though. You know, coming through for the rodeos or one of the festivals." He shook his head. "I can't guarantee you'll find something you like. Good luck."

The next stop was The Coffee Shop. As they stood in line waiting to place their order, Savannah realized how hungry she was. Nothing beat the smell of freshly brewed coffee—except maybe freshly baked goodies. There was a wide selection of kolaches, muffins, pastries, doughnuts, and several kinds of decorated Christmas cookies on display in the glass front counter. Her stomach grumbled.

Angus glanced at her, grinning. "I'm hungry, too. I'm tempted to get one of everything."

"Don't you dare. Or I'll have to help you eat them." She nudged him.

"You're eating for four." He nudged back.

She rolled her eyes. "I'll eat one. Maybe two. But that's all."

They got their order and found a small café table next to the front window.

Her delectable pecan roast latte was far more palatable than Angus's attempt this morning. Not that she'd ever say as much. "If you have work to do, I can shop on my own." Savannah had seen him check his watch more than once.

"I'd rather show you around and get you settled." Angus sat back in the chair. "With Christmas so close, things will be pretty slow until after the new year."

"If you're sure."

"I am." He unwrapped the pastries and put them on their plates. "Now eat."

She devoured the blueberry cream cheese Danish. "Oh, that was dangerously delicious."

Angus chuckled. "If I remember correctly, you've got a job? Do you need to let them know you've moved?"

She nodded, then shook her head. "I did." She pulled the wrapper off her gingerbread muffin. "I'm involved with several charities—charity work is important to me. But my day job was working for my father. Mostly press stuff—you know, for the Cougars football team. I also kept his schedule organized, meetings, events, that sort of thing." She managed a smile. "While he didn't specifically say as much, I assume I'm now unemployed. Is it wrong that I feel just the tiniest bit amused, imagining how lost he'll be without me to keep him on schedule?"

"Not wrong at all." Angus wasn't smiling anymore. His jaw was clenched, and his eyes had narrowed to slits. And, for some reason, he looked sexier than ever.

She tucked a strand of hair behind her ear. "I'll find something useful to do in Granite Falls." She split the muffin in half. "First, I need to find a doctor for me and the babies."

His expression softened instantly. "I can make a few calls, if you like? A couple of my friends are new parents. They'd probably know where to start."

"Yes, please." Having inside information on doctors would help but... "Will this cause you trouble? I mean, gossip and teasing? People talk, I know."

"Trouble? No. Gossip? Who cares." He shrugged. "We had some good luck, running into Dean. He'll make sure everyone in town knows you're here. Dean's mother is like the town crier."

"And that's a good thing?" She looked confused.

"It is." He was studying her with those brown eyes of his. "Why wouldn't I want everyone to know you're mine?"

The way he was looking at her had her insides melting. She should point out that she wasn't his, but the words got stuck in her throat. If Angus loved her and she loved him, she wouldn't mind being his.

"Hell, if I had it my way, we'd march on down to city hall and make it official." He picked up a sausage kolach. "I know you're against it, but maybe think about it. Savannah, after what happened with your father, I don't want you worrying about where to go or taking care of yourself and the babies. Let me help take care of you—of all of you. It's the least I can do."

Savannah wiped her fingertips on a napkin, her throat so tight she couldn't speak. Not that she had any words. Since she'd left with Angus, there'd been an underlying panic twisting her gut. She and Angus hadn't talked about how long she'd stay. Now she was here—with no place else to go. "I appreciate that, Angus. I know this isn't exactly what we'd talked about, but I don't have any place to go." She sniffed. Without Angus's kindness, her situation was pretty bleak. Pregnant and homeless and, for all intents and purposes, alone. As good as Angus was being to her, they were practically strangers. "But I'll do what I can around the place. I don't want to be a burden." Not that she knew much about horses or actual working ranches.

Angus studied her for a long moment. "I'll take you up on that—help get things more festive around the place." He paused. "But you should rest and take care of yourself and the babies. That's most important, don't you think? Take some time to figure out what you might want to do, a ways down the road, even. It'd be nice if it includes me and the babies, but I'll support you."

She laughed. "I'll try to pencil you all in."

He laughed, too. It was a rich and gruff sound that had her toes curling in her ankle boots. "You're making that face again." He sounded amused.

"I don't know what you're talking about." She turned her attention to her mostly pulverized muffin. Before she could think through her question, it was out there. "Why were you sleeping in the chair?"

It was silent.

She dared to look at him.

His jaw was rigid and there was a fire blazing in his eyes. "It would have been wrong. You'd had a hell of a night. I figured you needed sleep." He cleared his throat. "If I'd been in bed with you, I'm not sure either of us would have slept."

Warmth bloomed in her cheeks. It was all too easy imagining what would have happened. But he was right. She was a mess of emotions. Her poor heart ached for love—and Angus had made it pretty clear he wasn't interested in love. She was too fragile; it would be easy to confuse attraction for real affection. And that would lead to more heartache. "Thank you. I think you're right. It's been so much." She broke off. "I don't think… We shouldn't… Not for now."

His nod was tight. "Whatever you want, Savannah."

It wasn't what she *wanted*. She wanted Angus. But she had to protect herself—she had to be strong. "Thank you. For everything." His gentle smile stirred up all the want she needed to lock away. Wanting Angus McCarrick was oh-so easy. Something told her loving him would be, too.

"We will be there tomorrow." His mother's excitement was palpable. "It's Angus, Nola." She said to his hard-of-hearing aunt Nola, who wasn't on the phone. "Yes, it's Angus. And he has news. He's going to be a father." It wasn't uncommon for his mother to have more than one conversation at a time. "A father. Yes, a girl. And she's pregnant, Nola. I'm going to be a nanna."

Angus grinned. "Thanks, Ma. She could use some family support." Talking to his mother took some of the worry off his shoulders. "We knew her father wasn't going to like me being in the picture but disowning her—"

"Well, he's cut his nose off to spite his face. What sort of fool chases off his daughter and grandbabies." A pause. "Her daddy did, that's who. I know, Nola, but we can't call him that in front of Savannah, you hear?"

"What did Aunt Nola call him?" Angus loved how Aunt Nola didn't beat around the bush.

"I'm not repeating it. But it's another way of saying dumb donkey."

"*Dumbass* isn't so bad, Ma." Angus chuckled. "And it's a pretty spot-on description of the man."

His mother giggled. "Poor little thing."

"All things considering, she's holding up pretty well.

She's tough." But he suspected she was struggling far more than she let on. "Right now, she's taking a nap." Their shopping had been mostly a bust. She'd found some pajamas that had room to grow and some stretchy pants and a shirt that looked two sizes too big for her. But that was about it. By the time they'd gotten home, she was wiped out.

"Good. Growing babies is a lot of work. Heavens to Betsy, growing three at once?" His mother clicked her tongue. "She needs to get all the rest she can while she can." A pause. "Nola, we're gonna have to put off our cruise to the Bahamas so we can be there when those babies come home." Pause. "Yes, babies. She's having three."

There was a muffled exclamation.

"Nola, that mouth of yours." His mother sighed.

Angus chuckled. "Thanks for coming, Ma. I want her to make some new happy memories."

"We'll make sure of that." His mother was good at showering love on people. Savannah needed that. "Nola and I will spoil all of you. Is the tree up?"

Angus ran his fingers through his hair. "Nope. It's pretty much a blank slate."

"You boys." His mother sighed. "You make sure there's a tree ready and waiting to be decorated. We'll take care of the rest."

"Yes, ma'am." He listened as she rattled off a list of things she needed him to pick up before hanging up.

"She give you a to-do list a mile long?" Dougal sat on the opposite side of the kitchen table, a laptop open in front of him.

"More like a half a mile." Angus sat back. "I know Ma's a lot, and she and Nola were doing their own thing this Christmas, but I appreciate you not fighting me on this and letting them come spend the holidays with us."

"I get it. We're not exactly a barrel of laughs. Ma and Aunt Nola will definitely energize the place. Savannah's had a tough go and all." Dougal scratched the back of his head. "But it might be the right time for me to clean out the back shed."

"We need to get a tree." Angus rested both elbows on the table.

"Want me to cut down a cedar?"

"Nah, Aunt Nola is allergic, remember?" Angus would never forget that Christmas. Poor Aunt Nola's eyes almost swelled shut. He and Dougal had dragged the tree out while his mother had done her best to remove all traces of the tree from inside the house, but Nola had sneezed and wheezed until New Year's.

"Right." Dougal closed the laptop. "I'll head into town and see if there's anything at the Family Grocer's." The business line started ringing. "McCarrick Cutting Horses." Dougal listened, his gaze shifting to Angus. "I—" Dougal closed his mouth while whoever was on the phone kept talking. "Yes, ma'am, I—" Dougal sighed. "Ma'am, this is his brother." He held the phone out. "It's for you."

"Hello?"

"Angus? It's Chelsea."

"Hey there." He winked at Dougal.

"How is she? Are you two all right? I was calling and calling and thought she didn't want to talk to us. Then I found her phone." Chelsea paused. "Is she around? I'd really like to talk to her."

"She's sleeping. But I'll wake her up. She'll want to talk to you." Angus stood and headed down the hall. "How are things there?"

"A frigging nightmare. Momma's cried so much she's made herself sick so we're at the urgent care clinic. She says she doesn't want to go home. I think she might actually divorce my dad over this." Chelsea paused. "Which was sort of why I was calling."

"Go on." Angus had a sneaking suspicion where this was going.

"Can Momma and I come spend Christmas with you? I swear, if I have to look at Dad's face one more time…" She trailed off. "I'm worried about Momma, too. We've never spent Christmas apart—me, Momma, and Pickle, I mean. In case you were wondering, Momma does not agree with Dad or what he's done."

"I know." He stopped outside his bedroom door. "You're both welcome, of course. But I'd rather state troopers didn't show up to arrest me after your father accuses me of kidnapping you all."

Chelsea's laugh was flat. "No, we're telling him we're going to see Uncle Gene. Dad hates Momma's brother, they don't talk, so it'll be fine."

Maybe Richard Barrett didn't understand the way family was supposed to work after all.

"You have no idea what a relief this is, Angus. Seriously. Everything is falling apart here. Which serves Dad right. Dumbass. Anyway, I'm so worried about her."

He opened the door and smiled. Savannah was curled up on her side, sleeping. Gertie was balled up against Savannah's stomach and Willow lay across the foot of the bed.

"What are you two doing in here?" he whispered.

"Who is where?" Chelsea asked.

"The dogs. They've dumped Dougal and me for your sister." He chuckled as both dogs' tails thumped in greeting.

"Sister?" Savannah yawned.

"Yep. It's Chelsea." He handed her the phone and sat on the edge of the bed.

"Chels?" she gushed. "I know. I left my phone. Are you okay? Is Momma okay?" There was a long pause as she listened.

Angus was torn between giving her privacy and being there in case she needed him.

"How sick?" Savannah sat up. "Poor Momma." Gertie immediately wriggled her way onto Savannah's lap and curled into a fluffy ball. "She's brokenhearted." She scratched Gertie behind the ear. "I think we all are." There was another long pause. This time, she was looking his way. "When will you be here?" She sounded so damn happy he had to smile. "Really? Sounds good, Chels. Please tell Momma everything is okay and I'll see you all soon." She laughed. "Kisses back. I love you." She set the phone beside her and burst into tears.

"Hey, hey." It was the last thing he'd expected. "What's wrong?"

"You're so sweet, Angus. You've had, what, three days to get used to the idea of being a father and had to deal with all of this on top of that. My family. My father. Me, coming here. Now my mother and my sister are invading. And it's Christmas." She sobbed. "It's all so horrible."

"Is it?" Tears were one thing that made him feel useless. "I didn't think we were doing all that bad." He pulled a handkerchief from his pocket and dabbed her cheeks.

"No. No." She grabbed his arms. "Not *you*. You're wonderful. Everything else. I mean, not the babies. The babies are wonderful." She sniffed. "Mostly, my family. My father. I'm so ashamed and embarrassed. The things he said were awful."

"They were." But he couldn't leave it at that. She was

hurting. She needed comfort. "He was in shock and angry. People say things when they're in a state."

"You're so…so…kind. After all the things he said. How can you be so generous?"

"Believe me, it's taking effort." He shook his head, wiping away an errant tear from her face. "There's no point in wasting energy on something—or someone— that can't be changed."

She drew in a wavering breath, studying him closely. "I can't help but feel like…like I dumped all of this on you and made you take me in. And…and you've been so nice to me the whole time." She shook her head, sniffing.

"Gertie." He scooched the dog aside so he could get closer to Savannah. He couldn't take it if she started crying again. "You didn't make me do anything. As I recall, I was very willing." He pressed his hand against her stomach.

She gave him a watery smile. "Oh." She rested her hand atop his and pressed. "Can you feel that?"

He did. The slightest movement. So faint he closed his eyes to concentrate. "Barely." He chuckled. "Someone saying hello?" She was smiling at him when he opened his eyes.

She nodded. "You don't mind Momma and Chelsea coming to stay?"

"Nope." He kept his hand against her stomach. "I hope you don't mind my mother and aunt coming, too. They want to meet you and welcome you to the family."

"Really?" Her smile grew. "I can't wait to meet your mom. And your aunt."

"My aunt is a handful. I might need to apologize for her now." He was only half-kidding.

"You've met Chelsea." Savannah shrugged. "It sounds

like there will be a houseful for Christmas. Is Dougal okay with this?"

"Dougal is fine with it." He smoothed a strand of hair behind her ear. "It's Christmas, after all. The more the merrier."

"I'm sorry I get so emotional. I'm fine, and then, all of a sudden, I'm crying." She wiped at her cheeks with the back of her hand. "I guess it's part of the joy of pregnancy."

"You're doing a great job." Pregnant or not, she had plenty of good reasons to be emotional right now.

"It helps knowing you're in this with me, Angus. You're a good man." She took his hand in hers as her gaze locked with his. "Thank you."

The way she was looking at him scared the shit out of him. He liked living his life day by day, focusing on what was right in front of him, and doing what he pleased. He didn't relish the idea of being beholden to anyone or missing what he didn't have. But Savannah was changing that and he didn't know how to feel about it. Until now, he'd been perfectly content with one goal: making sure McCarrick Cutting Horses was the top operation in the Southern states. Anything beyond that hadn't really mattered. But now… Now he wasn't so sure that was true.

He was going to be a father. A father of three. He had a family to take care of, plans to be made, and hope for a future…one he'd never known he wanted. With Savannah.

Chapter Nine

"You are the prettiest thing I have ever laid eyes on." Orla McCarrick announced the minute she walked through the front door. She held both of Savannah's hands, not bothering to hide the thorough head-to-toe inspection she was making. "Sharp eyes and the sweetest smile. I'm tickled pink." She patted Savannah's cheek. "I do declare, Angus, you've done well for yourself."

"That's very kind of you." Savannah's relief was instant. Since Angus had announced his mother and aunt were coming, she'd been worried. Their situation wasn't exactly traditional. A lot of moms might not be pleased to learn their son was in the predicament Angus was in.

"Honest." Angus winked at her. "Ma's always honest."

"So am I. When are you going to shave off that beard? You look like a redneck caveman." Nola Cruz peered over her coke-bottle-thick glasses at Angus, shaking her head in disapproval.

Savannah hadn't meant to laugh, but the redneck caveman comment was too funny.

"Savannah, this is my aunt Nola. Nola, don't go running Savannah off now." Angus shook his head, but he was smiling. "If you don't like mine, you're going to hate Dougal's."

"Is he hiding somewhere?" Nola asked. "I think I scare the boy."

"You scare everyone, Aunt Nola." Angus kissed his aunt on the cheek in greeting.

"Smart-ass." But Nola was chuckling.

"Nola." Orla's disappointment was obvious. "Well, there goes a positive first impression." She looked at Savannah as she said, "You'll have to excuse her. She cusses like a sailor."

"I was married to one for thirty years. Don't blame me for picking up some of the lingo." Nola cackled. "Welcome to the family, Savannah."

"Thank you." Savannah shook the woman's hand. She couldn't wait for Chelsea and her mother to get here. Nola and Chelsea, together? That would be all sorts of fun.

"Where is Dougal?" Orla looked around the great room. "Land sakes, son, the place is short on holiday cheer. There's only six days until Christmas Eve. Six." She took off her coat and hung it in the foyer closet. She was barely five feet tall, but she had an energy that more than made up for it. "You know the red storage boxes have all the Christmas things in them."

Angus nodded. "I was getting them out when you pulled up."

Orla shook her head. "I'll tell you now, Savannah, you'll have your work cut out for you. The boys are just like their father. I'd have to make that man take time off for holidays and celebrations—and even then, I was lucky if he managed a whole day without wandering down to the barn. You might as well start putting your foot down now."

"Especially with those babies coming," Nola added. "You're going to need all hands on deck."

"My father is the same way." It slipped out before Savannah realized she'd said it.

Now all three of them were regarding her with sympathy and concern.

"Angus says your momma and sister are joining us? I'm so glad to hear it. Christmas is a time for family, I always say." Orla surprised Savannah by hugging her.

She hugged the tiny woman back. "I agree."

Orla patted her back. "Good." She stepped back. "Now. Where is the Christmas tree you promised me?"

"Dougal had to drive to Forrest Knoll." Angus ran his fingers through his hair. "They're all out in town."

"Because you waited so long," Orla chimed in.

"I got it, Ma." Angus chuckled. "Go easy on me, will ya? The last week has been an adventure." The way his brown eyes swept over her left Savannah aching.

Having separate bedrooms was the right thing—they both agreed on that. But that didn't mean she hadn't spent last night in bed, missing the stroke of hands on her skin, and the strain of his body against hers had her breathless.

"I'm not complaining." His gaze never left her face.

"I should think not." Orla glanced back and forth between the two of them. "You get a pass on the no decorations. This time."

"But next time, I expect to walk in to a Christmas wonderland." Nola rolled her eyes. "Just like your ma likes."

"Thank you." He hugged his mother, then his aunt. "I'll go get the red tubs."

"That's my boy." Orla waved him down the hallway. "Now, Savannah, you tell Nola and I what you need to make this Christmas special."

Savannah was so touched by the woman's offer. "It already is."

"Oh, now, that's hogwash." Nola wagged her finger at Savannah. "I saw an article in *Texas Monthly* that showed how fancy and posh your place was at Christmas. We might not be able to match that, but, with your mother and sister coming, we need to do something."

Savannah was laughing again.

"She did use the Google." Orla nodded. "Your family home is a showplace. I have to say, even when I've been at my decorating pinnacle, I never managed to make this place look that grand."

"You want to know a secret?" Savannah whispered. "We hire people to decorate. Momma does work with a designer for the layout, but that's about it. A whole team comes in for two straight days after Thanksgiving."

Orla and Nola exchanged a look.

"I can't remember the last time I decorated a Christmas tree. The most Christmas-y thing I do is bake cookies. But I do that well—decorate them, too. And it always makes me happy." Even with a chef on staff, she insisted on making cookies herself. And cleaning up the residual mess she inevitably left from her efforts.

"That we can do." Orla took her hand and led her to the kitchen. "Cookies are always a heartfelt welcome present, too. We'll make some and go calling so you can meet the good folk of Granite Falls."

"Some of them are good." Nola snorted. "Others…" She shrugged. "They don't deserve cookies."

"Nola Ann." Orla scolded.

Nola was a riot. The back-and-forth between the sisters had Savannah in stitches. They'd welcomed her into the family without hesitation, gone out of their way to put her at her ease, and wanted to make her holiday special. It didn't fill the hole her father had put in her heart, but it did ease the pain.

They'd almost reached the kitchen when the front door opened and Dougal came in, dragging a massive tree behind him. "A little help," he called out.

"Is it big enough?" Nola asked.

"It was all they had left." Dougal dropped the tree and crossed the room, scooping up Nola in a bear hug. "Good to see you, Aunt Nola."

"Get that scruffy thing out of my face." Nola batted at Dougal's full beard. "You got any wildlife living in there?"

"Not that I've noticed." Dougal released her and scooped up his mother next, giving her a spin. "Ma. You getting shorter?"

"Dougal." Orla giggled. "It's more like you're getting taller."

"What are you, seven feet by now?" Nola arranged her thick glasses and clicked her tongue. "That beard is an eyesore."

"I told you." Angus rounded the corner carrying two large red storage bins. "Mine looks downright refined now, doesn't it, Aunt Nola?"

"I wouldn't go that far." Nola shook her head. "But it's trimmed up nice without all that bushiness hanging off your chin. You need me to buy you a razor, Dougal? Now I know what to get you for Christmas."

"I'd rather have some new socks." Dougal winked. "Give me a hand, will ya, Angus? The damn tree's more fit for Rockefeller Center, but we'll make it fit."

"We'll have to wait on the baking just a bit. You sit,

darlin'." Orla waved Savannah into one of the leather recliners. "We'll need to supervise or they'll never get it right."

Dougal and Angus both shot their mother an offended look.

"I'm going to end up with a stomachache from all the laughing." Savannah was laughing all over again.

"Good. That's good." Orla patted her shoulder. "Laughter is good for those babies. If their momma is happy, they know it. And they're happy, too."

Savannah sat back in the recliner, Gertie appearing out of nowhere to wedge herself into the chair beside her. She patted the little dog while poor Dougal and Angus turned the tree one way, then the other, then back again. Nola and Orla preferred different sides and neither was willing to concede to the other. Dougal sat on the stone hearth while they argued, but Angus came to sit on the arm of her recliner.

"Were did you come from?" He scratched behind Gertie's ear. "Why do I get the feeling I'm being replaced."

Gertie yawned and settled her head on Savannah's lap.

"They're a pair, aren't they?" Angus shook his head, watching his mother and aunt walk around the tree, arguing.

"I like them." She smiled up at him.

"That's good to hear. 'Cause you're stuck with them through the holidays. All of us." He shook his head as the women kept up their back-and-forth on the right side of the tree.

She liked the sound of that. *Us.* Being a part of that us. She was happy. Really, truly happy. It had only been a couple of days since she'd arrived here, but it was enough to make a difference. Being here felt safe. There were still things that needed to be worked out, but right here and now, she was happy. The babies seemed happy, too, wiggling in her tummy. She placed his hand on her stomach. "I think they like your mom and aunt, too."

"I think they like it when you laugh." This was a new Angus look, one she wasn't sure how to decipher. He swallowed, his gaze falling to where his hand rested on her stomach.

The more time she spent with Angus, the more she cared about him. Despite all her best efforts, it was impossible not to feel something. And she was feeling all the feels for the handsome, burly man next to her. It felt a lot like the way she'd imagined falling in love would feel. Which was bad. Really, really bad. Especially since Angus had only ever said he wanted her. Was it too much to hope that she might affect his heart as much as she affected his body?

"How are you holding up?" Angus stood on the top of the ladder, sliding the cord onto the hook along the roof's eave.

"I haven't snapped yet." Dougal uncoiled another strand of outdoor lights.

"They've only been here six hours." Angus stifled a laugh.

"It's been a hell of a long six hours." Dougal glared up at his brother. "It'd be easier if Aunt Nola didn't keep poking about my beard." He ran a hand over the length of his facial hair.

"It's Aunt Nola. What did you expect?" Angus connected the new strand of lights Dougal handed him and went back to hanging them. "She's all about being clean-shaven, like Uncle Clyde was."

"Poor Uncle Clyde." Dougal sighed.

Angus laughed. Uncle Clyde had adored his wife. "I

don't think Uncle Clyde ever lost sleep over being beard-less." As far as Angus remembered, they'd had a good, long marriage.

"We'll never know now, will we?" Dougal snapped back.

"You gonna make it?" Angus paused, staring down at his brother. "Lana and Chelsea will be here tomorrow. Lana's on the quiet side, but Chelsea's like a younger version of Nola."

Dougal groaned. "Why'd you have to go and tell me that?"

"I figured I owed you a warning." Angus went back to hanging lights. "I appreciate the effort you're putting in."

"It's not right, what Savannah's father did. I can't imagine Pa ever doing something so…mean. He had his fits now and then, but he never used hateful words. You can't take that crap back."

Angus agreed. Choose Your Words Carefully. It was a motto he tried to live by. He'd swallowed plenty of choice words when Richard Barrett had gone on his tirade, but he'd managed to keep his mouth shut. If, no when, the man got his senses back, he didn't want to make that reconciliation more challenging than it was likely to be.

"You think he'll come after her?" Dougal asked. "Try to take her home?"

"I don't know." Angus climbed down and moved the ladder over. "Part of me hopes he does, for Savannah. An apology would go a long way. Though I'm not sure a man like Barrett ever apologizes or admits when he is wrong." He shrugged. "The other part is still tempted to land him on his ass."

"I don't envy you that. Having that rat bastard for a father-in-law."

"We're not getting married." One perk to her refusing his marriage proposal.

"That's just stupid." Dougal steadied the ladder while Angus climbed back up. "That light is upside down." He pointed at the one bulb pointed in the opposite direction from the rest. "You'll get an earful about it so you might as well fix it now."

Angus climbed down the ladder, dragged it back to where it was a moment ago, climbed back up, and fixed the bulb. "Good?"

Dougal gave him a thumbs-up. "I've been meaning to tell you we got a call from the Ramirez family in Dallas." He waited until Angus was on the ground before going on. "The January delivery."

"Five horses? I remember." Angus nodded. "It's a pretty penny."

"They canceled. Something about changing their mind." Dougal scratched his chin.

"Dammit." Mr. Ramirez served on the Fort Worth Rodeo board—the same board Richard Barrett chaired. The chances of this being a coincidence were slim to none. Barrett had said he'd do this. It looked like he was following through.

"Any others we should worry about? Other referrals from Barrett?" Dougal helped him move the ladder down.

"None that I can think of." He was done talking and thinking about Barrett. He switched gears. There was nothing his brother loved more than competing in one of the cutting horse shows. Dougal could talk about it for hours. "Still planning on competing in Arizona? Last I saw, it was a decent purse."

"I'm going." He glanced at the house. "Might be the only chance I have for some peace and quiet."

"I don't think they're planning on staying until the

babies are born." Angus frowned. "At least, I hope not. And they're not due until April. I think. I don't know how it works with triplets."

"Triplets." Dougal shook his head. "You're not scared?"

"Hell, yes." Angus climbed up the ladder. "I've never been so scared." His entire world was changing—there was a lot to be scared about.

"What are you scared of?" Their mother came out the front door, closing it behind her.

"You can't leave Savannah alone with Aunt Nola, Ma." Dougal pointed at the door. "She's liable to sneak out the back door and never be seen again."

"Oh, Dougal, she's not so bad." She waved Dougal's comments aside. "What's got you scared, Angus?" She took the steps down the front porch and came out into the yard, turning to assess their handiwork.

"Up to your standards?" Angus asked, lights in hand. "Tell me now, before I get even further."

"It looks great." She smiled. "Now stop dodging the question and tell me what's got you scared."

"What do you think?" Dougal nodded at the house.

She smiled. "You two seem pretty sweet on each other. That's a good place to start, if you ask me. There's no reason to be scared."

No reason? To start with, he *was* sweet on Savannah. He'd never been sweet on anyone before. Hell, more than sweet on her. It scared him how hard and fast he was falling for her. It scared him that this was turning into something more than doing the right thing. All of which was none of his mother's business. While he'd grown up with his family's unfailing support, they'd never been ones to talk about their feelings. "Nerves, I guess. Screwing up. That sort of thing."

"Nerves are to be expected, Angus." His mother's

quick reassurance didn't help. "You've always had good instincts. As long as you two communicate, you'll figure it all out."

Dougal rolled his eyes. "It's that easy?" Somehow, he always said what Angus was thinking.

"It's only as hard as you make it." Ma put her hands on her hips.

"That's another pearl of wisdom, there." Dougal chuckled.

"All right, you two. I appreciate the support." He went back to hanging lights. "Almost done."

"Good. Then both of you can come in and help decorate cookies." Ma clapped her hands together. "We've made about six dozen."

"I've got some work to do." Dougal shielded his eyes as he looked up at Angus. "Someone has to keep this place running."

"Remember that when you go to eat one." Ma wagged a finger at him before heading back inside.

"I'll eat as many damn cookies as I want to," Dougal mumbled, slinging another roll of lights onto his shoulder.

Angus laughed.

By the time the lights were strung, the sun was low in the sky and Dougal was officially out of patience. He headed for the barn while Angus went inside to check on Savannah.

The kitchen smelled delicious but resembled a battlefield.

On the table, cut-out gingerbread and sugar cookies were piled high on an assortment of festive trays. Aunt Nola sat at the head of the table sound asleep—head back, mouth open, and snoring up a storm.

Gertie and Willow were in a pile under the kitchen table. Savannah was wearing an apron and a fine coating of flour, humming along to the Christmas carols coming from the radio.

Ma was pouring candy into bowls on the kitchen counter.

"Think you got enough candy?" Angus peered into the bowls.

"Is something missing?" His mother frowned.

"I'm kidding." He shook his head. "What's all this for?"

"A gingerbread house." Savannah announced it with pure glee. "We're making one."

"She's never made one from scratch before." Ma was almost as excited as Savannah.

Angus sat on one of the barstools. "One year, we made a gingerbread castle."

"A castle?" Savannah's eyes went round. "I'm happy with a tiny cottage."

"I don't think Ma has ever made a tiny gingerbread house." Angus popped a chocolate-covered candy into his mouth.

"I didn't say *tiny*." His mother gave Savannah's shoulders a squeeze. "But we can make it a cottage."

It'd been a long time since he appreciated all the time and effort his mother spent to make the holidays special. Watching Savannah with his mother made him feel like a kid again. She was completely caught up in every little thing his mother did, nodding and standing at the ready to offer help.

"You want to make sure the frosting is thick so it'll hold the walls up." Ma laid down a thick stripe of white frosting. "Then you set up the house frame. Here are the walls." She pointed at the four sides of baked gingerbread. "Go ahead."

Savannah was so excited she almost dropped the gingerbread wall. "That would have been bad."

"Sugar, don't you sweat the small stuff. We can always bake more." His mother gave her shoulders another squeeze.

Angus could swear Savannah was holding her breath when she placed each wall—as if she was expecting them to topple over onto one another. They didn't. When she piped frosting between the cookie walls to cement them together, she was painstakingly slow.

"I've never seen anyone make such perfectly straight lines." His mother turned the stoneware lazy Susan to check the forming structure from all angles. "I mean perfect."

Savannah was beaming with pride.

"You got straight As in school, didn't you?" Angus ate another candy.

"I did." She glanced at him. "I was valedictorian of my class, too. High school and college."

"I knew it. Brains and beauty." He winked at her.

"I like understanding how things work. And getting things right," she explained. "There's something very gratifying about cooking. It's a lot like chemistry. I was good at Chemistry so I'd like to think I'd be a decent cook."

"You don't know?" his mother asked, filling the piping bag full of more frosting.

"No." She sounded so disappointed. "We have a chef. Two, actually. Daniella and Becky. They're both lovely, but the kitchen was their territory. I can boil an egg and make toast and bake cookies. But that's about it."

Thankfully, his mother didn't bat an eye. "Well, we can fix that. My meemaw expressed love through her cooking. Meaning, we were all a little soft around the middle. All of her recipes are good, hearty meals without a whole lot of fuss. I'd be happy to teach them to you. If you're interested, that is."

"I am." Savannah nodded.

"As long as you pace yourself." Angus didn't want to discourage her enthusiasm, but the little reading he'd done on a multiple pregnancy said to eat well, drink plenty of water, take walks, and rest.

Both the women were staring at him now.

"I will, I promise." Savannah's smile was sweeter than the candy he was eating.

"Savannah has a doctor's appointment tomorrow." His mother glanced back and forth between them. "I'm sure it'll put both your minds at ease."

It hadn't been easy to get Savannah in before the holidays, but due to the high-risk nature of her pregnancy, they'd squeezed her in. He didn't like how the term *high-risk* was used to describe her pregnancy, but it was standard for multiples. At least, that was what the nurse told them.

"And then your mother and sister will be here tomorrow afternoon." His mother twisted the piping bag closed and offered it to Savannah. "Tomorrow will be a big day. A good day."

Angus settled in as Savannah carefully attached the roof to the house. She was concentrating so hard that the tip of her tongue was sticking out of the corner of her mouth. It was the cutest damn thing she'd ever done. Today, at least. Every day, he found some new quirk or expression of hers that had him smiling like a damn fool. Not that he minded. Not in the least.

Chapter Ten

"I've washed my hands at least a half a dozen times and I still smell like frosting and gingerbread." She stretched. She was tired but content. "Then again, we did use a ton of both on the gingerbread house." Which she was ridiculously happy about. "It does looks pretty, doesn't it?"

"It's the prettiest gingerbread house I've ever seen." Angus sat on one of the bar stools that lined the long bar separating the kitchen from the great room. A laptop was open on the bar countertop in front of him and a plate of cookies sat beside that. He bit into an iced Christmas cookie, then used it to point at the gingerbread cottage. "I'm having a hard time believing you never made one before."

Savannah untied the apron, walked to the oversize pantry, and hung the apron on the hook inside—next to a collection of aprons. Orla and Nola had been so kind to let her come in and make such a mess. And they hadn't blinked an eye when she asked them about which cleansers and soaps to use in the dishwasher and on the marble countertops. She was mortified at her lack of basic common kitchen cleaning know-how and determined to learn to make up for it. Most people didn't have maids and chefs. She was now one of them.

"You know, I guess I have done it once before." She remembered the fancy children's event her parents had taken her and Chelsea to. She couldn't remember what charity it was—only that she'd been excited to decorate cookies.

"The truth comes out." He grinned. "It fell apart?"

She closed the pantry and frowned at him. "No. I remember it was a charity event we went to, as a family. I can't remember which charity." She paused, thinking, then shrugged. "It doesn't matter. Anyway, Chelsea and I were dressed up in these fancy white dresses. Mine had a red velvet bow and Chelsea's was green."

Angus was listening closely.

"I was so excited because I love to decorate cookies—"

"I sort of picked up on that today." He nodded at the cookies.

She smiled. "Anyway, it wasn't really a gingerbread house. It was a kit. One of those boxes that comes with everything. Cardboard-flavored cookies, prepackaged hard-as-rock decorating candy, and frosting that likely has a hundred-year shelf life."

"My mouth is watering." He finished off his cookie.

"Exactly. It doesn't really count. Then Chelsea started a gumdrop fight and our dresses got ruined and Dad was so mad he didn't talk to us all the way home." She shrugged.

"I can see why you'd remember it." He shook his head. "Chelsea's a piece of work."

"She is. And I wouldn't have her any other way." Savannah surveyed the day's accomplishments with pride.

A tray of gingerbread boys and girls with Red Hots buttons and raisin eyes. Two plates of sugar cookies with detailed frosting work and sprinkles. Peppermint double chocolate chip cookies with peppermint she'd broken herself. Raspberry and apricot thumbprint cookies. And shortbread—chocolate-dipped, plain, and lemon. "This was fun."

"I can tell." Angus was grinning.

"Oh?" She put her hands on her hips, waiting.

"You've got some flour, right...here." He pointed from her head to her toes.

"Do I really?" She reached up to smooth a hand over her hair.

He slipped off the stool and came around the bar into the kitchen. "Hold up." He ran the corner of a clean kitchen towel under the tap and approached her. "This might take a minute."

She laughed.

He stepped closer, running the towel along her cheek. "You smell good to me. Delicious, even." His smile was devilishly tempting.

She giggled, then covered her mouth. "You have to behave."

His gaze moved over her face, lingering on her lips. "Says who?" He dropped a kiss on her nose.

Her chest folded in on itself. "I do. Your mother is down the hall. And your aunt." She squeaked as his lips traveled along her neck.

"They're sawing logs, I guarantee it. They both turn into pumpkins at nine." He sucked her earlobe into his mouth.

"Angus." She shivered, pressing her hands against his chest. If he kept that up, she'd never be able to resist him.

Her body rebelled at the thought, but her mind was standing firm. "I...I thought we agreed we weren't going to—"

"Kiss?" He stopped kissing her. "Okay. No more kissing." He went back to wiping the flour from her face.

He was adorable. She could almost picture a little boy with the same concentration on his face. Or a little girl with his wide, clear eyes. She could imagine Angus playing with them and wearing that smile. This face. The warm brown eyes to the strong jaw. "We are going to have really beautiful babies."

He paused, a slow smile spreading across his face. "Yes, we are." He leaned back against the counter behind him. "You have a preference? Boys or girls?"

"Healthy." That was all that mattered. "You?"

"I wouldn't mind a little girl that looked like her mother." Then he shook his head. "Nope. Never mind. I don't think I'm cut out to be a little girl's father."

"Why not?" Savannah was surprised by the gruffness in his voice.

"I... I'd be worried all the damn time." He ran his hand along the back of his neck. "I'd have to wrap her in bubble wrap and get her a guard dog to keep the boys away—"

Savannah laughed. "Oh, Angus."

"What?" He looked downright afraid now. "Dammit all. I hadn't stopped to think..." He shook his head again.

She stepped forward and slid her arms around his waist. "Boys or girls or some of each, it will be a challenge."

His heart was thundering beneath her ear.

"But we will figure it out." She glanced up at him. "We will. Okay?"

He ran his hand down her back and buried his face against her neck. "Give me a minute."

She was in no hurry. The sound of his heart was strong

and solid and comforting. It wasn't the first time she'd felt true happiness since she'd arrived here. "Angus?"

"Hmm?" He didn't move.

"I know I've said it before, but thank you. For all that you've done for me. For us. We've invaded your life and you've made room for us, and acted like it was no big deal. I know it is."

He lifted his head then, searching out her gaze. "You're wrong, Savannah." He opened his mouth, then paused. "You haven't invaded, you… This is your home now." He had that look again, one that made her heart skip before picking up speed. "I know what you gave up when you chose to give us a chance. Having you, and them—" he glanced at her belly "—here is a damn big deal. I'll try harder to make sure you know that."

She wasn't sure what to say then. It was tempting to say more, to tell him that he was making himself at home in her heart, but the words wouldn't come. It wasn't fair to lay that on him on top of everything else. Her father's accusation that her hormones were affecting her emotions and decisions still lingered. If what she was feeling for Angus was colored by her pregnancy, she didn't want to say something she'd regret. They'd been honest with each other from the start. They'd agreed to try to be the family their children deserved. For now, that was more than enough.

The hunger in his gaze had her thoughts taking an immediate detour.

"You're so damn beautiful." His words were hoarse and raw.

Her lungs emptied and a bone-deep shudder ran the length of her spine. It was so new, this power he had over her. At times, like now, she was dizzy from it. Lucky for her, his arms kept her steady. She tore her gaze from his and drew in a deep breath. "I'm... I'm getting fat."

He cocked an eyebrow and released her. He scratched his chin, glanced at her again, then dropped to his knees. "Tell your momma she's supposed to be making room for you three." One big hand caressed the swell of her stomach. "It's not fat. It's all baby." He lifted her shirt, speaking to her stomach now. "Tomorrow, the doctor will tell her that, you'll see. I can't wait to see you three growing big and strong. Your momma will be more beautiful than ever because she's making you." He kissed her stomach three times. "I'll make sure to check in every night so you can tell me how things are going." He rested his head against her stomach and closed his eyes.

It seemed natural to run her fingers through his thick auburn hair. His close-cropped beard was rough against her skin, but she didn't mind. This was precious and intimate. This great, burly man on his knees, talking to his babies in her stomach. Her heart was so full. When the gentle roll in her belly made Angus chuckle and say, "There you are," she laughed, too.

When he looked up at her, her heart all but beat free of her chest. This was real—it had to be. What was bonding her to this man was solid and it wasn't just these babies. She did love him. She loved Angus McCarrick. The father of her babies. The man who said he wasn't the marrying kind.

"You're the doctor?" Angus stared at the man. Dr. Leland Wurtz was a lot younger than Angus had been expecting. He was more handsome than Angus had expected, too.

"Yes." Dr. Wurtz smiled. "Were you expecting my mother? She's still practicing, but I take on multiple and high-risk births." He waited, scanning Savannah's chart.

"Savannah is considered high-risk, but I can see if my mother has room in her client list."

"No, of course not," Savannah answered quickly.

Angus felt like an ass then. He wasn't the pregnant one. She was the one wearing a hospital gown with a cold white sheet draped over her lap, looking anxious.

"You're certain?" Dr. Wurtz asked him.

"Absolutely," Angus murmured.

"Not a problem." Dr. Wurtz sat on his stool. "Let's start with the basics." He referred to her chart. "It looks like you're about four months along?"

Savannah nodded.

"How are you feeling? Any complaints or concerns?" Dr. Wurtz set aside her chart.

"Not really. I'm tired and nauseous a lot of the time, but I know that's normal." She shrugged.

"What have you observed, Dad?" Dr. Wurtz turned to him. "Any concerns or observations?"

Dad. Right, *he* was Dad. He had a million questions, but one thing mattered more than all the rest. "I just want to know that Savannah and the babies are all healthy."

"Understandable." Dr. Wurtz nodded. "Let's find out. We're going to do a quick external ultrasound. We should be able to see all three babies and their heartbeats. In a few weeks, we'll get you set up to have a longer ultrasound. We'll check growth rate and the babies' weight then. Might even be able to see if you're having boys or girls or some of both. Let's set you back a little."

The moment he saw Savannah's face, he moved to her side. He wasn't the only one anxious about this visit. A surge of protectiveness rolled over him as he took her hand. She needed him to be strong for her. And, dammit, that was what he'd do.

Angus had plenty of experience with pregnancy—

when it came to horses. This was entirely different. The swell of Savannah's belly was covered in gel before the young doctor pressed the ultrasound transducer over her skin. On the monitor, shades of black, white, and gray appeared.

Savannah turned her head to look at the screen, her hand tightening on his when the first rapid thump-thump of a baby's heartbeat could be heard. The doc nodded, pointing at the screen. "One." He clicked a few buttons before moving the transducer down and to the left. "Two." Another heartbeat, a few more clicks on the keyboard. He moved the machine around, then back up. It took a minute. "Three. That one's shy." He sat back, smiling, and he typed in a few numbers.

Angus appreciated the heartbeat, but he was having a dickens of a time determining what was on the screen. He saw some shadows and movements, but not a lot that resembled a baby. Dr. Wurtz was pleased, though, and that was what mattered.

"Strong heartbeats. All of them." The doctor nodded, wiped off Savannah's belly, and wheeled the ultrasound cart back against the wall.

"That's good." Savannah sighed.

Angus helped her smooth her gown and sheet back into place. He needed to do something, dammit.

"It is." Dr. Wurtz sat on his stool again. "A few things. It's important you're eating enough. On average, we say to add about three hundred calories a day when you're expecting one baby. I'm not saying you need to add nine hundred calories a day, but you do need to up your caloric intake. For your height and build, your weight is on the low end."

"I'll try." Savannah wrinkled up her nose. "I'm still having a hard time with smells and throwing up."

"If it gets really bad, we might need to put you on some medication. Right now, taking your prenatal vitamins and making good, healthy dietary choices are key." He sat back. "Because you're carrying multiples, it's likely you'll experience stronger symptoms than someone carrying a singleton."

"Lucky you." Angus smiled down at her. "Anything else we should do? Or shouldn't do? Any restrictions? That sort of thing."

"Not really. I wouldn't take up training for a marathon or kickboxing, but a daily walk is a good idea." He picked up her chart. "I'm sure your last OB went over this with you, but there are a few increased risks with carrying multiples. Premature labor is one. With triplets, we'd like you to make it to thirty-two weeks. At least. Taking care of yourself won't guarantee you won't have any bed rest, but it's the best thing you can do for you and the babies. Finally, it's very important to reduce stress. Your body is already going through so much without adding the toll stress can take." He waited for them both to nod. "Good. I'd like to see you every two weeks—starting after your sonogram. We'll set that for twenty weeks. Any other questions?" Dr. Wurtz waited, then said his goodbyes.

When they left, they had an appointment card for their sonogram and a large Welcome Baby tote bag full of pregnancy and new baby items.

"You like him?" Savannah strapped her seat belt on.

"I do." Angus started the truck. "I guess I was expecting someone older." Less good-looking. He backed the truck out of the parking lot and navigated his way back to Main Street.

"Younger means he's up-to-date on all the newest and best techniques, right?" She rubbed a hand over her belly. "I'm going to get really big, aren't I?"

Angus grinned. "Probably."

"And that makes you smile?" She shook her head. "I already look big."

"Not according to the doc. As a matter of fact, I'm thinking about running into The Coffee Shop to pick up some more of those pastries you liked so much." He glanced her way. "I'll take that as a yes."

Savannah leaned back against the seat. "I did like them. And I didn't throw them up. If it's not out of the way—"

"Nothing is out of the way in Granite Falls, Savannah." He pointed down the street. "It's right there."

"Okay, then I'd love a pastry or two."

He was thinking more like a dozen. They did have company coming, after all. He parked in front of the shop. "I'll be back."

"I'll be here." She yawned, her head propped against the headrest. "I'll try to stay awake."

"Don't fight it. You heard the doc. Sleep." He rested his hand on her stomach. "Let her sleep."

She was smiling when he left her.

He heard his name called out as soon as he stepped inside the shop. There, huddled over cups of coffee and empty plates, sat his friends since childhood. Town veterinarian Buzz Lafferty, and the three Mitchell brothers—Hayden, Kyle, and John.

"You four sitting here thinking up trouble?" He glanced out the shop's picture window at his truck. He could make out Savannah, curled up on the front seat.

"From what I hear, you're the only one causing trouble." John Mitchell stood. "Gonna be a father, eh? Welcome to the club." He shook Angus's hand.

"When do we get to meet her?" Kyle Mitchell pointed out the window at his truck. "Or should we go introduce ourselves?"

"I'll get around to it. I haven't had time to catch my breath, let alone take her around meeting everyone." He ran a hand along the back of his neck. "We just came from a doctor's appointment."

"How'd it go? Like Dr. Wurtz?" Hayden Mitchell asked. "He took good care of Lizzie when she was pregnant."

"It went well. Three strong heartbeats for three babies." He appreciated that all four of his friends had the same reaction—a slow headshake. "Thanks again for the recommendation."

"Three?" John blew out a low whistle. "That's something."

"Go big or go home, I guess." Kyle laughed.

"I guess." Angus laughed, too. "I better get food and take her home."

"Duty calls." Hayden nodded. "If you need anything, let us know. We've got hand-me-downs by the box, if you're interested."

"So do we." Kyle raised his hand.

"Same here." Buzz nodded. "Boxes and boxes."

"I appreciate that. I'll let Savannah know." He'd grown up with these men and was glad he could still call them friends. There was a comfort in knowing they'd all been through what he was facing—well, close enough. Once things were more settled, he'd make sure Savannah got to know them and their families, too. "I'll see you."

Savannah was sound asleep when he got back to the truck. He put the box of pastries on the back seat, buckled in, and made the drive from town to the ranch. Winter, as mild as it was, had robbed the trees of most of their leaves and turned the grass to muted tones of brown and gray. Even so, Angus admired the scenery. The Hill Country was beautiful country—more so in the spring when the wildflowers were blooming. But spring was still months out yet. And with spring came the babies and a whole new set of challenges and changes. Good challenges. Good changes. All things to look forward to.

He glanced over at Savannah, his head sifting through the information Dr. Wurtz had mentioned. She needed to eat more and take care of herself. Which meant his job was to make sure both of those things happened. His mother had said today would calm his fears and make him feel better. Instead, alarming words like *premature birth*, *bedrest*, *complications*, *gestational diabetes*, and *high-risk* had him more on edge than ever. Not that he'd let on. All he could do was read the pregnancy book the good doctor had sent home with them so he'd know what to expect, what to look for, and how to make this as easy on Savannah and the babies as possible. If they were okay, he'd be okay. It was that simple. When that had come to be, he wasn't exactly sure. In less than a week, his reason for being had changed entirely. Did he have a real understanding of what was coming? Nope. Was he worried he'd screw something up? Absolutely. Was he concerned about Savannah and the babies' health? Hell, yes. Did he regret bringing her home or…falling in love with her? The realization was a lightning bolt to the chest. Shocking. Confusing. But true. He did. He loved Savannah. He took a deep breath. No regrets. Not in the slightest. He was happy she was pregnant—happy she was his. In time, he hoped she'd feel the same way.

Chapter Eleven

"Biscuits." Savannah secured the apron behind her. It had been a while since she'd been this excited. The kitchen had always been off-limits to her. Today, she was being welcomed and encouraged to try her hand at cooking. Orla and Nola, her teachers for the day, both felt biscuits were a solid starter recipe. Savannah was up for anything.

"Light and fluffy." Orla was putting bowls and measuring cups, spatulas, and canisters of spices on top of the marble countertop. "A good biscuit is the foundation for many a meal."

"That's true." Aunt Nola opened the refrigerator. "Don't forget the butter."

"You don't have to use butter." Orla set the butter aside. "Shortening works just as well. With buttermilk."

"If you want buttermilk biscuits." Nola shook her head, scooting the butter dish back into the middle of the counter. "Mine are lighter, flakier. And delicious."

Angus and Dougal sat on the other side of the counter, finishing off the stacks of pancakes Orla had made for breakfast. Savannah had managed to eat three of them and, so far, her stomach wasn't the least bit upset.

"Nola's biscuits are different than mine." Orla shook her head. "Different. Not better."

"Oh-ho, now who's getting all fired up?" Nola pushed her thick glasses up. "I say we make both and let her decide."

"Oh, come on now." Angus spoke up. "That's not fair, Aunt Nola. You can't put that on Savannah."

"Nope." Dougal mumbled around a mouthful of pancake. "They say they're not competitive, but that's a flat-out lie."

Savannah regarded the two women. "I'd love to try them both if you want to do that much baking. But I don't want to pick which is best."

"It's not too much work." Orla smiled. "We should take turns, though. We're supposed to be teaching her how to cook, Nola. Not judging a biscuit competition."

"Fine by me." Nola snorted. "We both know who makes the best biscuit anyway."

Savannah exchanged a look with Angus. What had she gotten herself into? When Orla and Nola learned she wasn't a cook, they'd been quick to offer her lessons. The idea of cooking lessons had been exciting. First, she'd always wanted to cook. And second, it would give her something to do beyond thinking about the babies and her growing infatuation with Angus. But now that they were all in the kitchen, her enthusiasm was cooling.

"You don't have to do this, Savannah." Angus's smile was sympathetic.

"No, I do want to learn." And she did. "I just don't want to cause any friction." She'd done enough of that lately.

"Ma. Aunt Nola." Angus sighed. "You two behave. Where's that holiday spirit the two of you were going on about?"

"You're right, Angus. I'm sorry, Savannah. We are, as Dougal said, a mite competitive. Both biscuits are delicious and both are handy to know." Orla looked and sounded repentant.

"But mine is better," Nola mumbled, but her smile was one hundred percent mischief.

It wasn't the first time Savannah saw a correlation between Nola and Chelsea. This was how Savannah pictured her sister later in life. Outspoken and stirring the pot. So, basically the same.

"Don't you two have something to do?" Nola peered over her glasses at Angus and Dougal.

"Yep." Dougal was up and gone before Angus could react.

From the little time Savannah had spent with Dougal, it was clear he preferred his peace and quiet. There was nothing peaceful or quiet about Nola.

Angus, however, didn't seem to be in a hurry. "I'll go when you promise to behave *and* not badger Savannah about this morning's doctor's appointment. We want to tell Savannah's mother at the same time."

It had been her request. She didn't want her mother and sister to feel like they were missing out. Hopefully, it wouldn't hurt anyone's feelings.

"I understand." Orla nodded. "And I think it's precious you want to share it all at once. Now." She waved her over. "Let's get started."

Savannah took another quick glance at the ingredients and tools assembled on the counter. "No recipe?"

Orla and Nola both tapped their temples.

"It's all in here." Orla smiled.

"A real Southern chef doesn't write down her secrets." Nola opened the flour. "It's all about keeping the family recipes a secret."

Savannah nodded, her confidence further shaken. No recipe. No notes. No problem. "Okay." She could do this. How hard could it be?

An hour later, Angus had gone out to work, there was a tray of Orla's biscuits in the oven, and Savannah was ready to admit defeat. Her two bowls of dough looked nothing like the dough in Orla's or Nola's bowls. And the two women noticed.

"Hmm?" Nola eyed the lumpy dough.

"I must have forgotten something." Savannah glanced back and forth between the baking powder and baking soda. "Or mixed them up?"

"That shouldn't make the dough look like…this." Nola pointed at her bowl.

"Nola." Orla chastised her. "It's a first attempt."

A terrible first attempt at that. Orla's dough was smooth and creamy. Nola's was rougher, but it didn't have the lumps of flour and butter that hers did. "What should I do?"

Orla and Nola exchanged a look.

"Let's start over." Orla patted her back.

"How about we bake up what Orla and I have made first, have a little snack, and then start again." Nola was already dumping Savannah's botched dough into the trash. "Nothing beats biscuits and honey. Or biscuits and jam."

Savannah's dough hit the bottom of the trash can with a resounding thud. It was biscuit dough. Not brain surgery. And yet, she couldn't manage it. It was enough to leave her deflated. Apparently, the others noticed.

"Don't you fret, sugar." Orla draped an arm around her shoulders. "It was your first try. It'll get better."

"You gotta get back on that horse." Nola nodded, patting her arm. "Shake it off. Have a seat." She pulled one of the kitchen chairs closer to the marble island where they were working. "Get off your feet and give those babies a rest. Those are the only buns in the oven that count."

Savannah was smiling when she sat.

"I remember being pregnant with Joseph. I have five boys, Savannah. Five." Nola was all business. She flipped the dough onto the well-floured counter. "And every time I got pregnant, my ankles would swell up like tree trunks. Big ol' things."

"I remember that." Orla laughed when her sister shot her a look of outrage. "My ankles were just the same."

Savannah looked down at her ankles. Was this something else she had to look forward to?

"Does Angus always hover that much?" Nola asked her, using a round cookie cutter to cut out biscuits.

"Hover?" Orla sounded offended. "He's only looking out for her. This might surprise you, Nola, but sometimes you say things that shouldn't be said."

Nola chuckled. "Guilty."

Savannah laughed. And it felt good.

"I'll say one thing, I've never seen my nephew so... protective." Nola rolled up the remainder of the dough.

Protective. Supportive. Generous. "He has been amazing." Which was one of the reasons she found him so irresistible.

"So, you don't mind him hovering?" Nola asked, assessing her with a mischievous grin.

Savannah's cheeks were blazing hot, an irrepressible smile spreading across her face.

Orla set the pan down and hugged her. "I can't tell you

how happy this makes me. All of it." She held Savannah away from her, her warm gaze locked with hers. "You. The babies. My boy finding someone. And seeing you light up when you think about him. That's all a mother wants for her child—happiness. You'll understand that soon enough." She patted her shoulders and let her go.

Savannah's chest compressed and her eyes stung. If only it was that simple.

"Don't you worry." Orla patted her cheek. "It will all work out just fine."

"Just like your next batch of biscuits." Nola put her tray of biscuits into the oven. "But first, let's eat some of Orla's perfectly-acceptable-if-not-perfect biscuits."

Savannah listened to the two of them carry on and enjoyed a pretty-close-to-perfect biscuit. Two biscuits in and she was feeling ready to try baking again.

"That's something else you have in common with Angus." Orla toasted her with a biscuit. "You don't give up. That'll serve you well in life. Especially when it comes to motherhood."

Motherhood. Her hand settled on her stomach and she took a deep, calming breath. She would be a good mother. A mother that could make homemade biscuits for her kids.

Angus sat on the top rung of pipe fence, watching a herd of young horses. They were full of energy, pawing the earth and tossing their manes.

"They look good." Dougal climbed up beside him.

"They should. We've worked hard to get here." And Angus was proud of the stock they were producing.

"We have." Dougal tipped his hat forward and scratched the back of his head. "I don't remember the last time I had a day off."

Angus pushed him. "There's no such thing as a day off in ranching." It was something their father said on a regular basis. He'd instilled a strong work ethic in them. If they didn't get up and do what needed doing, animals would suffer and the whole operation could hit a snag. Ranching was a lifestyle and Angus wouldn't have it any other way.

He hoped it wasn't too big a change for Savannah. On top of all the other changes. Try as he might, Dr. Wurtz's warnings cycled through his head again. Was he wrong to have left her with his mother and Aunt Nola? They could be a lot. But she probably wouldn't appreciate him following her around everywhere. Dougal sure as hell wouldn't appreciate him shirking his duties around the ranch to play Savannah's full-time shadow, either.

"Hello?" Dougal waved his hand in front of Angus's face.

"What?"

Dougal pushed him then. "Where'd you go?"

"Nowhere." He reached up and adjusted his cowboy hat against the breeze. "Is it my imagination or are we getting a cold snap?"

"It's your imagination." Dougal pointed at a pretty little roan. "That one, that filly over there."

Angus nodded. He'd noticed the animal. "She's got a good gait. Light on her feet." He pulled out his phone and made a quick note. He'd keep his eye on her.

"That one, too." Dougal nodded at a dapple-gray filly running along the far side of the pasture.

Angus studied the horse, then added it to his watch list. "We should start working with them in the spring."

"Yep." Dougal agreed. "Didn't you have a doctor's appointment this morning?" He glanced his way. "Is that what's eating you?"

Angus glanced at his brother. "Nothing's eating at me."

"Well, that's a pile of horse shit." Dougal shook his head.

Angus chuckled.

Every horse in the field turned his way, their ears pivoting in his direction.

"Everything okay? With Savannah and the babies?" Dougal's tone was gruff.

"They're fine." Angus took off his hat and leaned forward. "Good."

"Well, that's something, isn't it?" Dougal clapped him on the shoulder.

"It is." Angus slowly turned the hat, working the leather band back onto the crown of his well-worn brown felt cowboy hat. "I don't know what the hell I'm doing."

Dougal made a noncommittal sound.

"The doctor said some things that scared the shit out of me." That was it. He was scared for her and the babies. And there was nothing he could do. "This is a high-risk pregnancy—"

"What the hell does that mean?" Dougal was frowning.

"It means there's a higher risk of complications." He ran his fingers through his hair.

"Okay." Dougal blew out a long, slow breath. "Well, shit."

Angus chuckled. "Exactly. I don't want Savannah or the babies to be at risk." He spun his hat in his hands. "And I sure as hell don't like feeling…useless."

"You are pretty damn useless." Dougal shoved him again.

"Thanks." Angus put his hat back on and sat up. "You're a real ball of sunshine."

Dougal's eyes narrowed and he shook his head. "I'm

listening to your sorry ass, aren't I? That's about all I can do."

Angus felt like an ass. "Sorry."

"You should be. You're sitting there, thinking the worst. That's me, not you." Dougal slid off the fence. "The doc said good things, right? So, knock it off. Savannah doesn't need any of that mopey shit, either."

Angus nodded. "You're right."

"I'm what?" Dougal froze, cupping his hand around his ear. "Say that again."

Angus laughed, emphasizing each word. "You are right."

"Damn." Dougal pulled his phone from his pocket. "I'm putting that on the calendar."

"You should. I doubt it'll happen again." Angus jumped off the fence. "I'm gonna go back up to the house."

"Probably a good idea. Savannah probably needs rescuing from Ma and Aunt Nola by now." He shook his head. "I'm going to help Jack with that damn tractor. Again."

"Good luck." Angus headed back to the barn before he could tease his brother about the "damn tractor." Dougal had a hate-hate relationship with the machine. It was a perfectly good tractor—until Dougal used it. Every time he used it, something went wrong.

By the time he'd made it to the house, he was feeling more like himself. Dougal's advice was solid. Focus on the good. For all the warnings the doc had given them, he'd said all was well. That was good. No, that was great. He'd focus on that and make sure Savannah didn't pick up on his worries.

"Hey, Willow." He stooped on the back porch, scratching the Lab behind the ear. "You holding down the fort?"

Willow stood and stretched.

"Wanna go inside and see what they're up to?" he asked the dog, who was keeping pace at his side. He opened the back door and was greeted with laughter. "Sounds like they're having a good time." Which was a relief.

Gertie was a bullet, running across the room to leap into his arms.

"Hey, baby girl." He cradled the wriggling dog against his chest. "Let's go see Savannah."

"And then I heard this thump-thump overhead." His mother was talking and laughing. "And I looked at my husband and asked, 'Where is Angus?'"

He came around the corner to find Savannah perched on the edge of a kitchen chair, listening intently.

"He jumped up and ran outside. 'I left the ladder up,' he said." His mother started laughing again. "I ran outside, too, but I knew it was Angus on the roof. He was a little mountain goat. Sure enough, there he was. No fear. Just his red curly hair blowing in the breeze and his diaper slipping off."

Savannah shook her head.

"What can I say, I like living on the edge." Angus shrugged.

"You liked keeping your father and me on our toes." His mother wagged her finger at him.

"What about you, Savannah?" Aunt Nola was cleaning up. "Did you get into any mischief when you were a little thing?"

Savannah wrinkled up her nose. "Not quite like that but… I was in ballet when I was about five. I was going to play a dancing flower—"

"And I bet you were precious." Ma was beaming at her.

"I didn't like ballet." She shook her head. "I didn't want to be a dancing flower or perform in front of an audience.

If I was going to have to, I wanted to take my stuffed dog, Chance, with me. I took him everywhere." She sighed. "When the lights went down, our ballet teacher set us up on the stage, took Chance with her, and then the music started and the lights went up and I took one look at the audience and started sobbing."

His mother and Aunt Nola both "aww'd" over her story.

"I sat in the middle of the stage through the whole song, sobbing, while everyone else danced around me."

"That's sad." He didn't like the mental picture it conjured up. Little Savannah, sobbing for her toy under the bright lights. "There's no reason you couldn't have danced with Chance."

Savannah turned a huge smile his way. "My teacher said it would ruin the performance. Which I managed to do anyway."

"Chelsea, on the other hand, was aways up to something." Savannah shook her head. "She still is. I can't wait for you to meet her," she said to Ma and Aunt Nola.

Which was a reminder that Savannah's mother and sister were coming. Today.

"Is there anything I need to do to get their room ready for them?" Angus asked. Unfortunately, they were down to one guest room. Which meant Lana and Chelsea would have to room together.

"All set." His mother gave him a reassuring smile. "No need to worry."

Easy for his mother to say. She hadn't seen the Barrett home—or how the family lived. Now he was expecting Lana Barrett to share a bed with her daughter.

"Why are you making that face?" Aunt Nola wiped her hands on the kitchen towel.

"I'm not making a face." He forced himself to smile.

"All good. I should probably go wash up before they get here."

"Go on. We're making lunch." Aunt Nola shooed him away.

Angus glanced at Savannah—Savannah, who was studying him. So much for not adding to her stress. He headed from the kitchen, kicking himself. He needed to be more careful.

"Angus?" Savannah had followed him. "Is everything okay?"

"Yes." He smiled again.

"Are you regretting inviting my mom and sister?" Her gaze locked with his.

"No." He swallowed. "I'm… Well, it's not exactly what they're used to, is it? What you're used to, for that matter."

Savannah's brow furrowed. "Angus." Her hand gripped his arm. "Your home is lovely. Your family is lovely. *You've* made it possible for us to be together for the holidays after…" She broke off, blinking rapidly.

Dammit. He drew her into his arms. "You should be with your family during the holidays. That's what the holidays are for." He ran his hand down her back, savoring the feel of her. She felt so right in his arms. It felt so right to have her here.

"I only hope Chelsea doesn't do or say something that's too…Chelsea." She laughed.

His hold eased on her. "She can't compare to Nola." He was glad she was smiling again.

"Don't let her hear you say that. She'll consider it a challenge." She stepped away from him, but her gaze landed on his lips. And she was wearing that look. He swallowed.

"I'll go shower." He cleared his throat.

She nodded, still staring at his mouth.

"Savannah." His voice was all longing. He wanted to kiss her. Ached to feel the softness of her lips beneath his.

Her eyes met his and he all but groaned. The hunger on her face set him on fire.

"A cold shower." He spun on his heel and headed for his room.

Chapter Twelve

"I tried to pack as much as I could." Chels pointed at two bulging suitcases Momma was unpacking. "I didn't know what you'd want—you know, what might fit when you're the size of a hot-air balloon," she teased. "It might be my imagination, but you seem a little rounder than when you left." She cocked her head to one side and stared at Savannah's stomach.

"Really?" Savannah smoothed her soft cotton sweatshirt over her stomach.

"No." Chelsea hugged her. "You look exactly the same. A little less stressed—okay, a lot less stressed. Probably from all the sex you're having."

"Chelsea." Momma stopped unpacking and stared at Chelsea.

"Momma." Chelsea sighed. "How else do you think she got pregnant?" She patted Savannah's stomach. "There's no point in being a prude now."

Momma huffed and went back to putting Savannah's things away.

She'd dreamed of Angus every night since she'd arrived. Cuddling Angus. Kissing Angus. Making love to Angus. But the real thing? Not possible. She and Angus had honored their agreement that sex was off the table. It was the smart thing to do, but there were plenty of times throughout the day that she regretted ever suggesting such a thing. There was something about him, something virile and sexy, gentle and tender—basically everything about him appealed to her.

Savannah sat on the edge of the bed. "You don't have to do that, you know."

"I like doing." Momma smiled. "I like feeling useful."

"How are you feeling?" Savannah glanced at Chelsea, suspecting her sister would be more forthcoming than their mother.

Chelsea gave her a so-so hand wobble.

"I'm fine. I'm good." Momma zipped up the now empty suitcase and slid it under the bed. "I'm even better now that I'm here."

"What do you think of the place?" Savannah held her breath. Their mother had been born into wealth and spent every day since waited on, hand and foot. While the McCarrick ranch was by no means rough living, it wasn't what her mother was used to.

"It's charming." Momma stopped to look around the guest room. "Homey."

Chelsea nodded. "Who was the hunky gardener out back? Thick black hair. Wily beard. He could till my garden anytime."

"Chelsea." Momma's cheeks went red.

Chelsea giggled.

Savannah did, too. She couldn't help it.

"Momma, you didn't see those shoulders? I bet he's good with his hands and knows how to plant bulbs like nobody's business."

Momma was more purple now.

"And gives the ground a good soaking, too. To keep everything nice and wet." Chelsea kept laughing, watching their mother the entire time.

Savannah couldn't breathe; she was laughing too hard.

A little peep slipped from Momma, then she was laughing, too. "Chelsea, you are a mess." She sat between them, hugging them close. "Whoever thought gardening had so many euphemisms for…"

"Sex?" Chelsea finished. "Oh, I'm just getting started."

"No." Momma jumped up. "I can't take anymore. My ears will catch fire if you keep that up."

"I missed you two." Savannah sighed.

"Oh, sweet girl." Momma shook her head. "How can I ever apologize for…everything?"

Savannah was up then, taking her mother's hand. "You have nothing to apologize for, Momma. Nothing." She hugged her close. "Now you're here and we get to celebrate Christmas together."

There was a knock on the door. "You three doing okay?" Angus asked. "You need anything?"

"Hey, Angus." Chelsea smiled her mischievous smile. "I need your help. I was asking Savannah who your gardener was."

"Chelsea." Momma let go of Savannah. "Don't you dare."

"Gardener?" Angus scratched his jaw. "Dougal probably. Gardening is how he unwinds."

"A stress reliever, huh?" Chelsea was enjoying herself far too much. "It's important to let all that stress out."

"Exactly." Angus shot Savannah a questioning smile.

Savannah started laughing again. Her sister had no shame.

Angus looked from one to the other. "Do I want to know?"

"No." Momma held up her hands. "Goodness gracious, no."

"And who, exactly, is Dougal?" Chelsea was not about to be deterred.

"My brother." Angus leaned against the door frame. "He's washing up now. You'll meet him at lunch."

"Oh, goody." Chelsea rubbed her hands together. "I'm famished."

Savannah couldn't seem to stop laughing.

"Heaven help me." Momma pressed both hands to her cheeks. "Angus, thank you so much for having us. I hope it wasn't too great an inconvenience."

"You're family, Mrs. Barrett. You're always welcome here." When Angus was sincere, like now, Savannah was torn between adoring him and wanting to do things to him that would mortify her mother.

"You are a dreamboat, aren't you?" Chelsea shook her head. "Would you say you and Dougal are alike?"

Savannah hadn't had much one-on-one time with Dougal. He was more of a loner than Angus. Quieter. She didn't know what he'd do when Chelsea came for him. It would be interesting to watch, that was for sure.

"He's on the gruff side. Not as verbal." Angus shrugged. "But we're brothers so…"

"Oh, the strong, silent type?" Chelsea nodded. "Lovely."

Savannah's cheeks were beginning to hurt from all the smiling and laughing.

"Is there anything we can do to help with lunch?" Momma was edging toward the door, shooting warning glares Chelsea's way.

"No, ma'am. I think it's about ready." Angus cleared his throat. "We keep things casual around here so Ma, Aunt Nola and Harvey and Jack will be joining us."

"Who are Harvey and Jack?" Chelsea checked her reflection in the mirror, running her fingers through her platinum hair.

"Ranch hands. Good men. They've been with us for years—like family, really."

"I'm sure they're lovely gentlemen." Momma seemed calmer now. "Lead the way." She hooked arms with Angus, leaving Savannah and Chelsea to follow.

"Give me the scoop real quick," Chelsea whispered. "Is Dougal available? Straight? Interested?"

"I can't help you, there, Chels. I don't know."

"Too busy with all the sex?" Chelsea nudged her.

"Chelsea, we can hear you." Momma called back. "Please, please lower your voice."

Angus chuckled then.

"You're no fun, Momma." Chelsea didn't bother keeping her voice down. "I'm simply trying to determine whether or not Dougal is available for…private gardening sessions."

Savannah burst out laughing then. She was settling in here just fine, but having her mother and sister here made it really, truly feel like home.

"Gardening doesn't mean…gardening, does it?" Angus asked Savannah once they were taking their seats at the table.

She shook her head. "Not at all." She rolled her eyes. "I think she's just messing with Momma, but you never really know with Chels. I guess we're about to find out."

Angus sat beside her and rubbed his hands together.

"She'll keep him on his toes, that's for sure." He, for one, was looking forward to the show.

"You don't think you should warn him?" Savannah's hand covered his.

He liked that she reached for him—as if it was the most natural thing in the world. It was beginning to feel that way. He turned his hand over, threading their fingers together. "Nope. Dougal's a big boy. He can handle it." Maybe.

"I can see a family resemblance." Ma nodded. "Lana, you look like their sister, not their mother."

"You're too kind, Orla. But all the credit goes to my skin cream." Lana smiled.

"Good genes." Aunt Nola used her fork to point at the Barrett women. "Damn good genes."

"That, too," Lana agreed. "My mother still turns heads when she walks into a room."

"Oh, I do, too." Aunt Nola grinned. "And then, when they realize it's me, everyone scatters." She cackled.

Leave it to Aunt Nola to break the ice. Even Harvey and Jack seemed to relax a bit.

Lunch was family style—as was the normal. Angus tried not to think about the elegantly arranged plates and maids hovering to clear dishes that was the norm in the Barrett household. Funny how he'd never been troubled by such thoughts when it was just Savannah. Now that Lana was here, he saw everything through new eyes. The view left him torn.

"This is delicious." Lana took a bite of Aunt Nola's chicken church spaghetti. "It reminds me of something my meemaw used to make."

"She probably did." Ma sounded proud as she went on. "It's an old Southern staple. Chicken, canned mushroom soup, canned cream of chicken soup, spaghetti noodles. That's about it. Easy, cheap, and filling."

Angus winced at the *cheap* comment. Cheap, for his Ma, was a point of pride. The better deals or more coupons, the better. Cheap, for Lana Barrett, likely meant low quality or less than.

"Will you pass the rolls?" Savannah asked.

He was pleased, however, to see her enjoying every bite of her lunch. She took two rolls, slathered them both with butter, and smiled at him—looking a bit sheepish.

"What? I'm hungry." She shrugged.

"Nothing." He added a third roll to her plate. "I'm tickled pink." Her smile brushed aside all else.

"How did the doctor's appointment go?" Nola piped up, completely oblivious to the way Chelsea Barrett was sizing Dougal up.

"You beat me to it, Nola." Ma nodded. "I figured I'd wait to ply you two with questions until we were all together."

"I figured you'd pester Savannah until she cracked." Angus shot Savannah a smile.

Savannah smiled back, looking proud.

"We didn't ask." His mother sighed. "You wanted to wait until her mother and sister were here, so we did."

Angus was impressed—and surprised. His mother and Nola liked to be in the know about everything. "I appreciate it."

"You had an appointment this morning?" Lana's face lit up. "How are the babies?"

Savannah put her half-eaten roll on her plate. "They're fine. Three heartbeats."

"Strong heartbeats," Angus added. To him, the strong bit was important.

"That's good." Dougal served himself another large portion of chicken church spaghetti.

"What else did the doctor say?" Lana asked. "Don't spare a thing."

"We grammas want to know it all," Orla agreed, winking at Lana.

"We're scheduled for the big sonogram in a couple of weeks. They should be able to determine the size and weight of the babies." Angus looked to Savannah for anything he might be missing.

"And, maybe, the sex of the babies." Savannah eyed her roll. "I'm not sure I want to know."

"Nice to have a few surprises." Aunt Nola nodded.

"Not like there hasn't been plenty of those in, oh, the last month or so." Chelsea laughed.

For the first time, Dougal looked her way.

Savannah nudged Angus, hard. He nodded, watching to see what happened next.

Dougal blinked and went back to eating.

Chelsea was shocked.

And Angus almost choked on his food trying not to laugh. He got the feeling Chelsea Barrett didn't often get a brush-off. Not that that was what Dougal was doing. He was a cool character.

"Whatever you decide, of course." Lana Barrett smiled.

Ma hesitated before saying, "But I can see benefits to finding out."

"I can, too," Lana agreed.

"I just wanted to see what you'd say." Savannah smiled. "I don't think I could handle any more surprises. Like Chels said, we've all had more than enough."

"Oh, good." Lana pressed a hand to her heart. "I want to know."

"Right?" Ma giggled. "I can't wait."

"Are you two waiting to get hitched until after the babies are here?" Aunt Nola asked. "I know some folk frown on a pregnant bride, but I say that's hogwash. Plenty of marriages have started with a baby—good strong marriages, too. Nothing to be ashamed of."

And just like that, the table went quiet.

"We're not planning on getting married, Aunt Nola." Angus hoped his aunt would contain herself.

"What?" Nola stopped eating. "What, now? Why the hell not? What sort of nonsense is that?"

"Nola," Ma shushed her. "Eat and mind your own business."

Savannah had almost finished with the third roll, but she stopped and sat back in her chair. There was a green cast to her skin.

Dammit. He'd hoped her liking the food meant she'd tolerate it better. Instead, he'd fed her too much and made her sick. And he suspected his aunt spouting off and speaking her mind didn't help. "You okay?" he whispered.

She nodded, sipping her water. "I need a minute." She excused herself and left the room.

Which brought all conversation to an end.

"Is she okay?" Nola asked. "She's still getting morning sickness?"

"You didn't help, Nola." Ma sighed, shaking her head.

Angus nodded. "The doc says the symptoms a woman has with one baby are more intense with multiples."

"Poor Savannah." Lana put her napkin down and stood. "I'll go."

"Thank you, Lana." Angus was on the verge of following, but he let Lana go. Savannah wasn't feeling well, and she'd probably welcome her mother's care.

Lana gave him a gentle smile and left.

"I only said what we were all thinking." Nola shrugged.

Angus exchanged a long-suffering look with Dougal.

"How is Savannah doing?" Chelsea asked. "I'm no doctor, but she looks awful skinny."

"She needs to up her calorie intake, as tolerated." He left it at that.

"We'll just have to see what agrees with her." Ma stood, clearing plates. "Harvey, Jack, you two want more?"

"You're so quiet, I almost forgot you were sitting there." Aunt Nola frowned. "What's that mess hanging off your face, Harvey?"

"Watch out, Harvey. Aunt Nola isn't a fan of beards." Dougal shot his aunt a look.

"The lady has the right to her opinion." Harvey smiled. "It's wrong, but that's okay."

Aunt Nola cackled and passed the food.

Ten minutes later, Ma, Chelsea, and Aunt Nola had cleared the table, Harvey and Jack had gone back to the barn, but there was still no sign of Lana or Savannah.

Angus checked his phone as he paced the length of the great room. No messages or phone calls—nothing to distract him from worrying over Savannah.

"You're looking tense." Dougal stood at his side. "You're not saying all there is to be said."

Angus glanced at his brother.

"Talk, dammit. I can see something's eating at you."

"I'm in a tailspin." Angus ran a hand along the back of his neck. "All of this." He shook his head. He didn't even know where to start.

"Is it…bad?" Dougal's voice was low.

"I don't know." No, it wasn't bad. "If… If she weren't pregnant, none of this would be happening. She wouldn't be here." Which wasn't exactly a revelation. He wasn't making a lick of sense.

"Probably not." Dougal waited, his face clouded with confusion.

"*Definitely* not." He shook his head. "It'd be me and you, since Ma and Aunt Nola had made other plans for Christmas this year, and a whole lot of quiet." It sounded pretty damn depressing.

"You mean, back to normal?" Dougal sighed.

He nodded. Normal. Meaning, boring. He couldn't picture going back to that. Lucky for him, he didn't have to. But there was a hard jagged knot that stayed glued in the pit of his stomach. It was that knot, like a splinter beneath the skin, that he couldn't ignore.

"She wouldn't choose me, Dougal. There's something humbling knowing that, without fate forcing her hand, I wouldn't stand a chance with her." That was it. Now that he knew he loved her, he didn't want to be someone she'd had to settle for. He wanted her to choose him for him. To love him.

"Now you're being stupid." Dougal sighed. "You're gonna let that get in your way? You *do* have her. It shouldn't matter how you got her. If you're happy, if she makes you happy, then be happy. Screw the rest."

"That easy, huh?" Angus chuckled at his brother's straightforward advice.

"It should be." Dougal shook his head. "Damn, Angus, for a man who's got a good head on his shoulders, you're not thinking straight. See what's in front of you. Be happy."

"You're right."

"Of course I am." Dougal was frowning at him. "And if Ma and Aunt Nola weren't here, then there'd be no gingerbread and, dammit, I do like me some gingerbread." He grinned then.

Angus grinned back. "Speaking of seeing what's in

front of you. You happen to notice a pretty blonde giving you a certain look at the lunch table?"

Dougal was frowning again. "What the hell are you talking about?"

"I'll take that as a no." It was Angus's turn to sigh now. "Maybe keep your eyes open at dinner? You might like what you see." He clapped his brother on the shoulder and laughed. Dougal might have just knocked some sense into his head, but he had absolutely no awareness of Chelsea Barrett and the numerous times she'd batted her eyelashes his way. For Dougal's sake, it might be best if his brother didn't catch on. Unlike Savannah, Chelsea wasn't exactly long-term relationship material. It'd be a shame for his brother to take an interest only to have his heart broken. Just the thought of losing Savannah put him in a cold-sweated panic. He wouldn't wish that sort of pain on his worst enemy.

Chapter Thirteen

Plenty of marriages have started with a baby—good strong marriages, too.

Nola's no-nonsense words floated through her brain.

She'd thought there was nothing left to upset her stomach, but she was wrong. Nausea kicked in and sent bile flooding her mouth. With a groan, she pushed off the bed and headed back into the bathroom.

She sat on the mat in front of the toilet and leaned against the wall, resting her hands on her stomach. Nola hadn't meant any harm. She asked a question they'd likely get asked over and over again. Why the hell weren't they getting married? *Because I want it all.* Now that answer seemed insufficient somehow.

"Savannah?" Chels called out. "I'm coming to check on you so try not to throw up for a minute, okay?"

She didn't say anything.

"Are you alive?" Chelsea came into the bathroom and sat beside her on the floor. "What can I do?"

Savannah shook her head. "Ugh."

"Where's Momma?"

Savannah shrugged, not trusting herself to speak.

"I'm so sorry, Pickle." She rubbed Savannah's shoulder. "I can only imagine how miserable you feel."

Until Nola sounded off and the throwing up started, she'd been pretty content. Sitting at that table, Savannah had felt like she belonged. Like they were a family. And then she was reminded that they weren't—not really. Not the way she'd pictured her family, anyway. Angus cared for her, but he didn't love her the way she wanted. And without that, could they ever truly be a family? Or was she being ridiculous?

She was exhausted. She swallowed and rested her head on her sister's shoulder.

"Well, Angus's mom and aunt are awesome. That Nola is a hoot—if a little outspoken. I hope I'm half as cool a badass as she is when I'm her age." She rested her head on Savannah's. "Dougal, on the other hand, is completely disinterested. I swear, I have never had anyone look right through me like that. I'm not going to lie, my ego hasn't recovered."

Savannah smiled. "His loss."

"I know. But still. Does he not see what a hottie I am?" Chelsea laughed. "Here I was hoping to have a festive fling. I guess I'll have to get over that. Or give Harvey or Jack another look?"

"No." Savannah shook her head. "Harvey's attachment to his beard is concerning. I don't think Jack has said more than five words to me, but I think he's closer to Momma's age."

"I guess I'll have to jingle my own bells." Chelsea sighed.

Savannah laughed then. "You have a way with words, Chels."

"What can I say? It's a gift." She took Savannah's hand. "Feeling any better?"

She hadn't thought about throwing up for a whole two minutes. "I don't think my stomach is on the spin cycle anymore." Her heart, however, was another matter.

"Distraction. It's a very useful skill."

"Chels…" She took a deep breath.

"Yes, Pickle?" Her sister squeezed her hand.

"I think… I'm so confused." The words were a whisper.

"What do you mean?" Chelsea leaned back enough that Savannah had no choice but to sit up. "About what?"

"I… I…" She broke off. Chelsea was quick to fall in love, she always had been. And it never lasted. That wasn't the sort of love she wanted. She wanted the real deal—with Angus.

But Angus… Her heart hurt. He didn't want to get married. He didn't. He'd only proposed because it was the right thing to do. Doing the right thing was important. Knowing Angus, he'd marry her tomorrow because he still felt that way. She could marry Angus. But would that be enough for her? Would she be happy in a marriage knowing her husband didn't love her with every fiber of his being? Why was she even considering it?

"Pickle?" Chelsea sat forward, her eyes searching. "What's going on? And don't tell me nothing. Twin thing." She tapped her temple.

"Nothing worth talking about." Before she said or did a thing, she was going to think it all through and get some sleep. Once she clued Chelsea in, her sister would be like a dog with a bone. And while she loved her sister's ability to be single-mindedly focused, she wasn't sure she could take that kind of energy at the moment. "I'm tired."

"Um, you know there are three people growing inside of you right this very minute, don't you?" Chelsea's brows rose. "Three." She counted off on her fingers. "I'm tired just thinking about it."

"Will you stay in here with me?" Savannah asked. "I don't snore as loud as Momma. And I've missed you."

"Where did that come from?" Chelsea was back to studying her again. "I don't really want to be in the same room when Angus comes sneaking in for—"

"There won't be any sneaking in." Especially if Chelsea was sharing a bed with her. "Not with Momma here. It's too weird."

"Oh, please tell me you're not serious. You're too young to think like that, Pickle." Chelsea shook her head, disapproving. "Especially when you've got a big, strong, manly man waiting in the wings."

She didn't want to think about *her* big, strong, manly man at the moment. "Chels, please."

Chelsea's eyes narrowed. "You're really not going to tell me what this is about?"

"Like I said, I'm tired and I've missed you." She was pretty sure her sister wasn't going to buy it, but it was all she could come up with at the moment.

"And?"

Savannah shrugged. "That's it."

"You're going to tell me eventually, you know that. You might as well get it out now." Chelsea took her hand again. "I don't like it when you keep secrets from me."

"You keep secrets all the time." She tried to smile.

"Only because I'm afraid I'd shock you so badly you'd never speak to me again." It took a lot to make Chelsea blush, but she was blushing.

Savannah shook her head. "Nothing you could ever do or say would manage that, Chels. I promise." She didn't want to think about their father or all the hateful things he'd said and how it had made her feel. She could never, ever, do something like that to someone she loved.

"I know." Chelsea nodded. "Because you're the best sister anyone could ever wish for."

"I am." Savannah smiled. "Now I think I'm going to crawl to the bed and take a nap."

"Oh, Pickle. I'll crawl with you." She smiled.

"No, no. You need to go make yourself impossible for Dougal to miss. I have faith in you." Savannah waved her sister aside. "Go on. You know you want to."

Chelsea stood and held out her hand. "You know me so well. Come on, I'll help you to bed. We'll go really, really slowly."

Savannah took her sister's hand and her help to the bed. But once the lights were off and the door was shut, Savannah's mind refused to quiet.

Was Nola right? Was she being nonsensical? Should she set aside the love she craved and accept his marriage proposal? She was having triplets—the idea of doing every day alone was more than a little terrifying. She'd have Angus for her husband, even if she didn't have any claim on his heart. It did, in a practical way, make sense. Nola hadn't exactly been tactful, but she hadn't been wrong.

No. She couldn't do it. She couldn't settle. This was where she had to be now, and she was thankful, but her future wasn't set. Maybe having something more to think of, something beyond the pregnancy and the babies and Angus, would help.

Think, Savannah. She'd had a life before Angus; why was she basing all of her decisions on him now? Co-parenting was a thing. People did it all the time. She and Angus could make it work and she wouldn't have to live every day knowing her husband didn't love her.

Enough.

She was a strong, independent woman. It was time she started acting like it again.

She didn't need her father or her father's money.

She didn't need Angus or his money.

She had her untouched inheritance from her nanna and a perfectly respectable Public Service and Communication degree. She'd been the press secretary for the Austin Cougars football team for almost a decade and served on numerous nonprofit and charitable foundations—it shouldn't be too hard for her to find a decent job. She had Momma and Chelsea, too. She wasn't alone. She would be okay. *I can do this.*

When it came to the babies, things got a little complicated. She took a deep breath. But that's what co-parenting meant, sharing parenting duties. She and Angus would work that part out together. The fact that her heart would break every time she saw him didn't factor into it. This was about giving her babies the best: a mother and father that loved them unconditionally.

Angus tipped his black felt cowboy hat forward and shoved his hands into his coat pockets. The temp had dropped a good ten degrees over the last hour and the wind had a sharp bite to it. He glanced back at Savannah. The tip of her nose was red and her ears weren't covered, but she and Chelsea were laughing and talking—and that made him happy.

"There are over a million lights here on the courthouse lawn." Ma was pointing up into the branches of the trees overhead. "Isn't it beautiful?"

"It is." Lana Barrett was in awe. "It's a Christmas wonderland."

"People drive from all over to see all the lights." Ma nodded. "I think it gets better with each year."

"It's the same." Aunt Nola argued. "Every year, the same thing."

Angus chuckled.

"Nola." Ma sighed. "Well, *I* think it gets prettier every year."

"It's certainly impressive," Lana agreed. "I can't imagine it ever getting old."

Nola snorted. "I'm going for hot chocolate."

"Sounds good." Angus nodded. "Anyone else want some?"

"Me." Chelsea raised her hand. "And Savannah." She turned a dazzling smile on his brother. "What about you, Dougal? Are you a hot chocolate sort of man?"

Dougal blinked at Chelsea. "I'll lend a hand."

Angus turned on his heel before everyone saw him laughing. Either his brother was more clueless than imagined or he was in fact rattled by Chelsea Barrett. He managed to hold on until they were across the street at the hot chocolate stand operated by the high school agriculture club.

"You been kicked in the head recently?" Aunt Nola peered at Dougal over her thick glasses.

"No." Dougal frowned at her.

"You sure?" Aunt Nola's drawn-on eyebrows were almost in her hairline.

"I'm sure." Dougal sighed. "Is there a reason you're asking?"

Aunt Nola shook her head. "Where do I start?"

Angus was in danger of laughing, so he took a sip of hot chocolate. "Damn." He held the cup away. "That is hot."

"Still think I'm the one that's been kicked in the head?" Dougal shot Aunt Nola a look.

"I don't know. I can't account for either of you." Aunt Nola took an insulated cup in each hand. "You're both clueless, as far as I'm concerned. I guess that's why they say youth is wasted on the young." She carried the cups back across the street.

"What was that all about?" Dougal frowned after her. "I wasn't the dumbass surprised that the *hot* chocolate was *hot*."

"But you are the dumbass that has a woman doing her damnedest to catch your eye." Angus pointed at Chelsea with his cup.

"Savannah's sister?" Dougal appeared sincerely shocked.

"I didn't think I'd have to spell it out for you." At this point, Angus figured he might as well lay it all out there. "But yeah, Savannah's sister might have expressed interest in your clueless ass."

"Savannah's sister?" Dougal repeated, scowling across the street at Chelsea. "You mean… The pretty blonde?"

"Savannah's *only* sister." Angus shoved a cup into each of Dougal's hands. At least his brother had noticed Chelsea was pretty—that was something. "Now you know."

Dougal waited for Angus and walked back across the street with him. "Here." He held out a cup for Chelsea.

Chelsea lit up like a Christmas tree. "Thank you, Dougal. That's very sweet of you."

"Um." Dougal stared at her. "Yep." He turned and walked in the other direction.

"There is something wrong with that boy of yours, Orla." Aunt Nola sounded mighty disappointed.

"Is he okay?" Chelsea asked. "What's wrong?"

"Oh…" Angus stared after his brother. "He'll be fine. I think." With Dougal, it was hard to tell. "For you." He gave Savannah her hot chocolate. "Your nose is red. You warm enough?"

"Perfect." She didn't quite meet his gaze. "This is something. They really do this every year? Decorate all these trees?"

"It's right up your alley." Chelsea pointed at the sign. "All the money raised goes to help the local Christmas toy drive."

Savannah perked right up. "Oh, that's lovely."

"They're always looking for volunteers to help when Santa is here." Ma pointed at the empty gazebo. "He is here all day Saturday and Sunday, taking pictures with kids."

"You'd love that." Chelsea sipped her hot chocolate. "Goodnight, that *is* hot."

"That's what I said." Angus nodded. "Be careful, Savannah."

"I see how it is. I get to burn my tongue, she gets a warning." Chelsea stuck her tongue out and pretended to fan it.

"I do like her better." Angus shrugged.

Savannah glanced his way, but her smile faded quickly—and he didn't like it.

"That's fair." Chelsea laughed. "And as it should be. But man, that's, like, scalding hot."

"Maybe you should go warn Dougal." Angus pointed at his brother.

"You think?" Chelsea asked.

Angus nodded. Then he might be able to catch a second or two alone with Savannah.

"I'll be right back." Chelsea made a beeline for his brother.

"Good for her." Aunt Nola chuckled. "A woman who goes after what she wants."

"What are you talking about, Nola?" Ma asked.

"Well, now I see where the boy gets it from," Aunt Nola mumbled.

"Did you see the wishing tree?" Ma led Lana toward the Christmas tree on the far side of the lawn, with Aunt Nola following.

"Hi." Angus nudged Savannah.

"Hi." She seemed wholly focused on blowing on her hot chocolate.

"You good?" He could feel the tension between them. Ever since lunch, she'd seemed set on keeping distance between them.

"Yes." She glanced his way, then back at her cup. "Don't want to burn my mouth."

"Okay." He'd let it go for now. Instead, he moved on to a topic he knew she'd find impossible to resist. "Dougal had no idea Chelsea was interested."

"Really?" Savannah looked in the direction of Chelsea and Dougal. "I love my sister, but she's not exactly subtle."

"Oh, I know. I think everyone *but* Dougal picked up on that." Angus took a careful sip of his hot chocolate.

Chelsea was laughing, her hand resting on Dougal's arm.

"He looks like he's about to bolt." Savannah's head cocked. "Is he okay?"

Angus took a long look at his brother. "I don't know. I've never seen him act like that before." About that time, Dougal spilled his hot chocolate and jumped back. "Ever."

Chelsea stepped forward to blot Dougal's jacket, but Dougal took another step back, tripped over the curb, and fell over backward. All that was visible were his booted feet and Chelsea, looking down at him.

"Oh, damn." Angus chuckled.

"Poor Dougal." But Savannah was giggling. "She's got him all flustered."

"I'd say so." And it was hysterical.

But then Dougal was sitting up, his hand to his head, and Chelsea dropped to her knees, her face going white.

"Angus," Chelsea called out, waving them over.

"Damn." Angus hurried over, his amusement fizzling when he saw blood on his brother's head.

"You poor thing. Oh, Dougal." Chelsea had a hold of Dougal's arm. "I think you might need some stitches."

Angus pulled out his phone and shone a light on his brother's head. The gash wasn't all that long, but it was deep. "Probably wouldn't hurt." He held out his hand and pulled his brother up.

"I'll throw some superglue on it." Dougal wiped at his head. "I don't need anyone coming at me with needles."

He gave his brother a hard look. He was hurting, Angus could tell. But Dougal was a proud man, and falling, in public, was ten times worse than being in pain.

"Your head bounced off the concrete. It hit hard, Dougal. I heard it." Chelsea stopped Dougal from touching his head. "You could have a concussion."

It wasn't funny, but Angus was still tempted to laugh. "Hell, I could call Buzz and he could patch you up."

"Then I'd never hear the end of this." Dougal closed his eyes.

"Oh, that's never gonna happen, anyway," Angus mumbled.

"Angus." Savannah stared at him in shock.

"I can't believe you're teasing your brother." Chelsea looked like an avenging angel. "He is hurt. He's bleeding, for crying out loud."

Dougal was suddenly enjoying this—a whole hell of a lot. The sonofabitch was grinning.

"How are you feeling?" Chelsea had a hold of Dougal's hand now.

"Fine." But then he looked at Chelsea and went all deer-in-the-headlights dazed.

"You don't look so good." Chelsea patted his hand and held it against her chest.

"We should call for help." There was nothing funny about Savannah's disappointment in him.

"He's had worse." Angus pointed at the small grin on Dougal's face. "He's getting a kick out of you two ganging up on me."

"We are not ganging up." Chelsea frowned at him. "We're holding you accountable for unacceptable behavior."

Dougal nodded.

"I'll call 911." Savannah pulled out her phone.

Dougal wasn't smiling then. "Don't call 911." Because that would bring even more attention to what had happened. An ambulance would cause a scene and, in a small town, everyone would know about it. "I'll call Buzz." He glared at Angus.

What the hell? Like this was all my damn fault. Angus glared right back.

"Are you sure?" Savannah hesitated, glancing between Chelsea and Dougal.

"Buzz can take care of him. He's a vet, but he can patch up a cut as well as any doctor. And he's a friend." Angus was finding it less and less funny by the minute.

Dougal was already on his phone. "Buzz." He walked away, his conversation short and too muffled to hear. He called back, "I'm gonna walk over to the clinic."

"I'll go with you," Angus offered.

"I don't need a babysitter." Dougal brushed off his offer. "I'll see you at home." With an awkward nod for Chelsea, he set off down the sidewalk.

"Should he really go alone?" Chelsea was staring after Dougal, concerned.

"He didn't sound like he wanted company." Savannah took her sister's hand. "You can check on him later, Chels. Let's go find Momma." She yawned.

"It's getting late. And colder. We should probably head on home." Angus didn't want Savannah wearing herself out.

From the look they both sent him, he knew he was in the doghouse.

Growing up, he and Dougal had teased each other through broken bones, chain saw cuts, dislocated limbs, and more. It was what they did. He would have expected Dougal to do the same if their roles had been reversed. He knew better than to try to explain that to them now. When Dougal was patched up and they were all home, they'd all get a good laugh over it. And he could figure out what was worrying Savannah. She didn't need any extra stress. Neither did the babies. The four of them were what mattered most.

Chapter Fourteen

Savannah held her hands out to the fire. The fireplace was built into the far wall of the great room, all rocks of varying earthy tones and textures. Orla had told her the rocks had all been found on the property and set into the walls to remind the family of their ties to the land. The McCarrick family had a proud heritage and Savannah admired that.

After their eventful visit to the lights on the chilly courtyard square, it was nice to sit in front of the fire and get warm. Dougal arrived home not five minutes after they did with a bandage on his head and surlier than ever—preventing anyone from questioning him or bringing up what had happened.

"Cookies." Aunt Nola carried a large platter of Savannah's decorated cookies into the room and placed them on the large wooden coffee table. "Orla's making her world-famous hot chocolate."

"World-famous?" Dougal asked.

"Isn't that what they say on all those roadside signs? To get you to buy stuff? World-famous?" Aunt Nola shrugged. "Fine. It's damn good hot chocolate is all I meant."

Savannah smiled. Chelsea was right—the woman was a character.

"It's about time we got this tree decorated." Orla carried in a large insulated pitcher.

Her mother followed, carrying a tray stacked high with ceramic mugs and a bag of mini marshmallows. "Help yourself."

While everyone fixed their hot chocolate, Orla unearthed boxes of family ornaments—each of which seemed to have a story to go along with it. Savannah hung a few, but wound up sitting on the couch with Gertie in her lap. She propped her head on a pillow, loved on the little dog, and watched the tree come to life. There were strands of vivid-colored twinkle lights and bright white lights, too. Glass bulbs, handcrafted ornaments from the boys and small-framed pictures. In years to come, her babies would add to the ornament collection.

Would she be here to see the tree with those additions?

Now wasn't the time to get bogged down with that line of thinking. She'd rather enjoy the moment and the company.

"All done?" Momma stepped back, tilting her head one way, then the other. She'd seemed more invested in decorating the tree than anyone.

"It's lovely." Orla nodded. "You have a good eye, Lana."

Savannah and Chelsea gave two thumbs-up.

This tree looked nothing like the dramatic statement trees she'd grown up having. This tree was a personal reflection of the McCarrick family's love and history. To Savannah's eyes, it was perfect.

"Want some aspirin?" Aunt Nola asked Dougal. "Or a shot of whiskey?"

Dougal shook his head, winced, and said, "No. Thank you."

"It's just like old times." Orla shook her head. "I remember the time the two of you were playing with those yard darts. You remember that, boys?" Orla sat in the rocking chair by the fireplace. "Next thing I know, Dougal comes running in the house saying Angus was dead."

Savannah stopped munching on her cookie. "What happened?"

"Dougal had thrown the dart up and it had come down, smack, right into Angus's head." Orla pointed at the top of her head. "Sticking up like an antenna."

"I gave you boys those darts." Aunt Nola cackled.

"That sounds about right." Dougal sat in front of the fire on the floor. Willow joined him, putting her head in his lap.

Angus rubbed his head. "That one hurt."

"Lucky for him, his hard head kept it from going too deep." Orla picked up her knitting bag and pulled out the project she'd been working on since she'd arrived. "He had to stay in the hospital a few days so the doctors could keep an eye on the swelling. You know, make sure his brain was okay."

"Traumatic brain injury—by yard dart." Dougal chuckled. "That explains it."

Angus pointed at Dougal then. "See?"

Savannah hid her smile by taking another bite of cookie.

"There was always something." Orla took a deep breath. "It's a miracle they both survived childhood. Falling out of trees. Crashing tractors. Trying to ride the bull—how many times? Using gasoline instead of lighter fluid on a brush pile cost them both their eyebrows and eyelashes."

Savannah could picture the two of them, running wild and up to no good.

"And both of them would look you square in the eye and deny they'd done a thing wrong." Orla frowned at both of them. "I think the only reason that changed was because Angus almost died."

"A dart in the head sounds pretty lethal." Chelsea sat beside her on the leather sofa, spreading a fleece holiday throw over their laps. Gertie stood, stretched, then wedged herself between them and underneath the blanket.

"Not compared to the two of them jousting with pitchforks." Orla set her knitting aside. "It gets me choked up just thinking about it."

"Don't think about it, Ma." Angus moved to her side. "I'm fine. Dougal's fine. We're all fine." He kissed the top of her head.

"I do have a knot on my head and glue in my hair." Dougal reminded them all.

"Which I don't understand." Nola pushed her glasses up. "It's not like the place wasn't all lit up. You weren't stumbling around in the dark. I was wishing I'd had my sunglasses."

Savannah couldn't help but feel sorry for Dougal. There was no easy answer. She'd watched the odd exchange between Dougal and Chelsea that led to his fall and she still wasn't sure what, exactly, had happened.

"I've never seen anything like it." Momma sat on the fireplace. "The lights, I mean. It was truly breathtaking."

"You're right, Momma." Savannah yawned. Being tired was becoming her new normal. She yawned again—only to find Angus watching her.

Damn him and that smile.

How was she supposed to stop feeling for the man when his smile triggered an instant response in her? Warm and achy and molten. Want. And so much love. What she'd love right at this moment was to be snuggled up against his side—with his strong arms around her.

Don't. She mentally pleaded as he walked to the couch. If she wasn't so tired, she could scare him off with a scowl or something. As it was, she could only watch. *Please, don't.*

He sat on the other side of her. "You going to make it?"

She nodded.

"No one would blame you if you went on to bed." His voice was low and rich.

She hated that she loved the sound of it. "I don't want to miss anything."

His chuckle, a sound she equally loved, had Gertie waking up and wagging her tail.

I know how you feel. Savannah patted the little dog. *At least you know he loves you back.*

"What's wrong?" It was a gruff whisper.

"Nothing." She wouldn't look at him. She couldn't. Thankfully, Gertie decided to put both paws on her chest and give her an abundance of kisses. "Thank you, Gertie."

"I asked her the same thing." Chelsea leaned forward. "And she answered me the same way."

"Huh." Angus shifted so he could see her sister, but Savannah ignored them both.

"Don't worry. I'll get it out of her. Or I'll figure it out. Twin things." Chelsea sounded pleased with herself.

"How does that work, exactly?" Angus reached over and gently moved Gertie off Savannah's chest. "Behave, Gert. Don't stand on your momma."

Oh, no. She was not going to cry. Not again.

"I'm not sure." Chelsea sighed. "Even when we were kids, we had this sort of shorthand thing going on. Probably from being in such close quarters for so long when we were babies." She rested her hand on Savannah's stomach. "I bet these three will have it."

"I guess we'll see." There it was—that undeniable affection lining his every word.

"You realize you're talking over me?" Savannah hadn't meant to snap, exactly, but she was stressed and tired and sad and done.

"You're free to join in the conversation anytime, you know." Chelsea patted her stomach. "You need another cookie. You're getting all crabby. I'll be back."

"I apologized to Dougal," Angus murmured, draping his arm along the back of the couch. "If that's what's got you upset."

"Why do you think I'm upset?"

"Well, for one thing, you won't look at me." His hand rested on her shoulder. "For another, you're all tense and stiff."

Which was true. "I guess I'm just tired." She closed her eyes. If she pretended to sleep, everyone would leave her alone. Besides, she was tired. Very tired. Between Gertie curled up on her lap, the soft blanket keeping her warm, and Angus's undeniably delicious scent close enough for her to breathe in, it wasn't all that hard to pretend.

At some point, the conversation became a low murmur and she'd shifted against Angus. She knew this because she could hear his strong heartbeat. His fingers were sliding through her hair. And he chuckled. "Come on, Gertie. I like cuddling with Savannah, too," he whispered. "You're gonna have to share, okay?"

Savannah heard Gertie's grunt and smiled.

"I don't know what she's dreaming about, but she's smiling." Angus murmured.

Was this a dream? It could be. If it was, she could burrow into Angus—so she did.

"I'm sure she's dreaming about you and the babies." It was Orla. "She's a lucky girl, Angus, to have you."

"You got it backward, Ma. I'm the lucky one." It was the softest whisper. So soft and tender Savannah knew it had to be a dream.

Angus applied the slightest pressure with his left knee. The horse responded, turning left without missing a step. "Good." He kept his voice low and steady.

"He's coming along." Dougal rested his arms on the top rung of the fence.

"He's smart. Aren't you, Ranger?" Angus patted the horse. With the lightest touch, he used his right ankle. Ranger went backward until Angus stopped. "Good."

After spending a mostly sleepless night, he'd come down to the barn to work off some of his restlessness. Ranger seemed to understand his mood. He'd settled right in, listening closely to each and every command Angus gave him.

"What time did you get down here?" Dougal rested his chin on his arms.

He tipped his cowboy hat forward, keeping the morning sun out of his eyes. "I don't know." If he told his brother he'd been out here since sunrise, Dougal would start asking questions.

"Uh-huh. Are you thinking of coming up for breakfast? Or are you needing a break from all the women, too?"

He didn't need a break. If anything, he needed more time with one woman in particular. Lana and Chelsea

Barrett had been here for three nights now—and something had changed. Maybe he'd imagined it but, before everyone had arrived, the two of them had been building something good. He missed that. He missed her.

"I was thinking about going into town today. Doing a little Christmas shopping." Angus had Ranger do a sharp right turn and stop. "Good."

"I don't have to get presents for everyone, do I?" Dougal ran a hand over his beard.

"No." Angus grinned. "I'm only shopping for Savannah."

"Oh." Dougal shrugged. "I guess you have to, being that she's your…what? Your baby mama."

Angus frowned. He didn't like that. But technically, what was she? He walked Ranger to the gate.

"It's true, isn't it?" Dougal's brows went up. "Someone's touchy this morning." He opened the gate and stepped aside.

"I don't want people thinking of her as my baby mama." Angus slid from the saddle, choosing his words with care. "I want her to be my wife. I want people to know she's my wife. Respect her as such. It might seem like a little thing, but to me, it's not."

"And?" Dougal waited.

"She doesn't want to marry me," Angus snapped.

Dougal's brows rose. "Did she give you a reason?"

Angus tugged off his gloves. "She wants to marry for love." He cleared his throat.

"So, what's the problem?" Dougal crossed his arms over his chest. "You love her. I think she likes you well enough?" He paused. "Or not?"

Angus frowned. "I don't know."

"Well, maybe you should find out." Dougal shook his head. "And you say I'm clueless."

Angus chuckled at that. "Fine. I need a favor."

"Go on." Dougal closed the gate.

"You might have noticed Chelsea and Savannah are joined at the hip." He waited, but Dougal only shrugged. "I figure the four of us can go into town and you can keep Chelsea occupied while I get a few things sorted out with Savannah." Like making sure she understood how he felt and, hopefully, hearing she felt the same. Then he'd put a ring on her finger.

"Occupied?" The look Dougal shot him was all suspicion. "What the hell does that mean?"

Angus laughed. "I don't know. Buy her a coffee or a hot chocolate or something. What's your problem with Chelsea, anyway?"

"She makes me nervous." Dougal was scowling. "I don't like it."

If he thought Dougal would explain what that meant, he'd ask. But Dougal was Dougal and only offered up the bare minimum so he left it alone. "I'm asking for an hour. That's all." Angus sighed. "I'll owe you."

"I'll try... I don't know what I'll do with her for an hour." Dougal wasn't happy. "She talks a lot and is always looking at me."

"She likes you." Angus shook his head and put it all out there. "You could just grab her and kiss her and see where that gets you."

Dougal stared at him.

Angus stared right back. "If you're not interested in kissing her, introduce her to Dean—he's a talker and he'd probably take an interest in Chelsea."

Dougal kept on staring at him.

"What?"

"Nothing." Dougal led the way to the barn.

They stowed the tack, brushed and fed Ranger, and

made it all the way back to the house without another word. As soon as they opened the back door, they were greeted by the overlapping conversation of the women inside.

"That's another thing," Dougal grumbled. "The constant talking. What's wrong with a little peace and quiet now and then?"

"Guess they've got a lot to say." Angus shrugged, following the voices to the kitchen.

"All the time?" Dougal shook his head. "How is that possible?"

"There you are." Ma was standing behind the kitchen island. "We just made some gingerbread muffins. Correction, Savannah made them."

"Momma helped, too." Savannah was stacking muffins onto a tray. "I tried to make a casserole, too, but—"

"They didn't need to know that." Aunt Nola shook her head. "All they need to know is you made food for them and they'll be grateful."

"I'm sure they're very grateful." Ma glanced at them. He and Dougal nodded.

"See that, Savannah?" Lana asked.

Savannah glanced up and they nodded again.

"I'm taking notes." Chelsea was sitting at one of the bar stools along the island, an elbow propped up.

"You free to take us into town in a bit?" Aunt Nola didn't drive. Her license had been revoked after a run-in with a police officer. Nola argued the officer was too young to know what they were talking about and that she'd only been going ten miles over the speed limit, not thirty.

"Savannah signed up to work with Santa this weekend. We need to go pick up her elf outfit." Ma was super proud.

"She loves doing charity work. I don't know what the

foundation is doing without you there this year." Lana shook her head. "You do so much."

"I'm sure their people will step up." Chelsea hurried to reassure her sister. "You don't need to worry about it."

But Savannah looked like she was worrying about it. As a matter of fact, Savannah looked pale and tired and not like herself. He ignored the rest of the room as he headed straight for her. For three days, he'd kept his opinions to himself, believing everyone was just as in tune with her as he was. Now he was a man on a mission. "Savannah." He stopped at her side, taking both of her hands. "You look tired. Can I ask you to rest? Even for an hour?"

"You haven't eaten yet." Savannah nodded at the tray of muffins.

He grabbed one and took a huge bite. "I'll eat."

She looked up at him, the ghost of a smile on her lips.

"I'll eat the whole damn tray." Angus squeezed her hand. "If you promise you'll lay down for a bit?" He ignored the 'awws' from behind him, waiting for her answer.

"You're not eating them all." Dougal grabbed at least four. "That should do it." He grabbed another two. "Now. The rest are yours."

Angus shoved the rest of the muffin in his mouth, never breaking eye contact.

Her gaze fell from his. "I'm really—"

"I'm sure you are fine, but it'd mean a great deal to me if you'd lay down for a bit. Ma and Aunt Nola, Chelsea and your mom can take care of things for a bit." He wasn't asking. "Dr. Wurtz said you need to take care of yourself to take care of them."

"I'll lay down. For a little bit." She took a slow, deep

breath. Her hands slid from his and she untied and re-moved her apron.

"Thank you." He was glad she wasn't going to fight him on this. Did no one else see the dark circles under her eyes? "Dougal and I can go into town and get whatever you need."

"I can go on my own," Dougal offered. "If you want to keep an eye on her?"

"I don't need anyone keeping an eye on me." Savannah hung her apron in the pantry with the rest of them. "I'm going." She waved, the door swinging closed behind her.

He took a deep breath.

"You're really sweet on my sister, aren't you?" Chelsea was all smiles. "Like this isn't about you knocking her up."

"Oh, Chelsea." Lana pressed a hand to her forehead.

"I'll try again." Chelsea rolled her eyes. "You care about my sister. This isn't just about doing the right thing, here."

Well, damn, he was in the spotlight now.

"He's sweet on her." Dougal answered for him. "He damn near took my head off when I called her his baby mama. I think he's wanting to get married fast because he thinks she'll leave his sorry ass."

Angus shook his head and leveled a glare at his brother. "Unless you want me going around speaking for you, I advise you to go back to being the quiet one."

Dougal shook his head. "Whatever."

He didn't exactly want to pour his heart out to all of them—at least not until he'd told Savannah. At the same time, he wasn't trying to hide anything. "I do want to do the right thing by her and the babies. But I am sweet on her. I was hoping to tell her that and go into town to find her a ring."

Chelsea clapped her hands. "I knew it." She hugged her mother.

"Or you could use Meemaw's ring?" His mother sniffed. "Nola and I both want you to have it. If you want it?"

The family ring. It would mean the world to him. "I'd like that. I think Savannah would, too, knowing how strongly she feels about family."

"See," Dougal muttered, then glanced at Angus. "What? They can see you. It's all over your damn face. It's kinda—"

"The sweetest thing ever," Chelsea finished. "Someday, I hope a man will look like that when he's talking about me."

"The right man will." Lana slid an arm around her waist.

"Listen to your momma." Aunt Nola slapped the top of the kitchen island. "If he doesn't look and sound like a lovesick fool, you send him packing."

"I hate to admit it, but she's right." Ma chuckled.

"You heard that, right? Aunt Nola calling you a lovesick fool?" Dougal was laughing.

"Yeah, yeah." He didn't care. "I'd appreciate it if you could all keep this to yourselves until I get to talk to Savannah?" He waited for them to nod. "I'm going to go check on her." He'd feel better knowing she was getting some sleep. Still, deep down, he couldn't shake the feeling that something was off. If he ever got a moment alone with her, maybe he'd find out.

Chapter Fifteen

Her nose had gone numb a good hour ago. And, underneath the curling top of her green felt elf shoes, it was very likely her toes had frostbite. Not that she minded. How could she? The line of wide-eyed kids waiting for their turn on Santa's lap stretched from beneath the canopy of a million blue-and-white Christmas lights down the courthouse sidewalk and around the corner. She'd make sure to put her feet up and rest when she got home.

"Ho ho ho." Town veterinarian, Buzz Lafferty, was doing an admirable job as Santa. According to Angus, he'd always been loud—which was an asset in their current situation. "Merry Christmas. What's your name?" He regarded the little girl on his lap.

The little girl stared silently up at Buzz—er, Santa, with both awe and a small amount of terror. Her mouth opened, but nothing came out.

"Come on, Frannie." A boy stood at the front of the line. "Tell him what you want."

Frannie nodded, but never looked away from Santa. "Um…"

Savannah stooped beside the little girl. "I bet you'd like a…princess doll?"

Frannie shook her head.

"Some coloring books?" she tried again.

"Nope." Frannie sat up, smiling widely. "I want another bwothah or sistah."

Savannah laughed. So far, she'd heard requests for dinosaurs, big-wheel trucks, and vacations to see Mickey Mouse but this was the first sibling request.

"Frannie." The boy groaned. "You can't ask for that."

"Why not?" Frannie peered up at Santa. "Can I ask for that for Chwistmas?"

Buzz—Santa cleared his throat, shooting a desperate look her way. He was Santa, after all. He was supposed to make the kids happy. But this was a tall request—one Santa had no control over. Savannah didn't envy the poor man.

"Well, now," Santa murmured, stroking his massive fluffy white beard with one gloved hand. "That's a special request, one that only your parents can give you. Santa can't deliver babies."

Good answer. She shifted from one foot to the other.

"Oh." Frannie frowned. "Why not?"

"Um…" Santa cast another look her way.

"There's not room for them in Santa's bag of toys. It's not safe, you see." Savannah hoped the little girl would accept this. "Babies are very fragile."

"I know." Frannie sighed, looking deflated. "Okay. Then can I have a new pair of light-up sneakers?"

She heard Santa's relieved sigh and stood, smiling.

"I will put that on my list." Santa nodded. "Let's smile for the camera."

The photographer took a picture, Savannah helped Frannie from Santa's lap, and the boy hurried up to take his sister's hand.

"Here you go." She handed them each a candy cane. "Merry Christmas."

"Thank you." The boy nudged Frannie.

"Thank you." Frannie smiled. "Is that why the stawk delivahs babies, Gawwett?" Frannie was asking as they walked away. "Because they'd get squished in Santa's bag?"

"I guess." Garrett led her to a large family group, bundled up on a picnic blanket beneath the illuminated trees.

She suspected Frannie kept her family entertained. She watched, momentarily struck by the smiles and laughter and overall happiness that exuded from the group. She couldn't remember a time when her family had ever enjoyed one another like that. Not unless photographers or reporters were around, that is. Then the Barrett family was the picture-perfect family. A model family was a requirement for her father's career. Whether it was true or not.

"Savannah?" Buzz whispered. "Earth to Elf Savannah. I think you're being relieved."

"Really?" She shivered as another blast of cold air swept across the courthouse lawn. "Oh, good." She turned to find a teen wearing an identical elf outfit and handed off the stocking full of candy canes. "Hope you wore thermal underwear."

"I did." The girl took the stocking.

I wish I had. Now that her shift was over, she couldn't wait to find some hot chocolate and some comfy clothes. Red-and-white-striped tights were festive, but they didn't do much to keep the cold at bay.

She waved goodbye to Santa and headed straight for

the hot chocolate booth, texting Chels to let her know she was done. She was almost at the booth when her left stocking snagged on an especially prickly holly branch.

"Ow." She turned, reaching down to remove the branch—and turning so that her right leg snagged as well. "Really?"

"Need help?" The laughter in Angus's voice was insult to injury.

When had he gotten here? "No." She barely glanced his way. "I can...get it." She pulled the left leg free, leaving a large hole. "Dammit."

"Is Santa okay with that kind of language?" Angus shook his head.

"Santa is very understanding." She freed her right leg without tearing the stocking—but got one of the poky leaves stuck under her thumbnail. "Ow," she murmured, pulling out the dagger-like leaf and sucking on her thumb.

"I can help, you know." At least he wasn't laughing this time.

"You're always helping." And it bothered her.

"And that's a bad thing?" Angus walked along with her.

"That you think I always need help? Yes." She gathered up as much of her pride as she could and headed for the hot chocolate booth. "A large." She rubbed her gloves together. "With extra whipped cream."

"I'll have the same." Angus was regarding her closely. "There's not much else I can do at this point. Offering to help makes me feel like I'm doing something. I'm not, I know it. You're the one carrying our babies. I'm trying to...be here somehow."

Every one of his words had her heart surging with hope. She glanced up at him and instantly regretted it. He looked more delicious than ever. Warm, dark eyes. That strong, stubbled jaw. All cowboy. From his black felt cowboy hat to the well-worn brown boots, there was no denying Angus McCarrick was a very manly man. It wasn't quite so cold now. If anything, she was feeling warm.

Her not-so-subtle inspection earned her a crooked smile. "You're wearing that look."

Of course he'd notice. She'd spent the last few days trying to put distance between them, and now, with one look, she'd let him know she wasn't as indifferent as she'd been trying to be.

"Hold up." The teen boy inside the booth started banging on something. "It'll be just a minute."

Great. She could handle another minute of standing here—as long as she didn't do anything else to embarrass herself, that is.

"What did Frannie ask for?" Angus asked.

"You know Frannie?"

"She belongs to Buzz. Tonight's Santa." He paused. "Actually, Frannie and Garrett are Buzz's wife's younger siblings. But he and Jenna, his wife, adopted them so, yeah, she's his."

Savannah took a minute to make sense of what he'd said. "Oh. Well, that explains why Santa panicked a little." She smiled. "She asked Santa for a new brother or sister."

Angus was laughing then.

It wasn't fair how much she loved to hear him laugh. "He told her that was up to her mom and dad."

"I bet he and Jenna will be having an interesting conversation tonight." He took the hot chocolate. "Thank you." He handed one to her. "That's a lot of whipped cream."

"It's Christmas." She shrugged. And she was tired. Hopefully, the extra sugar would give her a little pick-me-up.

"How'd it go tonight?" He took a slow sip of his hot chocolate—and wound up with whipped cream in his mustache.

"It went well." She grinned, not saying a word about his new frothy adornment.

"Good." He smiled back at her. "I'm glad. You're the prettiest elf I've ever seen. Even if that holly bush did attack you." He tipped his hat back, revealing more of his devilishly handsome face—the whipped cream didn't do a thing to change that.

If anything, the whipped cream drew her attention to that smile. He had a nice mouth. Full lips. Kissable, even. Tempting.

Her phone vibrated. Chelsea.

Enjoy your bearded cowboy hottie. He's your ride home.

Chelsea texted, adding a string of winky-face emojis at the end. Get it? RIDE home?

She sighed and tucked her phone into her purse.

"Hey there, cowboy. You've got a little something right there." A very pretty blonde approached. "Looks like your mustache has a mustache."

Angus chuckled. "That was why you were smiling?"

"Guilty." She shrugged, feeling big and awkward next to the woman.

"Need a tissue?" The blonde dug through her purse. "Here." She offered him a tissue and regarded Savannah with open curiosity. "Are you going to introduce me, Angus?"

"Cassie Ford, this is Savannah. Savannah, Cassie. She's Buzz's sister."

And she was gorgeous.

"It's so nice to meet you. Finally." Cassie shook her

hand. "Sterling is around here somewhere. My husband."
She turned, scanning the crowd.

It came on so suddenly, Savannah wasn't sure what
was happening. One moment, she was fine. The next, it
felt as if all the blood in her body crashed into her feet.
A rush of cold followed. And the world began to spin.

"Angus?" she whispered. And the world went dark and
silent.

Everything shifted into slow motion.

Savannah's panic-filled voice.

The sheer terror on her face before she went deathly
white and she sort of folded in on herself. Some instinct
kicked in and he caught her before she hit the ground.

"Savannah?" He ran his hand along the side of her
face. "Can you hear me?" *Please, please say something.*
He scooped her up.

He was vaguely aware of voices and movement.

Buzz, in full Santa gear, was there, taking her pulse.
"She's breathing. Her pulse is okay." But his expression
didn't do a thing to put Angus at ease. "I'll drive you to
the ER."

He nodded, cradling her close and running to Buzz's
truck.

The hospital was at least ten minutes away, but they
made it there in half the time.

"Keep it together." Buzz gripped his arm. "We're here."

Angus carried her into the ER. "She's not moving. She
collapsed." He couldn't breathe. "Somebody do something." Anything. Dammit, just make her okay.

A nurse emerged. "What happened?"

"I don't know. She's pregnant." He sucked in a deep
breath. "Triplets. High-risk."

She nodded, listening to Savannah's chest with her

stethoscope. "Let's get her in the back for some tests, shall we?"

Tests? What sort of tests? "What's happening?"

"That's what we need to find out." She waved someone else with scrubs forward. "We're going to take her back."

"Where? I'll take her." Angus wasn't going to leave her.

"Angus." Buzz put a hand on his arm. "You'll get in the way. Let them take care of Savannah. Trust them."

He was just supposed to watch them take her away? Wait? Do nothing? Fear the worst?

"We need to take her now." The ER doctor pointed at the gurney. "The sooner we do the tests, the sooner we will have answers."

It made sense so he laid her on the gurney. But the minute they wheeled her behind those doors, he couldn't breathe. He bent over, bracing his hands on his knees, and did his best to keep it together.

"Breathe." Buzz placed a hand on his back.

He shook his head.

"Who should I call?" Buzz asked.

Angus ran a hand over his face. "Dougal." Think. "Get him to bring her mom. Sister."

"Will do."

He couldn't concentrate on anything. Buzz made phone calls, got him a cup of coffee, and tried to get him to sit. Angus couldn't sit.

Instead, he paced.

Buzz's phone rang. "It's Jenna."

Angus nodded and sat. There was nothing comforting about a hospital waiting room. Nothing. The massive clock on the wall was a constant reminder that time was moving on and he still didn't know what the hell was happening with Savannah.

He was on the verge of demanding the nurse get him some answers when Dr. Wurtz stepped into the hallway. He was up and met the doctor halfway.

"Is she okay?" Angus had to know. He had to know now.

"She's fine."

He blew out a slow breath and put a hand against the wall to steady himself.

"She fainted." Dr. Wurtz patted his shoulder. "It can happen. She's fine," Dr. Wurtz repeated. "How are you?"

"I've never been that scared in my life." His poor heart still hadn't recovered. "But if she's okay, that's all that matters." He shook his head. "The babies? They're okay, too?"

Dr. Wurtz nodded. "All three heartbeats are strong and accounted for."

"What happens now?" He straightened, steadier now.

"You can go sit with her, if you like. Let's keep her here for a couple of hours so I can monitor her, and then you can take her home. Sound good?"

"Are you looking for something specific?"

"No." Dr. Wurtz smiled. "But if she has another fainting spell, I'd like to see if there's a cause."

Angus nodded. That made sense. No reason for alarm. He needed to calm down. Doc said she was fine, and there was no reason not to believe the man. *Get it together.* The last thing she needed was him falling apart.

"I'll take you to her." The young doctor led Angus through a set of double doors and down a long hall. He stopped outside a hospital room and knocked. "Someone to see you, Savannah."

The moment Angus saw her face, all his good intentions went out the window. His heart couldn't handle her tears. "Hey." He sat on the bedside, drawing her into his arms. "You're okay. They're okay."

She clung to him. "I was so scared." Her words were muffled against his shoulder. "I didn't know what was happening."

"Doc says it happens sometimes." He spoke softly. "But if you can help it, I'd be okay with that never happening again."

Her laugh was unsteady.

Dr. Wurtz chuckled. "I've got a patient in labor upstairs. I'll check back in a bit."

"Thank you, Doc," Angus called out, too caught up in Savannah to say more. She felt so damn good in his arms. Even if she was shaking. "What can I do?"

"I can't stop shaking."

He slid onto the bed next to her and pulled her against him. "Warm enough?" There was an extra blanket at the foot of the bed. She nodded, but he pulled the blanket up and tucked it around her anyway. "Better?"

She nodded, resting her head on his chest. "Your heart is going so fast."

"It's slower than it was." He ran a hand over her hair. Touching her helped.

She yawned.

"Dr. Wurtz wants to keep an eye on you for a bit," he murmured, stroking her hair again. "Might as well get some sleep if you can."

"Will you hum something?"

"Hum?" He smiled. "Like what?"

"Anything." She shrugged.

Angus had hummed his way through several of Kenny Rogers's greatest hits when Lana Barrett tiptoed inside.

"She's sleeping," he whispered.

Lana whispered, "Is she okay?"

He nodded. "Fainted."

"Oh. I did that a time or two, with the girls." She pressed a hand to her heart. "My sweet girl." She tucked the blanket up over Savannah's shoulder. "Thank you for taking such good care of her, Angus. It does my heart good to see how well you treat her." She frowned then. "I hope you'll forgive me, but… When I heard that she'd been taken to the hospital, I panicked and called her father."

Well, dammit. Still, he didn't blame the woman. "He is her father."

"He is devastated." She cleared her throat. "I tried to tell him not to come but…"

Angus closed his eyes. "When will he get here?" Savannah didn't need additional stress. And he was pretty sure Richard Barrett was the epitome of additional stress.

"I don't know." She sighed. "Knowing him, as fast as he can. I did tell him he can't come in here and add to her stress. I made it very clear."

"I'm sure he'll do what's best for Savannah and the babies." He didn't believe a word of it. Richard Barrett would do what Richard Barrett wanted to. Angus would do whatever he had to to keep the sonofabitch in check.

Chapter Sixteen

All the cuddling and smiling and tender touches were going to make it impossible when everything fell apart. And it would. Her fainting spell had caused them both concern, but she'd be back on her feet in no time. Which was good—wonderful. She didn't want to be so reliant or needy. But when Angus was close, she was oh, so needy. Her fool heart seemed determined to hold on to him.

"You need anything?" Chelsea sat in a chair at the side of her hospital bed.

"Nope," she said again.

"How are you feeling?" Orla asked.

"Better." And she did, too. But she wasn't exactly moving.

When Dr. Wurtz had come in to release her last night, she'd stood up and her blood pressure had bottomed out. Dizziness had hit her hard and fast. But Angus had been there to prop her back against the elevated bed and murmur all sorts of reassuring things. He hadn't left her side all night. Once Dr. Wurtz had determined what was going on with her blood pressure, she could go home.

"Here." Dougal walked in, thrusting a large brown paper sack at Angus. "Wasn't sure what to get, so…"

"Thanks, Dougal. I'm sure we can find something in here that works." Angus was smiling at her, then.

And Savannah's heart instantly picked up. The heart monitor only added to her humiliation. Everyone in the room could hear it.

"What's in the bag?" Chelsea set her fashion magazine aside.

"Food your sister will enjoy." Angus handed over the bag. "You need to eat."

"It's not that I didn't want to." She'd actually been hungry when her breakfast tray had been delivered. One sniff set her stomach to churning.

"I almost turned green, too. And I'm not pregnant." Chelsea sat on the foot of her bed. "It was very sweet of your man to go out and find good food for you and the wee ones."

"Ahem." Dougal cleared his throat.

"Okay, it was very sweet of your man to send someone to go and find good food for you and the wee ones," Chelsea corrected, winking at Dougal.

Dougal flushed, backed into the wall, and mumbled something before leaving the room.

"So that's how he broke his head open." Nola glanced Chelsea's way. "It's your fault."

"I guess so. But I give up." Chelsea laughed, holding up her hands. "My pride has taken too many hits."

"His loss." Savannah reached for her sister's hand. "Want one?"

"You pick first." Chels patted her hand. "Otherwise, your man might not like me, either."

"Take at least two pastries," Angus interjected. "Or three."

She shook her head. "Three?"

"You are eating for four, Pickle." Chelsea pointed at her stomach. "Not that I need to remind you of that."

"The doctor did say you needed to eat more." Momma joined in. "We all heard him."

Savannah seriously regretted letting them all invade. Now it wasn't just Angus hovering, it was both mothers, her sister, his aunt, and Dougal—although she suspected he'd pretty much stay out of it.

"He did," Nola agreed. "We'll have you fat and happy in no time."

"I like the sound of that." Angus nodded.

"Okay, okay." She peered into the bag. "Did he buy everything?"

"The bag's not that big." Angus turned. "We don't have any—"

"Here." Dougal returned with a pile of paper plates and napkins. He sank onto the vinyl-covered sofa that ran the length of the wall, looking acutely uncomfortable.

"Thank you, Dougal." Savannah held out the bag. "Do you want one?"

"Those are all for you. All of them." He leaned back and crossed his arms over his chest. "You need to eat."

"You heard the man." Chels pulled the wheeled bedside table over and put a plate and several napkins on it. "Dive in."

She ate while the mothers discussed the pattern of Orla's knitting project. Once Momma had learned it was a baby blanket, she'd taken a keen interest in learning all about knitting. Orla was all too eager to share the process. Nola, however, was gleefully giggling over the tabloid paper she was reading.

A blueberry muffin and peach streusel later and Savannah was feeling much better.

Until she heard the unmistakable sound of her father's voice.

"Is that Dad?" Chelsea was up, off the bed, staring at their mother. "Momma, what did you do?"

The guilt on their mother's face said it all. "I was so worried. We all were. I know I shouldn't have involved him, but he is your father."

"According to him, he's not," Chelsea snapped. "Or have you forgotten his parting comments?"

Savannah hadn't.

From the stony set of Angus's jaw, he hadn't, either. Her father had been horrible to her, and the allegation he'd made about Angus had been beyond offensive.

"I'm sure he regrets all of that," Angus murmured, taking her hand. "Are you okay? You're the one that matters here. Not him." He was watching her intently. "I can tell him not to come in."

Would her father listen?

Dougal stood. "I can take care of that."

"Momma, I can't believe you." Chelsea ran a hand over her short platinum locks, a telltale sign that their father's presence stirred up her insecurities, too. "She's not just supposed to eat. She's supposed to avoid stress, remember?"

"I'll go talk to him." Lana stood. "Thank you, Dougal." She left the room.

Everyone fell quiet as an unintelligible conversation took place outside of her room. From the pitch and tone, her father sounded almost agreeable.

"Should we leave?" Orla stood. "I don't want to get into family business. But I sure don't want to leave you without backup."

"Dougal and I will stay." Angus spoke for his braced and ready brother. "You and Aunt Nola can go down to the cafeteria for a bit."

"Everything will be okay, sweetie." Orla patted her foot. "I'm hoping he's come to throw himself at your feet and beg for your forgiveness. He'd be a fool not to."

"I'd like to give the man a piece of my mind," Nola muttered as they left.

"You going to be okay, Chels?" Savannah could see how tense her sister was.

"You don't need to worry about me. Actually, I forbid you to worry about me." Chels came around to the other side of the bed and took her hand. "Angus is right. The only thing that matters here is you."

Chelsea was on one side, Angus on the other, and Dougal stood against the wall at the foot of the bed. "This is what it must feel like to have bodyguards." She tried to tease.

Angus squeezed her hand.

"Except we all love you. Which makes us ten times more dangerous than a hired bodyguard." Chelsea sighed.

She didn't dare risk looking at Angus then; her damn heart monitor was already letting them know she was flustered. Chelsea meant well, but it wasn't true. Angus cared about her well-being and the babies, but he didn't love her. He'd never said anything to lead her on or imply otherwise. She was the one who'd fallen head over heels for the man.

She smoothed the sheet over her stomach.

"Savannah?" Her father didn't sound like her father. He didn't look like his usual, put-together self, either. His hair was a mess. His shirt was rumpled. He hadn't shaved in some time. "You okay, sweet girl?"

She wasn't going to cry. She wasn't. He'd caused enough tears. He didn't deserve any more of hers.

He barely acknowledged Chelsea and entirely ignored Angus as he reached her bedside. "I know you probably don't want me here, but I had to make sure you were okay. I had to see it with my own two eyes."

She took a steadying breath. "I'm fine."

"You're strong." He nodded. "You always have been."

She was feeling anything but strong at the moment. Or fine. She was tired. Tired of pretending to be strong and okay. Nothing was okay. She had a sinking feeling nothing would ever be okay again.

Watching Richard Barrett walk into Savannah's hospital room was an exercise in self-control. He didn't want to physically attack the man, for the most part, but he was going to have to make an effort to school his features. One look or smirk or cocked eyebrow could trigger Barrett—just like it had the last time they were all together. Savannah didn't need that. Hell, Savannah didn't need any of this.

Damn Lana for bringing him here, and damn Barrett for coming. The man better have an apology ready to go.

"They taking care of you?" Barrett asked, scanning the monitors and equipment.

"She's getting excellent care." Lana smoothed the sheet over Savannah's feet.

"Good, good." He nodded. "I brought Dr. Garza, just in case. It can't hurt to have a second opinion."

Breathe. He could get upset at the bastard for meddling or be grateful the bastard was trying to give them all peace of mind.

"You think that's necessary?" Lana was studying Savannah.

"She's in the hospital." Barrett's gaze darted his way. "It seems appropriate."

The silence that followed thinned the air in the room until Angus knew he had to speak up. He could do this. "Your call, Savannah. It can't hurt to have a second opinion."

"No." Savannah pleated and unpleated the sheet with her fingers. "I guess not."

Barrett typed something on his phone, then nodded. "Okay. She's coming back now."

Dr. Garza was a middle-aged woman with a gentle smile. She shooed everyone out of the room and closed the door, leaving the hallway crowded and silent. Chelsea didn't last long, heading toward the cafeteria, mumbling something about a drink. Dougal stood, silent and imposing, like a sentinel beside Savannah's door.

He couldn't make out a single word they were saying, but it was impossible to ignore the heated conversation taking place between Lana and Richard. How Lana Barrett could tolerate the man was a mystery he had no interest in solving. She'd taken Savannah's side when it mattered. For Angus, that told him all he needed to know.

He stared up at the fluorescent lights overhead. What he wouldn't give for a walk in the open. Nothing but nature and fresh air. Which reminded him. "I was thinking we could use the tractor to cut a path around the fence line at the house? Give Savannah a level walking trail."

"Easy enough," Dougal agreed.

"A word?" Richard Barrett was standing before him.

"Richard." Lana Barrett's voice rose.

Angus took a deep breath. What more could the man possibly have to say? He didn't have the patience or the self-control to deal with the man.

Dr. Wurtz chose that moment to come around the corner. "Angus." He glanced at the closed door. "I was just coming to check in on Savannah."

"I appreciate that." Angus was about to make introductions, but Barrett beat him to it.

"I'm Savannah's father, Richard Barrett." His inspection of the young doctor wasn't exactly cordial. "And you are?"

"Savannah's doctor." He shook Barrett's hand.

"I see." Barrett's eyes narrowed as he gave the young doctor a more thorough inspection. "How long have you been practicing medicine?"

"All done." Dr. Garza opened the door. "You can come in now." She saw Dr. Wurtz and offered her hand. "Are you her attending physician?"

"I am." Dr. Wurtz was slightly irritated now. "Perhaps we could have a brief consultation aside?"

"Perhaps we could do the same?" Barrett asked Angus. "Lana can keep Savannah company."

If Barrett was going to push this, he might as well get it over with. "Fine." He followed the man to the end of the hall. A large window looked out on the view of the concrete parking lot below. No trees. No grass. He felt more fenced in than ever. It didn't help his mood.

"Nothing has changed?" Barrett clasped his hands behind his back and stared blindly out the window. "You're still determined to go through with this."

"This?" He wasn't in the mood to make this easy for the man.

"This…this charade of whatever this is." He gestured back down the hall they'd just come from.

"As in take care of Savannah and the babies?"

Barrett closed his eyes, his jaw muscle so tight Angus wondered he didn't hear bone cracking.

"Why are you so dead set against it?" Angus couldn't

stop himself. "I know I'm no Greg Powell, but I'm a good man. I will be a good father." And, if she'd have him, he'd try his hardest to be the best damn husband.

Barrett shook his head. "How long have you known my daughter now? Two weeks?"

Angus didn't answer. It wasn't relevant. Dammit, he knew what was in his heart.

"It takes more than two weeks for a banana to go bad. You can't expect me, or any sane person for that matter, to believe you know this is the life you want." Barrett still didn't look at him. "To understand what sort of life-long commitment this is."

"No offense, Mr. Barrett, but it wouldn't make a difference if it was two weeks or two years. There are no guarantees in life. Or time limits. There's choosing a path and sticking with it. That's what I'm doing." He didn't owe the bastard anything more than that. "I love her. I won't let her down."

Barrett shook his head. "You don't know what that means. If you did, you'd send her back home where she'd have round-the-clock medical care. The best of the best. Dietitians that ensure she's getting the proper nutrients for herself and this pregnancy. She wouldn't be overtired to the point of collapse." When he did look at Angus, it wasn't anger on the man's face, it was fear. "If you really loved her, we wouldn't be having this discussion. You would have called me, not Lana. Your damn pride and selfishness wouldn't stand in the way of giving her the best."

He was so rattled, it took a minute for him to find the right words. "You keep saying if I really love her, I'll do what's best for her. To you, that means I have to give her up." He wasn't going to let the man twist things around. "You could arrange for her to have the best no matter where she is. The doctors, the dietitians, all of it. What's stopping you? You want the best for her, so give it to her. Here. Where she wants to be." He was done. He didn't take kindly to being manipulated or made to feel lower than dirt. "How about we go and hear what the doctors have to say."

"Are you sure that this is still what she wants?" Barrett stopped him in his tracks.

Angus stared at the man. He couldn't decide which was stronger, pity or loathing.

"Let's ask her," Barrett continued. "If she does, I'll take care of everything. Just like I said. But if there's a doubt or hesitation, maybe you should do a little soul-searching."

"Fine." Angus wasn't worried. Anything to shut this man up. He didn't linger a second longer. He headed back to Savannah's room, doing his best to shake off the whole damn conversation.

Savannah was sitting up with her feet dangling off the side of the bed. "What took you so long?"

"What's the news?" He took up his spot at her side and smiled. "You've got some color in your cheeks."

"Is Mr. Barrett..." Dr. Garza paused as Barrett walked into the room. "Now that you're all here. I reviewed Dr. Wurtz's notes and, after my own evaluation of Savannah, I agree with his assessment and plan of treatment."

"We need to continue to monitor Savannah's blood pressure. She should take her time getting up to make sure she's steady on her feet. Eat more frequently, good calorie-dense food, and stay hydrated, too. She's borderline dehydrated. Which is why we've given her some IV fluids." Dr. Wurtz turned to Savannah. "We have her scheduled for a two-week follow-up and will continue to have appointments every two weeks moving forward."

Angus could breathe easier then. "That's good. All good."

"No cause for alarm." She smiled up at him. "And we can go home."

"I'll have her discharge papers signed shortly." Dr. Wurtz nodded. "Do you have any questions or concerns?" He glanced at Savannah's father. "Mr. Barrett?" Barrett shook his hand. "Well, Angus, Savannah, I wish you a Merry Christmas and I'll see you in the New Year. But if you have any concerns, you can call me."

"Thanks, Doc." Angus shook the man's hand.

"I should be heading home, too." Dr. Garza looked at Barrett expectantly. "Tomorrow is Christmas Eve."

"Yes. I'll take you to the helipad." Barrett was torn—it was written all over his face.

"I'll wait in the hall, then." Dr. Garza followed Dr. Wurtz out.

"Are you leaving, Dad? You don't want to wait for Momma? Or Chelsea?"

"I doubt either of them will be too distressed by my leaving." Barrett came to the side of her bed. "I know I said some hard things, Savannah. I crossed a line. I forced your hand and I've regretted that every second since you left."

Angus figured that was as close to an apology as it was going to get. But he waited, knowing there was more to come.

"A lot was said and done out of passion so if something has changed, you're always welcome home." He cleared his throat. "Is this, being here, still what you want?"

Angus almost felt bad for the man.

"I… I don't know." Savannah's answer knocked the air from his lungs. "It's all been so fast."

What was she saying?

"So much has changed." She shrugged, almost apologetically. "I don't know."

"That's okay." Barrett patted her hand. "I understand."

Angus didn't. What the hell was happening? He was glad there was a chair close by. Better to sit than to fall over.

"You think on it." Barrett kissed her temple. "I'd best get Dr. Garza back to her family." He gave her hand a final pat and left.

Angus didn't know if Barrett was gloating or not. He couldn't move. He sat frozen, willing his heart to slow and his lungs to work. He had to breathe. Be calm. They'd promised to be honest with each other and she had. She wasn't sure. That's why she'd been acting so differently. All the times she'd avoided looking at him. The times she'd slide her hand from his. It made sense now. And, damn, did it hurt.

Chapter Seventeen

Other than the snap and pop of the fire burning, the great room was quiet. She sat, cuddled up with Gertie, wishing she could absorb some holiday spirit from the Christmas tree or the stockings Orla had added only today. Tomorrow was Christmas Eve. It was her favorite time of the year and she'd never been more miserable.

After tossing and turning, she'd given up. Just because she couldn't sleep didn't mean poor Chelsea shouldn't.

She sipped her glass of milk and finished off her second Christmas cookie. The babies approved. There were all sorts of rolls and flutters.

Gertie's head perked up and she stared at Savannah's stomach. She stood, sniffed, and sat again, staring up at Savannah with her head cocked to one side.

"Did they scare you?" She rubbed the dog behind the ear. "They like sugar. Just like their momma." She cradled the dog's head between her hands and pressed a kiss to her nose. "What am I going to do without you, Gertie?"

Gertie gave her a big doggy kiss right on the nose.

"Thank you." Savannah laughed.

"You and Gertie having a midnight snack?" Angus asked as he came into the room.

"Yep." Savannah did her best not to stare, but it was impossible. His hair was ruffled. His white undershirt hugged every muscle of his chest and stomach, and his flannel sleep pants hung dangerously low on his hips. It would be so much easier if she could turn off her feelings. She didn't want to be happy that he was here. She didn't want him to sit by her or smile at her. And she certainly didn't want to ache at the thought of him pulling her into his arms—or how much she wanted to give his low-hanging pants a tug.

"Solving the world's problems?" He didn't sit beside her. He sat in the leather recliner opposite her.

That was good. If she couldn't touch him, she stood a chance of not getting distracted—as Chelsea put it. "No." She reached for the gingerbread cookie. "I guess the triplets gave Gertie a kick or something. She was showing her disapproval."

He chuckled. "I imagine those kicks are only going to get stronger, Gert."

She nibbled on the gingerbread man's leg.

"I heard what you said, about doing without her." He sat back in the chair, holding tightly to the armrests. "I'm guessing you're not staying, then?" His voice was flat.

How could she? The longer she stayed, the more she'd fall in love with him. The more her heart would break when he didn't love her back. Her throat was too tight to speak, so she nodded.

He sat there like a statue. His hands were tightly gripping the arms of the chair. "What changed?" He didn't sound like himself. Was he mad? Shouldn't he be relieved?

She set her cookie aside and took a sip of milk. It did nothing to ease her throat. "I think it all happened so quickly. We both sort of jumped in without really taking a look at the big picture. The idea is nice, but the reality is…different."

"Oh?" He cleared his throat then, his fingers biting into the leather.

"The whole attraction thing clouded things up, I think. Wanting doesn't last. And it can't sustain a family." She drew in a deep breath.

"I thought we agreed to give it, us, our all?" He sounded a little gruffer then. "We agreed to that."

"Angus…" She propped her head in her hands. "I'm not going to keep you from being their father. You don't need to worry about that. I give you my word."

"I was pretty sure you did that in the barn that night." He was definitely mad.

"We did. We *both* did." She shook her head. "Then things changed."

"What things, Savannah?" He was up, pacing in front of the fire. "I've been turning it over in my mind, and I can't figure out when, exactly, that change happened for you."

"Everything." She blurted it out, covering her face with her hands. She was not going to tell him how she felt. Being rejected would only make this ten times worse. "It doesn't matter, Angus. We'll still make co-parenting work."

Dougal came around the corner—it sounded like he was mumbling something about bears—and went straight to the kitchen. The door opened and closed and he didn't emerge.

"I don't understand, Savannah." Angus stopped pacing then. "What I wanted hasn't changed. It won't."

She stood slowly before she continued. "I'm giving you—both of us—what we want." She marched up to him, her temper flaring, while trying to keep her voice low. The last thing she wanted was the entire family involved. This was something that needed to be settled between the two of them.

"What are you talking about?" He shook his head.

"Just stop. It's okay. I get it. Neither one of us will be…brokenhearted if we call it quits."

"Savannah." He broke off and took a deep breath. "What makes you think you leaving is what I want?"

"Angus, you've never wanted to get married. Not ever. You point-blank told me you enjoyed being a bachelor." She wrapped her arms around herself. "Then everything happened with my dad and you had to take me in. It was so sweet of you. You are so sweet, Angus." She broke off before she could tell him she loved him. "But doing this, playing house, won't give us what we really want. You want space. I want love. Those things aren't compatible. And that's okay." It had to be okay. She couldn't change it. "We were going to be honest with one another. That's what we said."

"Playing house?" He stepped closer to her. "I'm trying to make sense of all this." He took a deep breath. "If I haven't been clear, then let me clear it up. All I want is you and the babies to be safe and looked after. I'm trying here—"

"I know." She sighed. "But it's not enough. Because of the babies, you're stuck with me." She was not going to cry. "I want more than that, Angus. I want to be someone's choice. And being here, settling, is a constant reminder that I'm not. It hurts…so much."

"I'll let you go if that's what you want, but that'll be your choice. Not mine. Every time, I will choose you." He cradled her face. "Dammit, Savannah, I want you. I want you here, with me, until you're old and gray and as obnoxious as Aunt Nola."

"But…you said…" Now she was confused.

"I should have said something, but I didn't know how you felt." His thumb traced along her jaw. "I was scared the only reason you were staying with me was because of the babies."

"Because you…" She broke off then, his words falling into place. "You… You choose me?"

"Always." He nodded. "It'll hurt like hell, but I'll respect whatever *you* choose. Even if it's not me."

She opened her mouth, but words failed her.

"If you need time—" his hands slid from her face "—you take whatever time you need. There's no pressure here. No stress." He shook his head. "Damn, stress is the last thing you need right now." He led her back to the couch. "Sit, put your feet up. I'll get you something to eat."

Dougal emerged from the kitchen, a pie dish in one hand and a carton of chocolate milk in the other. "The bear wake you, too? The damn wall's shaking, I swear it. How a person's supposed to sleep through that, I don't know." He sat in the recliner and started eating pumpkin pie. "Want some?"

Savannah sat and put her feet up, stunned. Gertie jumped up and turned in a few circles before curling up in her lap.

"No. She needs protein." Angus headed into the kitchen.

"To go along with your cookies." Dougal nodded at the remaining cookie. "Can't say that I blame you. They're good."

"Bear?" Savannah was still sifting through the whirl-wind in her head. "I didn't think there were bears here."

"Oh, there are. Few and far between, but I was talking about the bear sleeping on the other side of my bedroom wall. Aunt Nola. Snores like a damn grizzly bear. You really didn't hear it out here?" He shook his head. "Gonna start sleeping in here or in the barn if I'm going to get any sleep."

A few minutes later, Angus came back from the kitchen. "It's a ham and cheese croissant from The Coffee Shop." He set the plate on the table. "And water." He handed her the glass. "To keep yourself hydrated."

She took the glass.

"Where did you find that?" Dougal asked.

"I hid it. It's for Savannah." Angus didn't look at his brother.

"I just asked," Dougal huffed. "I did buy them for her."

Angus sat on the coffee table in front of her. "You can ask Dougal, if you don't believe me."

Savannah shook her head.

"You sure?"

"Ask me what?" Dougal yawned.

Savannah shook her head again.

"I'll say one more thing and let you have space." He cleared his throat, leaning closer to her. "Your dad wants you to come home." He ran his fingers through his hair. "I know he'll make sure you're taken care of. If you have to leave, I guess I'd rather you went there. Then I won't worry about you all. I mean, I will…" He stopped. "I love you, Savannah, and I want you to be happy. You deserve to be happy." He pressed a kiss to her forehead and headed back to his room.

"Yeah, go on and sleep," Dougal called after him. "In

your nice quiet room." He set the pie plate on the floor and leaned back in the chair.

Savannah went back to staring at the tree, hope and wonder and love rising up until her chest felt like it would burst right open.

"You better eat that or he'll be pissed off." Dougal pointed at her plate. "The only thing on his mind is making sure you eat and drink and sleep." He chuckled. "It's funny, seeing him like this."

Savannah took a bite of the croissant.

"I guess it's good practice for when the babies get here." He yawned and rubbed a hand over his face. "He's going to be insufferable, then."

She smiled, eating more of her croissant. "I'll take it."

"Thank goodness. If you didn't, he'd be like a lost puppy looking for someone to follow around and love all over." He shuddered. "Spare me from ever falling in love."

She laughed then, earning a look from Gertie. "It's not so bad, Dougal. Especially if they love you back. You should try it sometime." She ate the rest of the croissant and cuddled Gertie until long after Dougal was snoring— very bearlike himself—and the sun was starting to come up.

Angus hadn't bothered trying to sleep. It would be pointless anyway. Instead, he'd dressed and planned to head down to the barn. Instead, he'd taken a detour. Savannah was curled up on the couch, sound asleep— Gertie on her hip. He'd shooed Gertie aside, scooped her up, and carried Savannah to his bed. She sighed, rolled over, and buried her face in his pillow.

Damn, but she was pretty. Now all he had to do was get her to listen to doctor's orders and sleep. Of course, he needed to do the same.

He frowned as he tucked the blankets around her. Last night had cleared up a few things, but he'd gone about it all the wrong way. He'd dumped his wants on her long before he'd figured out what she wanted. That was something he'd learned about her—she put everyone else first.

He'd meant it when he said he wanted her to have what she wanted. He wanted her to be happy. He hoped like hell he could make her happy.

He crept out of the bedroom and headed down to the barn. If he couldn't sleep, he might as well find something useful to do.

He turned the horses out into the corral. They ran and jumped, happy to be out of their stalls and have a little freedom. They nickered and whinnied, as if saying their good mornings to one another. He smiled at the thought. Maybe he spent too much time with animals—Dougal more or less fit in that category. Animals were easy to read. People, not so much.

He headed into the barn, hung his coat on a nail, and started cleaning out the stalls. Harvey would be tickled pink to have a day's break and the physical work would do him some good.

It was Christmas Eve and, depending on what Savannah had to say, he had big plans. His meemaw's ring was in his coat pocket, ready to be put on Savannah's finger. But if she said she wanted to go home, he'd try not to beg her to stay. The very idea of her not being here was unbearable. He didn't know what the hell he'd do if that became his reality.

Not going to think about it.

He stabbed at the old hay with the pitchfork and threw himself into his work.

Christmas Eve had always been a big deal. It had been the same for as long as he could remember. All of Pa's favorites. Ma spent the day slow-roasting a turkey. She insisted on making the rolls from scratch, even though Nola swore store-bought rolls tasted just as good. There would be fresh green beans, glazed carrots, and butter-roasted potatoes for sides. And then there'd be the pies. Nola might suggest store-bought rolls, but she'd never forgive a person who served store-bought pie.

He'd have to make sure Ma and Nola didn't let Savannah do too much. She loved that they were giving her the chance to cook, and she was trying so damn hard. He'd managed to eat her undercooked chicken potpie without incident. He'd tried to feed Gertie the meat loaf, but even the dog tucked tail and ran. On both counts, Nola had taken a bite and announced neither was fit for consumption—scraping them both into the trash. But Savannah had taken it in stride and tried again.

No matter where he started, his thoughts always came back to her.

He pulled his handkerchief from his pocket and wiped the sweat from his face. The sun was up now, shining down so bright he suspected it'd be a warm Christmas Eve. He hoped Savannah wouldn't be too disappointed. She liked a more winter wonderland vibe.

His stomach was growling and he could use a cup of coffee, but he'd rather finish what he started. He took off his flannel shirt and hung it over his coat, then went back to work. He finished the stall and turned to find Savannah watching him.

"I brought you coffee." She held out a steaming mug. "It might not be as hot as you like it." She was in her green-and-red-and-white Christmas print pajamas—one of the things she'd been most excited about the day they'd gone shopping. Her hair was loose and her cheeks were flushed and his heart kicked into overdrive.

"Thank you." He set the pitchfork aside and took the coffee. "You warm enough?"

She nodded.

He sipped the coffee, uncertain. "Feeling okay?"

She nodded, smiling up at him. "Thank you for putting me to bed."

"You didn't look too comfortable on the couch. Plus, Dougal was snoring." Angus shook his head.

"I'm wondering how much of the snoring is Aunt Nola bear and how much is him." Savannah wrapped her arms around herself.

"Here." He pulled his shirt off the nail and handed it to her.

She slipped it on over her nightgown. "Thanks."

Watching her bury her nose in his shirt and smile gave him the courage to say, "If you don't want to talk about last night, just say so."

She looked at him, but her mouth stayed shut.

"I don't want to sway you one way or the other." He cleared his throat and stepped closer to her. "But I realized I didn't say something last night that I should have said a long time ago." He took another step.

She blinked, those big brown eyes watching his every move.

"I love you." He was close enough to touch her. "That's why I want you to choose what makes you happy. Because you being happy will make me happy—even if we're not together."

Her arms wrapped around his waist as she pressed herself against him. "I don't want us to be apart. I love you, Angus McCarrick." The words were almost a sigh. "I don't want to be anywhere other than right here. With you. I was only leaving because I wanted you to be happy."

"Good." He held on to her as if his life depended on it. "For all my big talk, I don't think I could let you go."

She laughed against his chest.

He pressed his nose to the top of her head, savoring her scent with every breath. Everything would be okay now. "Hold on." He moved closer to his coat, but he didn't let her go. "I'd come up with this big plan for tonight." He reached into the coat pocket and found the ring. "After you told me you were staying, which I've been praying for, I was going to lead you to the Christmas tree and drop down on one knee. But I'm not ready to let go of you just yet, so…" He took her hand and held it up. "Will you marry me, Savannah?"

Her smile lit him up from the inside. It was pure joy and love. For him. "I will marry you, Angus."

"Will you marry me? Soon?" he asked, sliding the ring on her finger. "One of the Mitchell brothers is licensed to do weddings…" He stopped. "I understand if you'd rather something big and fancy—"

"I can't think of anything I want more than to be Mrs. McCarrick for New Year's." She stood on tiptoe to kiss him, but paused. "You feel that?"

It was a solid thump against his stomach. "I do." He chuckled.

"They're just saying good morning to their daddy." She stared up at him.

"Something to look forward to every morning." He brushed the lightest kiss against her lips. "And that." He kissed her again. "And having you in my arms. Where you belong."

"I love you, Angus," she breathed. "You've given me everything I've always wanted."

"Damn straight." He pressed a hand against her cheek.

"I'll try to make you happy every damn day." He kissed her again, letting his lips cling a little longer.

"Angus." She gasped.

"Mmm?" he murmured, his mouth sealing with hers until she melted into him.

"Don't be mad at me, but..."

He lifted his head. "But what?"

"It's not that I don't want to kiss you—I do." She smiled. "But I'm *really* hungry."

Angus threw back his head and laughed.

"You're not mad?" She laughed, too.

"No, ma'am." He slid his arm around her waist and led her from the barn. "Feeding you and those babies takes priority."

"But after breakfast—"

"There will be a whole lot of kissing." He nodded.

"And then we'll be married tonight." She leaned her head against his chest. "So, I'll be back in our bed."

"I can hardly wait." His heart was thundering. "But I know it's worth waiting for." He pressed a kiss to her temple. "Everything about you is worth waiting for."

"Tell me again that you love me."

"I'll tell you again. You're going to get sick of hearing it."

"I won't. I promise. I love you." There was so much tenderness on her face he didn't doubt it.

"I love you." He kissed her again. "So damn much."

Epilogue

"You don't look like you gave birth six weeks ago." Chelsea hugged her sister. "You look gorgeous."

"You're lying. But I love you anyway." Savannah was exhausted. Even at the end of her pregnancy, she'd never been so tired. Or happy.

"Where are the wee ones?" Chelsea scanned the room. "I was expecting lots of screaming and chaos."

"Angus and Dougal are taking them for a walk. It's part of the daily routine." And it was adorable. Who knew Dougal would be such a pushover when it came to the triplets? "Overall, it hasn't been that bad, really. Orla and Nola and Momma have been amazing." Which was true. The three of them took shifts, making sure Savannah and Angus had time to sleep and bathe and have a minute to themselves—little things that made such a big difference. "Dad's tried, too. I think it's given him a whole new appreciation for Mom."

"That's good. She deserves it. Dad changing diapers. I can't picture *that*."

"Oh, I didn't say he'd changed any diapers. He gets greener than I did when I was pregnant."

Chelsea laughed. "That I can picture. So, are you excited about your date?" She bobbed her eyebrows. "You know, some quality couple time."

"I am." Savannah bobbed her eyebrows right back.

"Look at you, being all naughty." Chelsea laughed. "I approve."

"Well, that can't be good," Dougal said as he walked through the front door. "Chelsea."

"Oh, hush. I'm not here to see you anyway." Chelsea brushed him aside, cooing, "Ooh, they're so big. How did you three muffins get so big in two weeks?"

"Lots of eating and sleeping and loving." Savannah scooped up little Henry from the old-fashioned pram and handed him to Chelsea.

"Don't forget the diapers." Angus chuckled. "So many diapers."

"Who's my favorite nephew? You still look like an old wise man, Henry." Chelsea cradled him close. "I just know you're already full of insightful things to say. When you start talking, that is."

Tabitha squeaked.

"I got you." Dougal picked up the pink-swaddled baby girl. "You're fine."

"They do like this stroller better." Angus smiled as he lifted little Emilia up. She was wriggling and squirming in her blanket. "I guess it's because you're all next to each other. Makes you feel like you did with your momma." He pressed a kiss against the top of Emilia's head.

Savannah hadn't thought it was possible to find her husband more handsome or sexy. The moment he looked at his babies, she knew she'd been wrong. Somehow, some way, Angus got sexier with each passing day. It was the way he loved them. And not just the babies, but her, too. He didn't shy away from showing or verbalizing his love. Nothing made her happier than seeing the joy on his face when he was spending time with them.

"I know that look." Angus was smiling—that devastating smile.

She didn't bother denying it. She was definitely thinking about how nice it was going to be to have a whole night alone with him. Assuming they could stand being away from the babies for a whole night. It wasn't that the babies wouldn't be loved and coddled and more than taken care of, it was that they hadn't been away from them that long since they were born.

She leaned against Angus's side, reaching up to tuck the blanket beneath Emilia's chin. "She's pretty perfect, isn't she?"

"They all are." Angus kissed her temple. "You did good. More than good."

"I had a little help." She smiled up at him.

"Okay, you two, the sweetness factor is getting a little nauseating in here." Chelsea shook her head. "Put poor Emilia in the bouncy seat. Dougal and I've got this covered. So, shoo."

"Nola's asleep. Orla and Momma should be back from the store any minute now." Savannah watched Willow take up her spot beside the bouncy seats. She'd transferred her devotion to the babies now, following them wherever they went and alerting the closest adult if they squeaked or fussed or needed something.

Gertie, on the other hand, still preferred being the baby. She took every opportunity to claim a lap. Currently, she was squeezing in between Dougal and Chelsea on the couch.

Angus finished buckling Tabitha into the bouncy seat and stood. "Need anything?"

"We've got this. Go on, Pickle." Chelsea didn't even look up. She was too besotted with Henry.

"I know their schedule." Dougal nodded, patting Tabitha on the back and using his foot to rock Emilia's bouncy seat.

Angus took her hand. "You going to make it?"

"Are you?" Savannah asked, squeezing his hand.

"A night alone with you?" He scratched his well-groomed beard. "Hell, yes." He pulled her against him to press a gentle kiss against her lips.

"Seriously, guys." Chelsea groaned. "Your bags are in the truck. Go on. Just don't get pregnant again for a while, okay?"

Dougal chuckled then.

"Oh, Chels." Savannah tugged Angus after her. "Bye."

They could hear Dougal and Chelsea laughing as Angus pulled the front door closed behind them.

"Now, where were we?" Angus pulled her close, his kiss more insistent this time.

She melted into him. It had been so long. "It's weird not to have a massive belly separating us."

"I didn't mind the belly." He rested his forehead against hers. "I guess we should hit the road before Ma and Lana get back."

Savannah slipped free of his hold and led him to the truck. "Excellent point. We'd lose a whole hour, at least."

"Why, Mrs. McCarrick, you in a hurry?" He was grinning.

"Only to get there. Then I want to take everything nice

and slow." She hopped into the truck's passenger seat. "Is that okay with you, Mr. McCarrick?"

He kissed her once, then again. "It is. I like the way you think, Mrs. McCarrick."

"Good, because you're stuck with me." She counted her blessings every day.

"Damn straight." He kissed her again. "You know I wouldn't have it any other way."

* * * * *

Chapter One

"You're really going to go in there. Alone. Just before dark?" The low, masculine voice came from somewhere behind her.

With the brisk January wind cutting through her clothes, Tess Gardner paused, house key in hand, and turned toward the Laramie, Texas, street. Senses tingling, she watched as the man stepped out of a charcoal-gray Expedition, now parked at the curb. He wasn't the shearling coat-wearing cowboy she had expected to see in this rural southwestern town she was about to call home. Rather, he appeared to be an executive type, in business-casual wool slacks, dress shirt and loosened tie. An expensive down jacket covered his broad shoulders and hung open, revealing taut, muscular abs. Shiny dress boots covered his feet.

Had it been any other day, any other time in her recently upended life, she might have responded favorably to this tall, commanding man striding casually up the sidewalk in the dwindling daylight. But after the long drive from Denver, all she wanted was to get a first look at the home she had inherited from her late uncle. Then crash.

The interloper, however, had other plans. He strode closer, all indomitable male.

Tess drew a bolstering breath. She let her gaze drift over his short, dark hair and ruggedly chiseled features before returning to his midnight blue eyes. Damn, he was handsome.

Trying not to shiver in the cold, damp air, she regarded him cautiously. Drawing on the careful wariness she had learned from growing up in the city, she countered, "And who are you exactly?"

His smile was even more compelling than his voice. "Noah Lockhart." He reached into his shirt pocket for a business card.

Disappointment swept through her. She sighed. "Let me guess. Another Realtor." A half dozen had already contacted her, eager to know if she wanted to sell.

He shook his head. "No." He came halfway up the cement porch steps of the century-old Craftsman bungalow and handed over his card, inundating her with the brisk, woodsy fragrance of his cologne. Their fingers touched briefly and another tingle of awareness shot through her. "I own a software company," he said.

Now she really didn't understand why he had stopped by, offering unsolicited advice. Was he flirting with her? His cordial attitude said *yes*, but the warning in his low voice when he had first approached her, and had seen that she was about to enter the house, said *no*.

He sobered, his gaze lasering into hers. "I've been trying to get ahold of you through the Laramie Veterinary Clinic," he added.

So he was *what*? Tess wondered, feeling all the more confused. A pet owner in need of veterinary care? A potential business associate? Certainly not one of the county's many successful, eligible men who, she had been teasingly informed by Sara, her new coworker/boss, would be lining up to date her as soon as she arrived.

Curious, she scanned his card.

In bold print on the first line, it said:

Noah Lockhart, CEO and Founder

Okay, she thought, so his name was vaguely familiar. Below that, it said:

Lockhart Solutions. "An app for every need."

The company logo of intertwining diamonds was beside that.

Recognition turned swiftly to admiration. She was pretty sure the weather app she used had been designed by Lockhart Solutions. The restaurant finder, too. And the CEO of the company, who looked to be in his midthirties, was standing right in front of her. In Laramie, Texas, of all places.

"But even though I've left half a dozen messages, I haven't gotten any calls back," he continued in frustration.

Tess imagined that wasn't typical for someone of his importance. That was just too darn bad.

Struggling not to feel the full impact of his disarming, masculine presence, Tess returned his frown with a deliberate one of her own. She didn't know if she was relieved or disappointed he wasn't there to ask her out. She did know she hated being pressured into anything. Especially when the coercion came from a place of entitlement. She propped her hands on her hips, the mixture of fatigue and temper warming her from the inside out. "First of all, I haven't even started working there yet."

His expression remained determined. "I know."

"There are four other veterinarians working at the animal clinic."

"None with your expertise," he stated.

Somehow, Tess doubted that. If her new boss and managing partner, Sara Anderson McCabe, had thought that Tess was the only one qualified to handle Noah's problem—whatever it was—she would have called Tess to discuss the situation, and then asked Tess to consult on the case. Sara hadn't done that. Which led Tess to believe this wasn't the vital issue or "emergency" Noah deemed it to be.

More likely, someone as successful as Noah Lockhart was simply not accustomed to waiting on anyone or anything. That wasn't her problem. Setting professional boundaries was. She shifted the bag higher on her shoulder, then said firmly, "You can make an appointment for next week."

After she had taken the weekend to get settled.

Judging by the downward curve of his sensual lips, her suggestion did not please, nor would, in any way, deter him. His gaze sifted over her face, and he sent another deeply persuasive look her way. "I was hoping I could talk you into making a house call before that." He followed his statement with a hopeful smile. The kind he apparently did not expect would be denied.

Tess let out a breath. *Great.* Sara had been wrong about him. Noah Lockhart was just another rich, entitled person. Just like the ridiculously demanding clients she had been trying to escape when she left her position in

Denver. Not to mention the memories of the ex-fiancé who had broken her heart...

Determined not to make the same mistakes twice, however, she said coolly, "You're still going to have to go through the clinic."

He shoved a hand through his hair and exhaled. Unhappiness simmered between them. Broad shoulders flexing, he said, "Normally, I'd be happy to do that—"

And here they went. "Let me guess," she scoffed. "You don't have time for that?"

Another grimace. "Actually, no, I—we—likely don't."

"Well, that makes two of us," Tess huffed, figuring this conversation had come to an end. "Now, if you will excuse me..." Hoping he'd finally get the hint, she turned back to the front door of the Craftsman bungalow, slid the key into the lock, turned it and heard it open with a satisfying click.

Aware that Noah Lockhart was still standing behind her, despite the fact he had been summarily dismissed, she pushed the door open. Head held high, she marched across the threshold. And strode face-first into the biggest, stickiest spiderweb she had ever encountered in her life!

At the same time, she felt something gross and scary drop onto the top of her head. "Aggghhh!" she screamed, dropping her bag and backing up, frantically batting away whatever it was crawling through her thick, curly hair...

This, Noah thought ruefully, was exactly what Tess Gardner's new boss had feared. Sara Anderson McCabe had worried if Tess had seen the interior of the house she had inherited from her late uncle before she toured the clinic and met the staff she was going to be working with, she might change her mind and head right back to Denver and the fancy veterinary practice she had come from.

Not that anyone had expected her to crash headfirst into a spiderweb worthy of a horror movie.

He covered the distance between them in two swift steps, reaching her just as she backed perilously toward the edge of the porch, still screaming and batting at her hair. With good reason. The large, gray spider was still moving across her scalp, crawling from her crown toward her face.

Noah grabbed Tess protectively by the shoulders with one hand, and used his other to flick the pest away.

It landed on the porch and scurried into the bushes while Tess continued to shudder violently.

"You're okay," he told her soothingly, able to feel her shaking through the thick layer of her winter jacket. She smelled good, too, her perfume a mix of citrus and patchouli. "I got it off of you."

She sagged in relief. And reluctantly, he let her go, watching as she brushed at the soft cashmere sweater clinging to her midriff, then slid her hand down her jeans-clad legs, grimacing every time she encountered more of the sticky web.

Damn, she was beautiful, with long, wildly curly blond hair and long-lashed, sage-green eyes. Around five foot eight, to his own six foot three inches, she was the perfect weight for her slender frame, with curves in all the right places, and she had the face of an angel.

Not that she seemed to realize just how incredibly beguiling she was. It was a fact that probably drove all the guys, including him, crazy.

Oblivious to the ardent nature of his thoughts, she shot him a sidelong glance. Took another deep breath. Straightened. "Was it a spider?"

Noah had never been one to push his way into anyone else's business, but glad he had been there to help her out, he said, "Yes."

Her pretty eyes narrowed. "A brown recluse or black widow?"

He shook his head. "A wolf spider."

"Pregnant with about a million babies?"

He chuckled. "Aren't they always?"

She muttered something beneath her breath that he was pretty sure wasn't in the least bit ladylike. Then, pointing at the ceiling several feet beyond the still open front door, where much of the web was still dangling precariously, she turned back to regard him suspiciously. "Did you know it was there? Is that why you told me not to go in alone?"

He held her gaze intently. He hadn't been this aware of a woman since he'd lost his wife, but there was something about Tess that captured—and held—his attention. A latent vulnerability, maybe. "It never would have occurred to me that was what you would have encountered when you opened the door."

Squinting, she propped her hands on her hips. "Then why the warning about not going in alone?"

Good question. Since he had never been known to chase after damsels in distress. Or offer help indiscriminately. He had always figured if someone wanted his aid, that person would let him know, and then he would render it in a very trustworthy fashion. Otherwise, he stayed out of it. Tonight, though, he hadn't. Which was interesting…given how many problems of his own he had to manage.

She was still waiting for his answer.

He shrugged, focusing on the facts. "Waylon hadn't been here for at least a year, before he passed four months ago, and he was never known for his domestic skills." So he honestly hadn't known what she would be walking into.

She scanned the neat front yard. Although it was only a little past five o'clock in the afternoon, the sun was already setting in the wintry gray sky. "But the lawn and the exterior of the house are perfectly maintained!"

"The neighbors do that as a courtesy for him."

"But not the interior?" she persisted.

"Waylon didn't want to trouble folks, so he never gave anyone a key."

Tess turned her gaze to the shadowy interior. All the window blinds were closed. Because it was turning dusk, the inside of the home was getting darker by the minute. And the mangled cobweb was still dangling in the doorway.

Noah knew it was none of his business. That she was an adult, free to do as she chose. Yet he had to offer the kind of help he knew he would want anyone in his family to receive, in a similar situation.

"Sure you want to stay here alone?" Noah asked.

Actually, now that she knew what she was facing, Tess most definitely did *not* want to stay here tonight. "I don't have a choice," she admitted with grim resignation. "I don't have a hotel room. Everything in the vicinity is booked. I guess I waited too long to make a reservation."

He nodded, seemingly not surprised.

"The Lake Laramie Lodge and the Laramie Inn are always booked well in advance. During the week, it's business conferences and company retreats."

"And the weekends?" she queried.

"On Saturdays and Sundays it tends to be filled with guests in town for a wedding or family reunion, or hobby aficionados of some sort. This weekend I think there's a ham-radio conference… Next week, scrapbooking, maybe? You can look it up online or just read the signs posted around town, if you want to learn more."

"Good to know. Anyway…" Tess pulled her cell phone from her pocket and punched the flashlight button. Bright light poured out. "I'm sure I can handle it. Especially if we turn on the lights…"

She reached for the switches just inside the door. To her surprise, neither brought any illumination.

Noah glanced at the fixture on the ceiling inside the house, then the porch light. "Maybe the bulbs are just burned out," he said.

Stepping past the dangling web, he went on inside to a table lamp. She watched as he tried it. Nothing.

Still wary of being attacked by another spider, she lingered just inside the portal, her hands shoved inside the pockets of her winter jacket. The air coming out of the interior of the house seemed even colder than the below-freezing temperature outside. Which meant the furnace wasn't on, either. Although that could be fixed.

Noah went to another lamp. Again, nothing happened when he turned the switch. "You think all the bulbs could be burned out?" Tess asked hopefully, knowing that at least that would be an easy fix.

"Or…" He strode through the main room to the kitchen, which was located at the rear of the two-story brick home. She followed him, careful to avoid plowing through another web, then watched as he pushed down the lever on the toaster. Peering inside the small appliance, he frowned.

Anxiety swirled through Tess as she wondered what she had gotten herself into. "Not working, either?"

"No." Noah moved purposefully over to the sink and

tried the faucet. When no water came out, he hunkered down and looked inside the cabinet below. Tried something else, but to no avail. As he straightened, three small mice scampered out, running past him, then disappeared behind the pantry door. Tess managed not to shriek while he grimaced, and concluded, "Both the electricity and water are turned off."

Which meant the mice and the spiders weren't the worst of her problems. "You're *kidding*!" After rushing to join him at the sink, she tried the ancient faucet herself. Again…nothing.

Noah reached for the cords next to the window above the sink and opened the dark wooden blinds. They were covered with a thick film of dust. As was, Tess noted in discouragement, everything else in sight.

Plus, the spiders had had a field day.

There were big cobwebs in every corner, stretched across the ceiling and the tops of the window blinds, and strewn over the beat-up furniture. Worse, when she looked closely, she could see mice droppings trailing across much of the floor. Which could mean she had more than the three rodent guests she had already encountered. *Ugh.*

"Seen enough for right now?" Noah asked.

Tess shook her head in dismay. She'd had such dreams for this place. Hoped it would give her the kind of permanent home and sense of belonging she had always yearned for. But while she was certainly taken aback by what they had discovered here tonight, she wasn't going to let it scare her off. Besides, in addition to the property, her late uncle had left her the proceeds of his life-insurance policy, with the expectation she would use the funds to fix up the house. "Maybe the upstairs will be better…"

Unfortunately, it wasn't. The single bathroom looked

as if it hadn't had a good scrubbing in years. Two of the bedrooms were filled with piles of fishing and camping equipment. The third held a sagging bed, and heaps of clothes suitable for an oil roughneck who spent most of his time on ocean rigs.

On a whim, she checked out the light switch, and the sink in the bathroom, too. Neither worked.

Noah was gazing at her from a short distance away. "Well, that settles it, you can't stay here," he said.

Tess had already come to the same conclusion.

Although, after two very long days in her SUV, she wasn't looking forward to the two-hour drive to San Antonio for an available hotel room.

He met her gaze equably. "You can come home with me."

Chapter Two

Noah might as well have suggested they run away together, given the astonished look on Tess Gardner's pretty face. Then, without another word, she brushed by him and headed down the staircase, still using her cell-phone flashlight to lead the way.

Noah followed, giving her plenty of space. He had an idea what she was feeling. He had been orphaned as a kid and had lived in three different foster homes over a two-year period, before finally being reunited with his seven siblings and adopted by Robert and Carol Lockhart. So he knew firsthand what it was like to be alone, in unfamiliar circumstances, with those around you offering help you weren't sure it was safe to take.

If he wanted to help her, and he did, he would have to make sure she knew his intentions were honorable.

Being careful to avoid cobwebs, she walked out of the numbing cold inside the house and onto the front porch, breathing deeply of the brisk air. Slender shoulders squared, she swung back to him. "Why would you want to do that for me?"

It wasn't lost on him that for a fiercely independent woman like her, an offer like this probably wasn't the norm. But for someone like him—who had finished growing up here—it was. Patiently, he explained, "Because this is Laramie County, and neighbors help neighbors out here all the time. Plus—" he winked, teasing, as if this was his only motive "—maybe it will give me an in with the new vet. But if you want, you could always call Sara Anderson McCabe—" their only mutual acquaintance, that he knew of, anyway "—for a character reference."

The mention of the other Laramie County veterinarian had Tess relaxing slightly. "First, I already did Face-Time with her earlier today. Both her kids are sick with strep throat. And on top of that, between the construction for the new addition on her house, the extra work at the veterinary clinic since the founding partner retired five weeks ago and the fact she is seven months pregnant, she is completely wiped out. I'm not about to add anything to her already full slate."

Noah admired Tess's compassion. That she was willing and able to put others first, even when her own situation was far less than ideal, spoke volumes about this newcomer. Perhaps Sara had been right. Even though the two of them had kind of gotten off on the wrong foot, his gut told him that Tess was going to fit right into this rural community.

She studied him even more closely, then after a pause, admitted wearily, "And second, it's not necessary. I already know what Sara's going to say when it comes to your character. Since you were first on the list of eligible men she thought I should meet."

Noah frowned. His old friend had already been match-making? This was news to him. But perhaps not such an unexpected occurrence for the gorgeous woman standing opposite him.

He studied the guileless look in Tess's light green eyes.

"Initially, I sort of assumed that was why you were here," she continued dryly, with a provoking lift of her brow. "To get a jump on the competition?"

Glad to know he wasn't the only one who routinely tried to find the irony or humor in every situation, Noah stifled his embarrassment and scrubbed a hand over his face.

As long as they were going to talk candidly...

He met her casually probing gaze. "Ah, no." Romance had most definitely *not* been on his mind when he had stopped by the house on a whim, to see if she had arrived or if there was anything he could do for the town's newest resident. "Since my wife passed a couple of years ago, I've had my hands full with my three little girls. And I don't see that changing anytime soon."

Her eyes widening in obvious surprise, she stepped toward him. Up and down the block, the time-activated streetlamps suddenly switched on, spreading yellow light through the increasing winter gloom and enabling her to peer at him even more closely. She tilted her head up to his. "So, you're *not* interested in dating?"

He shook his head. A woman like this... Well, she could make him forget his new, more cautious approach to life. And that was something he just couldn't risk.

She sighed in obvious relief and stepped back.

He watched the color come into her high, sculpted cheeks. "And you?" Noah asked.

"No," she said emphatically. "I'm definitely not on the market."

Their eyes locked.

"Although I am interested in meeting new people…" she said, then paused. "Making friends," she added eventually.

Noah exhaled. "Can never have enough of those," he said, meaning it. It was his friends and family who had helped him through the past few tumultuous years.

And would continue to help him.

Because as rough as it had been to weather the emotional impact of losing the first and only love of his life, it was even harder to face life as a single dad.

"So about that offer to bunk at your place tonight…" Tess said, pacing the length of the porch, squinting to evaluate. "It really wouldn't be an inconvenience?"

Wanting to give her the kind of small-town Texas welcome his friends Sara and Matt McCabe had wanted for her, Noah shook his head. "Nah. I've got a big house with a nice guest suite. But if you get there and you're not comfortable with the setup for any reason, you could always take refuge at my folks' ranch house just down the road. They are babysitting my three girls this evening, so you'll have a chance to meet them, too." He released a breath. "And if you're *still* not comfortable with that option, my mom is a social worker for Laramie County, so it's possible she might be able to pull some strings and find you a place to bunk for the night."

Tess pursed her lips. "Like where?"

"Uh… I honestly don't know," he admitted. "Maybe there's an on-call room at the hospital that's not being used?"

She ran a hand through her thick mane of curly hair. "This is getting ridiculously complicated."

"You're right. And it doesn't have to be. So what do

you say?" he asked her gruffly. "How about you lock up here, and we head out to my place?"

When she still looked a little hesitant, he added, "You can follow in your Tahoe. Check out the accommodations. And we can take it from there."

Fortunately, the drive was an easy one. And fifteen minutes later, Noah was turning his charcoal-gray Expedition onto a paved driveway off the country road they'd been traveling on, winding his way past the mailbox. Tess was right behind him in her red SUV.

The black wrought-iron archway over the entrance proclaimed the property to be the Welcome Ranch. Which was ironically appropriate, given the circumstances, Tess couldn't help but think.

Neat fences surrounded the manicured property. In the distance, a sprawling home could be seen. The impressive two-story abode featured California architecture, with an ivory stucco exterior. There were plenty of windows, and the first floor was all lit up. In the distance she could also see a grassy paddock and a big, elegant barn that looked as if it had been recently built.

She didn't notice any livestock grazing in the moonlit pastures. But she supposed there could be horses stabled in the barn.

Noah parked next to an extended-cab pickup that was in front of the four-car garage. Tess took the space next to that. As they got out, the front door opened, and a handsome couple in their midfifties stepped out and stood beneath the shelter of the portico.

He fell into step beside her. "My folks," he explained as he ushered her toward them. "Mom, Dad, this is Tess Gardner, the new veterinarian at the Laramie clinic. Tess, my parents, Robert and Carol Lockhart."

"Oh, you're here to see Miss Coco!" Carol Lockhart exclaimed, making an incorrect assumption. A slender woman with short dark hair and vivid green eyes, she was dressed in a cashmere turtleneck, tailored wool slacks and comfortable-looking winter boots.

Her tall, dark-haired husband had the year-round tan and fit appearance of someone who spent his life working outdoors. He nodded at Tess in approval. "Mighty nice of you."

Noah shifted closer to Tess and lifted a halting palm, before any further assumptions could be made. "That's not happening tonight," he said definitively, looking chagrined at the way his parents were jumping to conclusions. "Tess isn't starting work at the clinic until Monday, and she has had a really long day. Or actually, probably a couple of very long days."

He was right about that. Tess's muscles ached from the two-day, 800-plus-mile drive from Denver to Laramie County. Some of it over mountain roads. Much of it in inclement weather. Still, she didn't want anyone making decisions about what she was or wasn't up to. Curious, she turned back to his mother. "Who is Miss Coco?"

Carol explained, "Noah and the girls' miniature donkey. Noah's been worrying nonstop about her the last few weeks. So when he heard you had cared for a lot of mules back in Colorado during your fellowship, and were considered quite the expert, he was ecstatic."

Noah exhaled. He sent his mother a look that said he did not appreciate Carol speaking for him. "I wouldn't say ecstatic, exactly."

"Relieved, maybe?" his dad suggested.

"Something like that," Noah murmured.

Frowning in confusion, his mom turned back to him. "So if Tess isn't here to see Miss Coco tonight, then…?"

"I'm afraid I didn't plan my arrival very well," Tess admitted, chagrined. "I thought the house I inherited from my uncle would be clean and empty. It was neither. There's also no electricity or water."

Noah added matter-of-factly, "Unfortunately, as you know, the offices that can turn the utilities back on won't be open until Monday. All the lodging in the area is booked. So I offered to let her bunk here temporarily."

Carol and Robert both smiled, understanding. Before they could say anything else, he asked, "Were the girls well-behaved for you?"

His parents nodded. "They went to bed at eight o'clock and went right to sleep," his dad said.

The interior of the house did seem quiet.

A lethargic chocolate-brown Labrador retriever ambled out on the porch. Recognizing an animal lover when he saw one, he went straight for Tess. She kneeled to greet him, letting him sniff her while she scratched him behind the ears. With a blissful huff, he sat down next to her, leaning his body against her legs.

"You know…we could stay a few more minutes if you all want to walk out to the barn, just for a minute," Carol suggested hopefully.

Tess had the idea that the older woman was worried about the miniature donkey, too. Although no one had yet said exactly why…

Her fatigue fading, the way it always did when there was an animal in need of care, she turned back to Noah. A little embarrassed she hadn't been more helpful when he had tried to talk to her earlier, she asked, "Is that where Miss Coco is housed?"

Noah nodded.

"We could stay with the girls until you're back from

the barn," Carol offered. "And I know Noah would feel better if you just took a quick peek at Miss Coco."

So would Tess. Appreciating the unexpectedly warm welcome from both Noah and his folks, she smiled. "Just let me get my medical bag out of my SUV."

"You really don't have to do this," Noah said as they took off across the lawn toward a big slate-gray barn that looked as new as the house.

He paused to slide open the door and turn on the overhead lighting. The floor was concrete and there were a half-dozen stalls made of beautiful wood, and a heater was circulating warm air. He motioned for her to come inside.

Aware how comfortable she already felt with him, Tess smiled. "The least I can do, given how truly hospitable you have been."

Their eyes met. With a brief businesslike nod in her direction, he pulled the door shut to keep in the heat, and led the way forward.

Tess had to quicken her steps to keep up with him. As she neared him, she caught another whiff of his woodsy scent, and something else, maybe the soap or shampoo he used, that was brisk and masculine.

A tingle of awareness surged through her. She pushed it away. She had mixed work and pleasure once, to heartbreaking results. She couldn't allow herself to react similarly here. Especially to a man whose heart was ultimately as closed off as her ex's had been. "So what has you so concerned?" She forced herself to get back to business. "Can you give me a little history…?"

He paused and placed one hand over the top of the middle stall on the right. "Eight months ago, I went to the local 4-H adoption fair with my oldest daughter, Lucy."

He eased open the stall door, gazing tenderly down at the miniature jennet curled up sleepily on fresh hay. "She fell in love with Miss Coco the minute she saw her..."

Tess gazed down at her new patient, entranced. "I can see why. Oh, Noah. She is beautiful!" With a light brown coat the color of powdered cocoa, a white stripe that went from her ears down her face, to the base of her throat, and white socks and tail, Tess figured the miniature donkey measured about two and a half feet tall. Her eyes were big and dark, and she was watching them carefully.

"Luckily, she has a personality to match. The problem is, I didn't know she was gestating when we adopted her. I just assumed her belly was a little swollen from lack of care. By the time I found out it wasn't an issue of malnutrition or lack of exercise, Lucy—my oldest—was already very attached."

Tess kneeled next to Coco, petting her. "And you don't want two donkeys." She opened up her bag.

"It's not really that. As you can see, I obviously have space for them. It's my three-year-old twins I am worried about. Lucy's eight. She can follow directions and understands there is no negotiation when it comes to the safety and welfare of animals in our care. The rules are the rules. Period."

Tess examined Coco's belly and the area around the birth canal, finding everything just as it should be. She reached for her stethoscope, pausing to listen to the strong, steady beat of Coco's heart, the breath going in and out of her lungs. Then she listened to the foal nestled inside. All was great.

She removed the earbuds and turned back to Noah. "And the twins...?"

"Are still at an excitable age. Angelica is sweet and mellow most of the time. A follower. Avery, on the other hand, has a real mind of her own. When she sets out on a mission, whatever it is, it can be hard to rein her in."

Tess laid the stethoscope around her neck and resumed petting Coco. She gazed up at Noah, who was still standing with his back to the side of the stall, the edges of his jacket open, his arms folded in front of him. He had the kind of take-charge, yet inherently kind, aura she admired. And if she were emotionally available, she'd be a goner. "Are you worried the twins will be too rough with the foal and that the baby's mama might be too protective and hurt them?"

He nodded with no hesitation. "Both—if the twins get too wound up. But I heard about something called imprint training, where you teach an animal from the moment they are born to trust and love the human touch. Which really gentles them. Sara said you gave classes in it, back in Colorado."

The ambient lighting in the stable made him look even more handsome. Which was definitely something she did not need to be noticing. Any more than how good he smelled. Or how strong and fit his body looked in business-casual clothing.

Fighting the shiver of sensual awareness sliding through her, she forced herself to smile back at him. "I did."

His gaze sifted over her, igniting tiny sparks of electricity everywhere he looked. "And you plan to give them here?"

Tess nodded. "When I get settled in, yes."

His expression fell in disappointment.

"But I could help show you what to do, in the meantime, so you will be prepared."

He cocked an eyebrow, his good humor returning. "Private lessons?"

One lesson, maybe. Ignoring the potent masculinity and charisma radiating from him, she returned dryly, "I don't think it will take you all that long to get the hang of what to do. In the meantime, Miss Coco and her baby are doing fine. Everything is as it should be."

"Any idea when she will go into labor and deliver?" he asked, concerned.

She studied the conflicted expression on his face. "I'm guessing you heard that a miniature jennet's gestation period can last anywhere from eleven to fourteen months."

He nodded.

"Right now, I'm guessing it will be another one to two weeks." Tess put her stethoscope back in her vet bag and closed the clasp. She rose to her feet. When her shearling lined boots unexpectedly slid a little on the crushed hay, Noah put out a hand to steady her, the warmth of his hand encircling her wrist. His gentle, protective touch sent another storm of sensations through her. She worked to hold back a flush.

Gallantly, he waited until he was sure she had her footing, then let her go slowly. He stepped back, folding his arms across his chest once again. The warmth inside her surged even more as he looked her in the eye. "How will I know when it's time?" he asked.

She replied in the same serious tone. "A number of things will happen. The foal will turn and move into the birth canal. Miss Coco'll be restless and may even look thinner. And she'll be holding her tail away from her body to one side. At that point, she will need to be closely monitored 24/7."

Noah began to look overwhelmed again.

Together, they walked out. "What about being here when Miss Coco's foal is born?" He paused just outside the barn doors. "Will you do that for us, to make sure everything goes all right?"

Tess nodded. "Be happy to," she promised with a re-assuring smile. Ushering new life into the world was the best part of her job.

As they reached the porch, the fatigue hit her hard. Noah went to get her two bags out of her Tahoe, while Carol showed her where to wash up and poured her a hot cup of tea. By the time he'd returned, his parents were already half out the door.

He regarded her sympathetically. "What else can I get you?"

Her hands gripping the mug, Tess shook her head. "Nothing. Thanks. All I want is a hot shower, and a bed. Time to sleep."

He gave her an understanding look. "I'll show you the guest suite."

She followed Noah as he led the way up the stairs, then past two rooms, where his three daughters could be seen snuggled cozily in their beds, sleeping in the glow of their night-lights.

Tess couldn't help but think how lucky he was to have such a beautiful family and nice home, as the two of them moved silently past his girls to the very end of the hall.

Oblivious to her quiet envy, he showed her the nicely outfitted guest suite with a private bath, chaise lounge just right for reading and comfortable-looking queen-size bed. He set her bags down just inside the door, in full host mode. "If there is anything you need that's not in the bathroom, let me know." He stepped back into the hall, and as their eyes met, a new warmth spiraled through her. He continued in a low, husky voice calibrated not to wake his daughters. "The kitchen is fully stocked, so make yourself at home there, too."

"Thank you," Tess returned just as softly, marveling at his kindness, even as she reminded herself he had already stated that, just like her, he was not emotionally available. For anything more than a casual friendship, anyway. "I will."

"Well…" He cleared his throat, suddenly looking as reluctant to part company as she was. Which made her wonder if the latent physical attraction went both ways.

Giving no clue as to what he was thinking, he nodded at her. "See you in the morning."

A distracting shiver swept through her once again.

Working to slow her racing pulse, she responded with an inner casualness she couldn't begin to feel. "Sure, see you then." She smiled as he turned to walk away. And just like that, she was on her own for the rest of the night.

Chapter Three

Hours later, Noah was awakened from a deep sleep. "Daddy, there was a pretty lady in the kitchen, and she said to give you this when you waked up," Lucy said importantly. She and her twin sisters climbed onto his bed, the twins on one side, Lucy perched on the other.

Damn. He'd overslept. Noah scrubbed a hand over his face. *Not exactly the way he wanted to start the day.*

"Are you awake now?" Avery asked. "'Cause we want to know what the letter says. And Lucy still has trouble reading cursive."

"Okay." Noah sat up. A piece of paper was pushed into his hand. "'Noah,'" he began, reading out loud. "'Thanks so much for all your help and hospitality last night. Tess Gardner.'"

Nothing about seeing each other again.

Noah felt a wave of disappointment move through him. He couldn't say why exactly, but he had expected a little more. Something warmer or more personal. But then, she'd said she wasn't looking for anything more than friendship. Same as him. And she did have a lot on her slate.

A lot of which she was still going to need help with.

He thought about the look on her face when she'd run into that giant spiderweb, how it had felt to step in to rescue her, and feel her brush up against him, for one long incredible moment. He swallowed, pushing aside another wave of unexpected yearning.

He hadn't been close to anyone since Shelby had died. Hadn't wanted to be. Initially, it had been because he was still grieving and couldn't imagine anyone ever taking her place. Later, because he didn't want to risk the pain that came with a loss like that. He'd also known he hadn't the time or energy to try and incorporate someone special into his life. Never mind worry about how his girls would react if he did ever start dating again. So to feel fiercely attracted to Tess now was…well, unexpected, at the very least.

Feeling like the worst host ever, he swallowed. "Did she leave?" *Please tell me she hasn't gone yet.*

"Uh-huh. But she said to tell you that she looked in on Miss Coco and she's fine this morning, too. And also she took Tank out to the barn with her, so he probably won't need to go out for a while, although he will need to be fed. She gave him fresh water."

Pleased by the unexpected help, he smiled, ruminating softly. "That was nice of her…"

"Who is *she*?" Lucy queried, looking protective. She flung her long, tangly hair out of her eyes. Hair she did not brush nearly enough. Unlike her twin sisters, who were always brushing and styling each other's hair. "And why was she in *our house*? And why didn't we ever see her before this morning?"

Unable to get out of bed with the girls perched on either side of him, and unwilling to make them move just yet, Noah pushed up so he was sitting against the headboard. He figured this was as good a time as any to have this conversation. "The nice lady's Dr. Tess Gardner. The new veterinarian I was telling you girls about. The one who knows a whole lot about taking care of miniature donkeys and their foals. She just moved here yesterday, and she came by last night to check out Miss Coco for us." At least that was what had ended up happening. Which was a good thing. It had given them a chance to get to know each other a little better, and see each other in a different light.

As he had watched Tess care for their miniature donkeys, it was easy to see why Sara had been so determined to get Tess to accept a position at the vet clinic in town. Tess was a very skilled clinician. Gentle. Thorough. Kind. And professional.

All were traits he considered essential.

In a veterinarian.

In a friend…

And of course she was very beautiful, and sexy in that breezy girl-next-door way, too.

Not that he should be noticing…

Exhaling, Noah continued, "Dr. Tess checked on Miss Coco's baby foal, too. And it was all good. Both were healthy as could be."

His three daughters readily accepted his explanation, for why Tess had been in their kitchen so early in the morning.

Although, Lucy gave it more thought, and her eyes widened. "She watched over Miss Coco *all night*? In the stable?"

Noah shook his head. "She slept in the house."

"Why?" Lucy's scowl deepened.

Patiently, Noah explained, "There was an unexpected mess-up with Dr. Tess's plans. Her house didn't have any power or water. The hotels were full, and she needed a place to sleep, so I offered her our guest room."

His eight-year-old folded her arms in front of her and her lower lip slid out into a pout. "Only our grandma and grandpa sleep in the guest room," she reminded him archly. "Or our aunts and uncles."

"Well, last night it was Dr. Tess."

Lucy continued to mull over that fact, not necessarily happily. Since all seven of his siblings had found love and gotten married recently, she had made it clear on numerous occasions that she was worried he would do the same. While she liked the attention of adult women, and the feminine, maternal perspective they brought, she didn't want anyone taking her late mother's place.

Initially, he hadn't, either.

But lately…seeing the rest of his family all paired up and so happy, he had begun to realize just how lonely he was. Having kids was great.

It was even better when you had someone to share them with.

But the woman who took his late wife's place in their lives was not going to be just anyone.

She'd have to be full of life and love. Independent. Kind. Giving.

Sort of like…Tess Gardner. Hold on! Where in the hell had *that* thought come from?

Lucy was frowning. "Hmm."

Figuring a change of subject was in order, Noah motioned for the girls to move. As soon as they hopped off the bed, he threw back the covers and swung his legs over the edge. "Who wants to go with me to give Tank his breakfast and then run down to the barn and check on Miss Coco?"

"Me!" all three girls squealed in unison.

"Then get your barn boots on," he said, shoving aside all thoughts of Tess and the impact she'd had on him in only a few glorious hours. "And I'll meet you in the kitchen."

"Well, what do you think?" Sara Anderson McCabe asked, after she had shown Tess around the veterinary clinic, and introduced her to all the staff before weekend office hours started at nine o'clock on Saturday morning.

The effervescent managing partner walked Tess into the small room with a desk that would serve as Tess's private office. With its polished linoleum floor, and standard office desk and chair, it was nothing like the luxurious office at her job in Denver. Yet, somehow, it was so much warmer.

"Are you going to be able to be happy here?" Sara asked, squinting at her.

Tess nodded. "I'm sure I will be." Everyone was just so darn nice. Including, and especially, Noah Lockhart. Not that she should be thinking of him...

Sara rested her palm on her pregnant belly. "Did you find a hotel to stay in until the movers get your belongings here from Denver? Or were you going to just go ahead and move into the house you inherited, as is?"

"Well, there was a slight problem with that." Briefly, she explained about the lack of utilities, and abundance of spiders and mice.

"Oh, no."

Oh, *yes*...

Sara shook her head, not looking all that surprised, now that she'd had a moment to think about it. "Well, Waylon wasn't known for his housekeeping. Not that he was ever home for long. When he came in off the oil rigs, all he ever wanted to do was go fishing until it was time to head back to the Gulf." She sighed. "But I had no idea he turned all his home's utilities off during his absences. Although I suppose it makes sense. Financially, anyway." She gave Tess another thoughtful squint. "So what did you do?"

"Um…"

This was a rural county. Sara was bound to find out, anyway. Not that it had been a secret.

Tess swallowed. "Noah Lockhart offered to put me up last night, at the Welcome Ranch."

Sara did a double take, unable to completely contain her pleased look. "You met Noah?"

"Yeah. He stopped by while I was looking at my Uncle Waylon's house." *And gallantly saved me from more than a few spiders.*

The woman's eyes lit up hopefully. "What did you think?"

That she had never met anyone who could take her breath away with just a look, the way he could.

Aware Sara was still waiting for her reaction, Tess shook her head, struggling for something she *could* say. Finally, she sobered and managed a response. "He's, um, very tall." About six foot three inches to her own five foot eight. *And handsome.* "And, uh, helpful." Oh, Lord, what was this? When had she ever been so tongue-tied? Or felt like such a teenager? One with a secret crush?

Sara laughed. She lifted a halting palm. "Okay, I won't pry. Moving on. So what's your plan now?"

That was the problem. Tess didn't really have one. Yet. "Well, I can't get the power and water turned on until their offices open on Monday. But I have an exterminator meeting me at the house this afternoon. And I'm going to spend the rest of the day just getting my bearings and figuring out what I need."

Concern radiated from Sara. "Do you have a place to stay in the meantime?"

Tess nodded. "I made a reservation at a River Walk hotel in San Antonio for the next two nights." Although she was hoping not to need to drive all that way if she could get her new home clean enough to camp out in for the next few days.

"Somewhere with spa services, I hope?" the other woman teased.

Tess chuckled in response, then grabbed her purse and keys. "Anyway, I better get going."

Sara walked her as far as the employees' entrance. "Let me know if you do need anything. Including a place to stay. Matt and the kids and I can always make room."

Tess knew that. She just didn't like depending on others for anything. It was always much better when she could handle things on her own. Which was exactly what she planned to do.

Several hours later, Tess had everything she needed for the cleanup of her new home to begin. She headed for Spring Street. No sooner had she parked, than a now-familiar charcoal-gray Expedition pulled up behind her.

Noah stepped out.

Unlike the evening before, when he'd been garbed in business-casual, he was dressed in a pair of old jeans and a flannel shirt, as well as a thick fleece vest and construction-style work boots.

He looked so good he made her mouth water.

Pushing away the unwanted desire, she met him at the tailgate of her Tahoe. Despite herself, she was glad he had come to her rescue again. She tilted her head back to look into his eyes. "Seriously, cowboy, we have to stop meeting like this."

He grinned at her droll tone. His midnight blue eyes took on the sexy glint she was beginning to know so well. "I figured you were going to need help."

He had figured right. What she hadn't decided was if it was a good idea or a bad idea to allow herself to depend on him. Especially because she had been down this road before, only to have it end disastrously.

Pushing all thoughts of her ex and their failed relationship away, she opened up her tailgate. Determined now to focus on the gargantuan task at hand.

He saw the big box. "A wet-dry vac. Good idea."

His approval warmed her. Why, she didn't know. She inhaled the masculine scent of his soap and shampoo. "It will be when I finally get electricity on Monday."

At least she *hoped* it would be on Monday.

Out here in the country, there was no guarantee they offered same-day service, for an extra fee, the way they did in the city.

Grateful for his lack of recrimination or judgment, with regard to her lack of proper planning, Tess let Noah help her slide the bulky box onto the ground. He smiled genially, as relaxed as she was stressed.

Nonsensically, she chattered on. "I figured it was the fastest way to get up all the crud inside and dispose of it."

He scanned her work clothes and equally no-nonsense boots. Her own quarter-zip fleece jacket.

"In the meantime," she sighed, lifting out the rest of her purchases, "there's the old-fashioned way of broom, dustpan and trash bag."

Noah stepped closer, inundating her with the heat and strength of his big masculine body. Then he rubbed his hand across his closely shaven jaw, before dropping it once again. "Actually—" he let his gaze drift over her face before returning to her eyes "—we could use your shop vac today. If you don't mind borrowing some electrical power from a neighbor."

He really knew how to tempt her. But... "I can't ask someone I don't know."

He chuckled, a deep rumbling low in his throat. "Sure, you can," he drawled, surveying her as if he found her completely irresistible. Another shimmer of tension floated between them and she felt her breath catch in her throat. What was it about this man that drove her to distraction? "Neighbors help each other out around here. Remember? But I can understand your reluctance to ask for a favor, when you meet the new neighbors for the first time. So if you want—" he placed a reassuring hand on her shoulder, the warmth of his touch emanating through her clothes "—I can rustle up some outdoor extension cords, go next door and set that up for you. As well as help you put the wet-dry vac together."

The part of her that wanted to keep her heart under lock and key responded with a resounding *No!* The temptation to lean on Noah Lockhart was too strong as it was. But the more practical part of her felt differently. She had to be at work at her new job, seeing patients, forty-eight hours from now. And right now, like it or not, the house she had inherited was definitely not livable.

She drew in a deep, enervating breath and dared to meet his eyes, trying not to think how attracted she was to him. She swallowed hard. "Sure." She forced herself to sound casual. As if she was used to such random kindness in her life. She took out the rest of the cleaning products and microfiber cloths, and shut the SUV tailgate. "Thanks... I would really appreciate that."

He picked up the bulky box and easily carried it up the front steps to the porch. "Now we're talking."

She followed with the bags. When they were face-to-face again, she tilted her head at him, curious. "Not that I'm not grateful for the help, but don't you have responsibilities of your own to tend to?"

He came near enough that she could feel his hot breath fanning against her skin. "My girls are on a play date with their cousins over at my parents' ranch."

He whipped out his cell phone, punched a button on the screen and began typing. To whom, she didn't know.

"I'm supposed to join them at six this evening, for dinner," he explained.

But until then, the implication was, he was free to do whatever he felt like doing.

"Nice." She set down her things, then fished around in the front pocket of her jeans for her keys. Unable to help herself, she added with an appreciative smile, "Your daughters were very cute, by the way."

The proud, affectionate look on Noah's face told her he knew he had hit the jackpot when it came to his kids. She could not help but agree.

Wistfully, once again, she wished she had a few of her own just like them. In fact, as far as timing went, she had thought she would be married, with at least one child by now. But she had fallen in love with someone who ultimately hadn't felt the same, so...

He finished texting. Glancing up, his eyes scanned her face, his expression serious now. "I hope they were polite to you this morning."

Tess reflected on the three pajama-clad little girls, with their pink cheeks and tousled hair. The three-year-old twins had their daddy's deep blue eyes. Their big sister, Lucy, was lovely, too. Albeit observant and intuitive. Guarded. Aware he was waiting on her reply, she said finally, "I think they were more shocked than anything."

He lifted an eyebrow. Urging…no, more like demanding that she go on.

Tess cleared her throat. "Lucy made it clear women did not spend the night at the Welcome Ranch, unless they were family." *Which I am definitely not.*

"Ah, well…" He slid his phone into his pocket. "As I said, I'm not looking for a new woman in my life."

Which should be reassuring.

It had been yesterday.

Now, that knowledge just left her feeling off-kilter. The way she always did when she allowed herself to want something that was not likely to happen. Like she had with her ex. Thinking that time—and increasing intimacy—and a more settled lifestyle after the super demanding years of vet school and residency—would ease them into a blissful future. And give them both the lifelong commitment and family that she had yearned for.

Unfortunately, her ex had other ideas. And priorities.

Noah's phone tinged, signaling an incoming text. He pulled it out and looked at the screen. Smiled, as he announced, "My brother Gabe lives a few blocks over. He's got a few outdoor extension cords we can borrow. He's going to bring them right over."

Another pleasant surprise. She could so get used to this. "That's nice of him."

"Yeah."

Tess unlocked the front door and carefully led the way inside. It was as icy cold and musty-smelling as the day before. To the point that all she could think was *ugh*.

Eminently calm, Noah looked up. "The spiders were busy."

The cowboy standing beside her was right. New webs were everywhere. Tess sighed. She hoped this wasn't an omen. "They certainly were."

Chapter Four

"Want to take a break?" Noah asked an hour later.

Looking even more overwhelmed than she had when they had first walked in, Tess nodded. She sighed, completely vulnerable now as she met his gaze, seeming on the verge of tears.

It was easy to see why she was so demoralized, Noah thought. While the exterior of the brick home was pristine, the interior of the house looked like something out of an episode of *Hoarders*. And though they had been knocking webs down from the ceiling and windows with the broom, and vacuuming up dirt and debris, there was still so much to do.

Tess shoved a hand through her wild butterscotch-blond curls. Her elegant features were tinged an emotional pink. He moved close enough to see the frustration glimmering in her eyes. "I mean, it helps to have some of the dust and gunk gone," she said, flashing him a grateful half smile, "but I still kind of feel like all we're doing at the moment is rearranging the deck chairs on the *Titanic*."

"Yeah. I can see that analogy." He stepped nearer. It was all he could do not to take her in his arms and comfort her. But he knew that could lead to trouble with a capital *T*. "Do you think it would help if we cleared out a room or two? Just made some space?"

Her teeth raked her plump lower lip. "Probably, yeah." A look of relief flashed on her face.

Next question.

Savoring her nearness and the pleasure that came from being alone with her like this, he asked, "Is it going to be difficult for you to sort through this stuff?"

She shoved her hands in the pockets of her jeans. The take-charge veterinarian was back. "No. There are only two things I'm keeping. The first is that rusted-out cast-iron skillet in the kitchen that I'm pretty sure belonged to my grandmother. The second are the fishing lures my uncle made, and one of his tackle boxes to keep them in. Everything else that can be donated will be. The stuff that can't will be trashed."

He liked her decisiveness. "What is your timetable for getting this all done?"

Another shadow crossed her face. Their eyes locked, providing another wave of unbidden heat between them. "Ah, yesterday," she joked, running her hands through her hair again.

He noticed how the midday sunshine, which was flooding in through the grimy windows, caught the shimmer of gold in her blond hair.

He reached over and took her hand in his, wondering what it would take to make her feel as crazy with longing and giddy with desire as he did at this moment. "What would you say if I could make that happen?"

She peered at him, the corners of her luscious lips turning up slightly. *"Are you serious?"*

Pushing aside the primal urge to kiss her, he took a deep, calming breath and watched her retreat into scrupulous politeness. "Well, not the yesterday part. I haven't mastered time travel yet," he quipped, letting go of her hand and once again giving her the physical space she seemed to require. He curtailed his own rising emotions. "But I *could* probably get this place cleared out for you today."

"How?" She folded her arms against her middle, the action pushing up the soft curves of her breasts. "Do you have trash haulers and charity pickup on speed dial?"

He had been ready for this kind of reticence, given how high she had her guard up. "Close. Six of my seven siblings live in Laramie County. And the sister who doesn't is visiting with her husband and twins this weekend. So they're at my parents' ranch."

"Still—" another beleaguered sigh "—it's pretty last-moment."

He wondered what it would take to begin to tear down the walls around her heart. And allow his own to come tumbling down in the process. "Let me guess. You don't want to impose."

She winced, looking uncomfortable again. "I really don't."

He locked eyes with her. "How about this, then? I'll send out a Lockhart family text, asking for volunteers. And we'll see what happens."

"Un-be-liev-able!" Tess said five hours later. She waved at the pest-control associate, who was backing out of her driveway. Then turned to Noah, unable to help but smile, as the two of them walked back inside the house. The rooms had been completely cleared out of all debris

and swept clean. She went from room to room, amazed at how spacious the house seemed, now that the rooms were empty. "I can't believe this was done in just five hours!"

"I know." Noah glanced around appreciatively, too. "Isn't my family fantastic?"

"They certainly are." They'd started showing up minutes after he'd sent out his SOS text. His sister-in-law Allison, a lifestyle blogger, had instinctively known what could be repurposed and what could not. His brother-in-law Zach had brought his Callahan Custom Carpentry delivery truck. Others had pickups and SUVs. The women sorted stuff inside, and the men carried things out. All of them talking and joking, and warmly welcoming her to the community.

For the first time in her life, Tess had a glimpse of what it would be like to be part of a big, loving family. To have people you could count on to be there for you, even on short notice. Growing up the only child of a single mom, with her only other blood relatives—the uncle and grandmother she never really knew—in Texas, Tess'd had to learn to rely mostly on herself, and her mom, when her mom was around. After her mom had died, she'd had her ex. But since she and Carlton had split, she had only her casual friends, who were just as caught up in their busy lives as she had been. To suddenly be surrounded by so many warm and generous people was a revelation.

And in Laramie County, Texas, apparently the norm.

Achingly aware of how cozy and enticing this all was, she took a seat next to him on the staircase steps. Somehow, they managed not to touch, but barely, given how big and manly Noah's tall frame was. They each held chilled bottles of water that had been donated by one of his sibs. "But you're not really surprised at the quick way they accomplished this, are you?"

He turned to her, his brawny shoulder nudging hers in the process. "They did the same for us, when the girls and I moved back from California a few years ago. They had us all unpacked and everything organized and put away, in less than a day. So—" he shrugged amiably, pausing to take another long, deep drink "—I knew if we all worked together we could get it done. Even if my available siblings and or their spouses only came in for an hour or two each."

"Do they still help you, too?" Tess asked. Aware she had met all of his siblings except Mackenzie, who had been helping his mom with preparations for the family dinner scheduled for that evening.

"Yeah. We all help each other, although I think, at least for now," he frowned, "with me the only parent on scene for my three little girls, I'm doing more taking than giving." He exhaled, his expression turning more optimistic. "Although in time, I think that will change, and I'll be able to pay them back for all the help they give me every week."

She studied his handsome profile. "What sort of things do they do?"

"My brothers help with any chore that requires more than one person—like putting up outside Christmas decorations or hauling hay for the barn. My sisters assist with clothes shopping. Which," he made a rueful face, "can be a hysterical mess if the girls think I don't understand what is pretty and what is not!" He tossed his head in mock kid-drama.

She laughed at his comically indignant tone.

Having met his three girls, she could see each of them doing just that.

Resisting the urge to take his hand in hers, she prodded softly, "What else?"

"Oh. Well. They all carpool with me so I don't have to

go into town twice daily on weekdays. My parents and sibs also take turns making an extra casserole or dinner, and drop one off with me, for our dinner. They have the girls over for sleepovers or playdates. Stuff like that."

"It sounds wonderful."

He nodded. "It is."

Feeling very glad he was there with her, despite herself, she got to her feet once again. Still tingling with awareness and something else—some other soul-deep yearning she chose not to identify—she began to pace. "Well, I'm going to have to figure out a way to thank them all."

He moved lazily to his feet. Tossed the empty bottle into the box earmarked for temporary recycling. Then, rocking forward on his toes, he hooked his thumbs into the loops on either side of his fly. "They don't expect anything in return except maybe a word of thanks, which you already said to each of them."

Tess knew that. She also knew she would feel better if she did more than that… But there was no time to figure that out now.

"So what's next?" Noah said.

It was five o'clock. Which reminded her… Tess dragged in a breath and retrieved her phone. "I need to cancel my hotel reservations in San Antonio." She pulled up the website and let them know she wouldn't be coming. "Done!"

He looked at her as if he could read her mind. Then quirked an eyebrow. "You're going to stay here tonight?"

Tess walked over to the fireplace and kneeled in front of it. She didn't have any wood, but she knew where the firewood-sales stand was. Her self-sufficient nature came back full-force. "That's the plan." She reached around for the handle that would open the flue. It seemed to be…stuck.

"Here. Let me." Noah kneeled beside her and easily

managed what she had been unable to. The damper opened with a rusty screech.

Tess winced. "That doesn't sound good."

"No kidding." Still hunkered down on the hearth, he pulled out his phone, turned on the flashlight and aimed it up the chimney. A loud fluttering sound and several chirps followed. They both ducked in response. But fortunately, whatever bird, or *birds*, that had been there went up, not down into the house. Probably because the down exit had been blocked, and they likely assumed it still was.

"Come take a look," he said.

Curious, Tess leaned toward him and followed the beam of his light. "Oh, no. A nest." It looked as if the visitors had really made themselves at home for some time now.

"Yep." Noah aimed the beam across the interior walls. "And quite a bit of soot, too." He frowned in concern. "You're going to need to get a chimney sweep out here to clean it before you can safely build a fire in this."

Sitting back on her heels, Tess moaned and buried her face in her hands.

There went one of the most important parts of her plan.

He gave her a curious sidelong glance and shut the flue. Moving smoothly to his feet, he chivalrously offered her a hand up.

Tess accepted his help, only because it would have been awkward not to, after all they had been through. Ignoring the sparks that started in her fingertips and spread outward through her entire body, she disengaged their grip, then took a big gulp of air. "Well, maybe I won't need to make a fire in there tonight," she mused, trying to look on the bright side, "if I can find a warm enough sleeping bag at the super store."

Somehow, he wasn't surprised to see her thinking

about roughing it until she could get all the utilities turned on, and her belongings sent down from Denver.

"Or," he said, regarding her amiably, "you could stay with us again until your place is livable and all your stuff gets here."

He had no idea how tempting that idea sounded. Especially given the kindness of her host.

He winked at her playfully. "Unless the Welcome Ranch is too 'California' for your taste. And you need accommodations that are more Texan."

Tess rolled her eyes at his teasing. "You know it's not that," she drawled right back.

True, the style of his home was unexpected for this neck of the woods, where southwestern and southern decor reigned. But it was beautiful and quite comfortable nevertheless.

She bit her lip and let out a long-suffering sigh. "I just don't want to impose."

"So—" he spread his hands wide "—we'll barter, to make things even. *You* check on Miss Coco and her foal, two times every day, until her little one is born and doing well. And the girls and I'll give you the shelter you need and all the privacy you want."

She chewed her lip, deliberating. The last thing she wanted was to be an imposition, and this arrangement he'd proposed was hardly a fair exchange. But there was no denying that it would be wonderful not to have to worry about making the house livable while simultaneously starting her new job.

Tess studied him intently, aware that they had known each other just twenty-four hours now and she already felt closer to him than most people she had known all her life. "You know, of course, that you are likely talking several weeks?" Which was a long time for a house-guest, especially one who was still a relative stranger.

He tilted his head, his seductive lips curving up in an inviting smile. "At least."

Oh, this could be trouble.

So much trouble, if she ever gave in to the attraction simmering between them and did something really crazy like kiss him…or let him kiss her.

And yet, with so few options, could she really afford to quibble? They were both adults, responsible ones at that. She could handle this. They both could.

"Well…?" he implored softly.

Her heartbeat kicked into high gear. "You really wouldn't mind?"

He sobered, then responded quietly, "I wouldn't offer if I did."

Silently, she went through all the rest of the reasons why and why not. Found, in the end, she was still leaning toward staying with him and his three adorable little girls. "And you really think that would be an even trade for several weeks of lodging…?"

He chuckled. "Given how nervous I am about birthing my first and probably only miniature donkey?" he said in a low, deadpan tone. "I sure as heck do."

She couldn't help but laugh at his comically feigned look of terror. She held up a palm. "Okay, I accept. But we do our own thing. You carry on as normal with your family and I will try not to get in the way."

He paused, as if trying to figure out how to phrase something. "That sounds fine," he said eventually. "In the meantime," he continued matter-of-factly, "you have been invited to my folks' ranch for dinner with the family. Most of whom you have already met."

The part of Tess who had become acquainted with

most of his siblings and their spouses, and knew how nice they all were, wanted to accept the invitation. However, the other part of her that needed to take a breath knew what a bad idea it was.

She'd gotten romantically attached to a guy before because she had found herself in a challenging situation and needed emotional support. Same as him.

While their relationship had continued through vet school, residency, and into their first jobs after graduation, their engagement had not ended well.

She had no intention of making the same mistake.

"Thank you, but I have a lot to do this evening. Laundry and a few other chores…so if that's okay I'll pass on the offer." Then she realized she was being a little presumptuous. "But, um, if you'd rather I not use your washer and dryer, I saw a Laundromat in town. I could easily stop there…"

"Don't be silly. When I said make yourself at home, I meant it."

"Daddy, you are *not* being fair!"

Uh-oh, Tess thought as the shrill voice came her way.

Lucy stomped closer, bypassing the laundry room, where Tess had been working, through the back hallway, and into the kitchen, where she was now seated. Checking her email on her laptop computer. "My bedtime is *always* a half hour later than the twins!"

"Under normal circumstances, yes," Noah returned calmly as he shut the back door behind them and ushered the weary-looking twins forward. He had a backpack slung over his shoulder, and a big foil-wrapped package in his hands that she guessed was dinner leftovers.

Avery and Angelica turned and gazed up. Their dad

was so tall they had to tilt their heads way back to see his face. "Do we have to get a bath tonight?" Avery asked.

Noah set the platter on the kitchen island, then came back to the twins. "Do you want one?"

The three-year-olds looked at each other, deliberating. Avery stifled a yawn. "No. I just want to wash my face and brush my teeth and get in my pajamas."

"I want to do that, too," Angelica said, following her twin's lead.

Meanwhile, Lucy was storming the back hallway, her arms crossed in front of her. She was so worked up that steam was practically coming out of her ears.

Noah looked at Tess. "Sorry," he mouthed.

She gave him a smile and a nod, letting him know it was okay. Then watched as he pulled out a computer tablet from the *Family* backpack of all their stuff. "All right, Lucy, you can have twenty minutes of screen time. But then you're going upstairs and going to bed with no more argument. Understand?"

Rather than looking appeased, Lucy's sulky expression deepened. "Yes."

He pointed her in the direction of the great room. Sent another apologetic look at Tess and disappeared with the twins.

Trying not to imagine what it would be like to be part of a family like this, instead of coming home every day to a solitude that often seemed far too lonely, Tess returned to the laundry room. She continued pulling her clothes out of the dryer, then proceeded to deposit them in the wicker basket. She was just going to be here for a short while, she reminded herself. And she and Noah had agreed they would each do their own thing, without getting in each other's way. So there was no reason to offer to help him with anything. Except...

Lucy was back. Standing in the doorway. Tablet in her arms. In that moment, she looked very much like her take-charge daddy. "Aren't you coming?" she demanded.

Tess stood. She settled the basket on her hip, doing her best to exude the kind of casual tranquility she was pretty sure Lucy needed in this moment. "You want me to sit with you?" she asked as if it was no big deal. When it felt like a big deal to her. After all, what did she know about caring for kids?

"Well, duh."

"Um, sure." Making certain to give the child her space, Tess followed her to the big U-shaped sectional. She sat on one end. Still looking mighty unhappy, Lucy settled on the other, making no move to turn on her tablet.

Tess was surprised by the girl's attitude. She had been as welcoming as her two sisters, when they'd encountered her in the Welcome Ranch kitchen that morning. What had changed to make her resent Tess so? The fact that she was back? Intending to stay for a few weeks, at Noah's request? He had to have told them something. None of them had seemed shocked to see her there, sitting in front of her computer. Or doing her laundry.

Then again, maybe it's not about me. Maybe it has to do with someone or something else.

Tess favored Lucy with a gentle smile. "Did you have fun at the Circle L?"

She received another resentful scowl in return. Lucy peered at her suspiciously. "How do *you* know where we were?"

"Your dad told me."

Lucy got up and went over to a table in the foyer. She came back with two framed pictures. The first was a wedding photo of Noah and his late wife. Noah looked about a decade or so younger. His wife seemed to be about the same age. The other was of their family of five, when her mom had still been alive, and Lucy looked to have been around four or five, while the twins were still at the age where they weren't yet walking.

"This is my mommy," Lucy declared. "Her name is Shelby. She loved us very much. Especially my daddy."

"I bet she did. She looks very beautiful." So beautiful in fact, it would be hard for any woman to compete with that.

"Yes. Which is why you should leave," Lucy continued.

"Lucy!" Noah's voice sounded from the top of the stairs. He came down swiftly. "You know better than to be rude to our guests."

Lucy sighed and stood. "Tess needs to go home, Daddy. 'Cause it is really late."

"Past your bedtime, certainly," Noah agreed sternly. He held out his hand to his oldest daughter. "Let's go."

She shuffled to obey. "What about the twins?"

"They are already tucked in. Now what do you say to our guest?"

"Sorry."

She clearly did not mean it.

But to Tess's relief, her dad let it go.

The two moved back up the stairs. Her heart went out to the petulant child. It couldn't have been easy, losing her mother at such a young age. Lucy probably still missed Shelby terribly, just as Tess still missed her own mother, close to a decade after her mom's death. The last thing Tess wanted was to somehow make things worse for Lucy. If her presence here was going to be a problem for the grieving child, she knew she would have to find other accommodation. But in the meantime, there were still chores to be done. Tess finished folding her laundry, and then went into the kitchen to check on the cast iron skillet she'd put in the oven. To her delight, the re-seasoning process was finished and it was ready. She pulled out the baking sheet that the heavy skillet was sitting on and set it on the stove.

Once again, Noah was back, looking embarrassed. "Sorry about what happened earlier," he said gruffly.

This time, Tess's heart went out to them both. Not sure whether or not he wanted to talk about it further, she lifted a hand and said, "Totally understandable—no apology necessary."

Not surprisingly, he still seemed to think there was. Noah let out what might have been a sigh, then scrubbed a hand over his face, before once again meeting Tess's eyes. "I'd like to say it's just because she is overtired tonight," he said candidly, "but the truth is—" Noah paused and frowned again "—Lucy can be pretty mercurial."

Was that a warning of more temper tantrums to come? Tess wasn't sure. She did need to ask. "Is my being here going to make things more difficult for her—or you? Because if it is…" Tess paused sincerely. "I'm sure I can find somewhere else to bunk while still checking in on Miss Coco, twice daily, like we agreed."

Noah vetoed that idea with a shake of his head. "That won't be necessary," he told her gruffly. "Lucy knows very well that no matter how grumpy or out of sorts she might be feeling, she still has to treat others kindly and use her manners, and I promise you, even if I have to gently remind her at times, that she will."

His weary expression had her feeling empathy for him, all over again. Struggling against the need to comfort him with a touch, she gave him her most understanding smile. "And I promise you, I won't take offense. I know she is just a kid, and she's doing the best she can, the way we all are."

He nodded and drew another breath. "Thanks."

Tingling from the near contact, Tess turned back to the stove. Suddenly wondering, she asked, "Is it okay if I leave this skillet here on the stove until it cools? It's going to take a while."

"Sure."

Noah followed her gaze to the gleaming black cast-iron skillet. Then his eyes widened in surprise. "That can't be the one you rescued from Waylon's home."

It had been such a sentimental find for her, refurbishing it had been at the top of her list of chores. Tess smiled, relieved to have something a little easier to talk about. "It is, actually."

The awkwardness between them faded as he surveyed the pan from all angles, clearly impressed. "I can't believe it. It looks brand-new."

"Doesn't it?" Tess said proudly.

He moved closer, inspecting it with interest. His tall body radiated both heat and strength. He sent her an approving sidelong glance before moving away once again. "How did you get all the rust off?"

She watched him go with just a tinge of disappointment. "I used table salt and steel wool, and a lot of elbow grease. Then I seasoned it with oil and put it in the oven to cure."

Looking finally ready to hang out and take a breath, he sprawled in a kitchen chair, long legs stretched out in front of him. "Amazing."

Trying not to think how sexy he looked, even doing practically nothing, she tilted her head at him. Refusing to notice how attracted she was to him, she asked, "You've never cooked in cast iron?"

"No." He lifted his arms over his head, stretched languidly. "My mom and sisters do, but I never knew how they cleaned them up." Lazily, he dropped his arms to his sides. Smiled. "You obviously do."

Tess roamed the large state-of-the-art space restlessly, not sure what she should do now that he and the girls were home again. Hide in her room? Or stay downstairs and finish her laundry? Because she still had a load in the dryer...

Figuring the best thing to do was just play it casual, too, she continued, "My mom was an executive chef for some of the best restaurants in Denver. Mostly French cuisine. All very chichi. But when she was home, which wasn't all that often, she often talked about the food she'd eaten, growing up, that her mother had prepared in her cast-iron skillet."

Noah tilted his head in the direction of the stove top. "You think that's the one?"

"I do. I just think it hadn't been cared for properly or used in a very long time. Which is a shame." Hence, she had needed to bring it back to life, ASAP, as a way of honoring both her grandmother and her mother.

He pushed out of his chair, sauntered over to the fridge and pulled out a beer. Wordlessly, he offered her one. She shook her head. He shut the door behind him and twisted off the cap. Lounging against the counter, he asked, "So you know how to cook in it, then?"

"Oh, yeah. My mom had a whole set of cast iron, and a nice set of stainless-steel cookware, too. Plus, chef's knives, and so on. I inherited it all when she died of pneumonia, my first year of vet school." A lump rose in Tess's throat. Tears stung the back of her eyes. Funny, how things could still hurt. Even nearly a decade later.

He put his drink aside and moved to give her a comforting hug. "Sorry." He squeezed her shoulders companionably, then admitted thickly, "I know firsthand how hard it is to suffer a loss like that. I lost both my parents, too."

It took a moment for what he had said to sink in. Tess did a double take.

He picked up his drink and took another sip. "My sibs and I are all adopted. Our biological parents perished in a fire after lightning struck our home in the middle of the night, when I was about Lucy's age."

And she thought *she'd* had it bad. She gave in to impulse and hugged him, too, just for a moment. "That sounds really traumatic," she murmured, stepping back.

He nodded in confirmation, then continued reluctantly, "My parents got us all out to safety, but then went back in for a few things after the rain put the fire out...or so they thought. A spark ignited the gas water heater, which was in the attic. The whole place exploded. They were killed instantly."

"Oh, my God, Noah, I am so sorry."

He moved out of touching range, took another long sip of beer. "It was a long time ago."

"Still, it must have been really tough."

Sorrow came and went in his eyes. Replaced by cool acceptance. "You're right. It was." His expression became even more bleak. "All of us kids were split up into different foster homes, and it was a few years before Carol and Robert were able to get permission from the court to adopt us all."

He shook off his low mood and straightened. "Anyway, that's one reason I don't ever like to put off until tomorrow anything that could be done today. Like," he said, his expression turning warm and welcoming once again, "ensuring you're comfortable. So what else do you need to really settle in? Dinner? Because my mom sent a huge plate of leftovers in case you hadn't eaten."

It was going to be really hard to keep her guard up, if he was so generous and helpful all the time. She reminded herself this was a short-term arrangement. Meant to be kept businesslike. So why was it feeling like it could be something *more*?

She flashed a smile. "Thanks. That was nice of her. But I'm good. I stopped for a sandwich on my way out of town."

Without warning, his brow furrowed. "Did you have a chance to check on Miss Coco?"

His concern for the animal was laudable. "Yes. She's doing fine."

His eyes turned a mesmerizing blue. "Looking any closer to…?"

Tess cut off his question with a definitive shake of her head. "I still think what I did last night, that it will be another week or two. Possibly even a little more. We will just have to wait and see."

Noah, who was so calm and competent in all other situations, abruptly looked tense and ill-at-ease. Knowing he was as out of his element birthing pets as she was caring for kids, she touched his arm, her fingers curling around his biceps. "It really is going to be okay," she soothed.

He leaned into her grip. "Promise me?" he rasped.

Trying not to imagine what it would be like to have those strong arms wrapped around her, Tess said, "I promise."

Don't miss
A Temporary Texas Arrangement
by Cathy Gillen Thacker,
available January 2024 wherever
Harlequin Special Edition books and ebooks are sold.
www.Harlequin.com

#3031 BIG SKY COWBOY
The Brands of Montana • by Joanna Sims

Charlotte "Charlie" Brand has three months, one Montana summer and Wayne Westbrook's help to turn her struggling homestead into a corporate destination. The handsome horse trainer is the perfect man to make her professional dreams a reality. But what about her romantic ones?

#3032 HER NEW YORK MINUTE
The Friendship Chronicles • by Darby Baham

British investment guru Olivia Robinson is in New York for one reason—to become the youngest head of her global company's portfolio division. But when charming attorney Thomas Wright sweeps her off her feet, she wonders if another relationship will become collateral damage.

#3033 THE RANCHER'S LOVE SONG
The Women of Dalton Ranch • by Makenna Lee

Ranch foreman Travis Taylor is busy caring for an orphaned baby. He doesn't have time for opera singers on vacation. Even bubbly, beautiful ones like Lizzy Dalton. But when Lizzy falls for the baby *and* Travis, he'll have to overcome past trauma in order to build a family.

#3034 A DEAL WITH MR. WRONG
Sisterhood of Chocolate & Wine • by Anna James

Piper Kavanaugh needs a fake boyfriend pronto! Her art gallery is opening soon and her mother's matchmaking schemes are in overdrive. Fortunately, convincing her enemy turned contractor Cooper Turner to play the role is easier than expected. Unfortunately, so is falling for him...